Black Road

Black Road

a novel

NANCY ZAFRIS

UNBRIDLED BOOKS

UNBRIDLED BOOKS
Copyright © 2022 by Nancy Zafris
PAPERBACK: 978-1-60953-150-8
e-book: 978-1-60953-151-5

1 3 5 7 9 10 8 6 4 2

First Printing

Book Design by Claire Vaccaro

For all of my friends. Thank you.

Cast

HIGH SCHOOL

Travis Hicks

Hannah Kirkpatrick, head cheerleader

Anisha Devajaran, 1st cornet in marching
band

Corbin Greesley, drum major and brother
of Josh

Chieko Watanabe, Japanese exchange
student

Mr. Hurd, marching band director

Miss Stacy, assistant marching band director

Miss B, English teacher

VICTIMS OF PRANK

Bratley and Kirk

HIGH SCHOOL DEFENDANTS

Jared Overholser, quarterback

Josh Greesley, wide receiver and younger
brother of Corbin

Dustin Crosby, tight end

Tyler Newton, non–football player

Clay Rhinehart, non–football player

COURTROOM

Honorable Merle Herrick, local judge

Honorable Javier Tanguay, outside judge

Shawna, security officer

John Willis, security officer

Roxanne Burker, clerk of courts, high
school mom

TOWNSPEOPLE

Henry and Ginny Zimmerman, owners of
deer decoy

Danny Zimmerman, AWOL adult son of
the Zimmermans

Jackie Hicks, AWOL mother of Travis

Erly Johnson, police officer

Mrs. Atkins, troublemaking mom

Freddy Burker, husband of Roxanne

Dr. Devajaran, mother of Anisha

AMISH COMMUNITY

Amos Goetz, teenage friend of Travis

Yoder, elderly neighbor of Travis

Keim family, neighbors of Travis

GREEK CHORUS

Apollo

Artemis

Black Road

I.

PRESENT & PAST

I recognized the

spot as soon as I arrived. I had followed her.

She was cautioned, my sister. For many swipes of the moon, she was repeatedly warned. Our father kept her under surveillance. But always she strayed from her assigned orbit. Always among all the sky creatures and their havoc, she was the panic.

To ask me if I was weary of the minding I was charged with is the equivalent of ducking under our round planet and inquiring of Atlas if the globe of the universe that he bore upon his shoulders was growing heavy. I fumed over my sister's antics. Sometimes she merely exasperated. Other times, much worse. Either way—for endless years—I was pulled from my own life and my own duties, which loomed far more important in their daily necessity than anything she might idly light upon during her irresponsible days. Each of her blank mornings offered the possibility of an amusing quotidian happenstance she could turn into an unceasing disaster.

In my head I practiced the speech I would give to Father about severing my obligation to her. I practiced my responses to his expected replies: that I was the only one swift enough to keep up with her, the only one who could battle her and survive—here he would sweep his arm to illuminate in the murky distance a swath of the Elysian Fields and the bloodied souls who had once challenged her and then with another gesture return them to their darkness. Yes, he would agree, my sister was temperamental and disobedient and haphazardly violent; she was immature, petulant, fraught with jealousies—but who didn't love these aspects of her? Hadn't we all, if we were to be completely honest, fallen in love with her idiosyncrasies and beauty? And I? I would barely register Father's usual arguments, still reeling as I was from the grisly sight of my boyhood hunting partner now a resident of the Elysian Fields; meanwhile, my father's quick amnesia about the tormented souls he had seconds earlier revealed to me was in keeping with the narcissism of his daughter. My father had moved on, undisturbed by the carnage both he and she had enkindled. They were too alike, father and daughter, for him ever to stop excusing her.

A warrior was all she ever wanted to be. At the same time she could be a mawkish fool who cried often and expected me to be at the ready with my sleeve. This, her wayward sentimentality, made her even more dangerous.

So here we were, my sister and I, traversing her old memories on a whim, which found us back at a locale the paltriness of which cannot be overstated. This was not Asia Minor or Sicily; this was not Sparta or Athens. This was not even Xi'an, not Arles or Salamanca. This was an insignificant town in the twenty-first-century New World, and the great battles now being fought came in the clash of airwaves as powerful and invisible as we once were, yet she behaved still as if the world proceeded as before, with spears and metal smithing, and as if history would continue to record us as heroes.

It had been over two hundred years since we had last visited this open hectare with its even sentry line of trees standing guard. Despite the addition of a nearby town, a recent occurrence from a century past, this particular spot remained as before. Every detail from that day 250 years earlier coursed back. How a colder clime had meant the rich odor of pine trees. How at once I felt invigorated and relaxed, how my muscles slackened and I dropped against a peeling beech and let my jaw hang loose. The light was different here, aslant and shadier, and I let it drift through me. On that first occasion I remember thinking perhaps it was not such a bad idea that my sister had chosen a journey across the sea. Our usual hunting grounds had been overtaken by cities and megaliths of stone and timber. Where once I had harvested salt and fishes from a lagoon, there was now the interference of Venice. In place of flowered hills to nap upon were the towns of Spello and Cortano. This land here in the New World, however, was uncorrupted by human trespass. The silence was vast. The virgin woods untroubled. Without the sun in high command, a comforting visit of melancholia fed the quiet inside me. I leaned deeper into the white trunk of the beech.

It was then, upon this first visit two centuries and more ago, that a mortal man burst through the treeline. Here was a land I had believed untouched. I had let my guard down, falling into slumber while my sister went off into the woods on a hunt. I burst awake. The mortal leaped over my crossed legs without breaking stride. He actually lifted his legs rather than stumble through me. He did not tense at the halo of bristling air the poets had correctly learned to recognize as a sign we were near. Their gift of divining had alarmed Aristotle enough to denounce all poets as misleaders of Truth. But the bards were right. This man who was leaping over me with a burning rifle in his hand and the smell of stag upon his skin was no poet, yet he turned in full stride and seemed to recognize me. He sent over a smile as one would to a little boy right before performing a trick.

And tricks did he perform.

On the dead run, he loaded his long rifle, then turned and aimed toward me from three hundred meters away. A gunshot cracked the stillness. The lead ball zipped into the woods over my head. Before I could wonder whether the lead ball was meant for me, a second mortal breaking through the treeline landed at my feet. The felled man's visage stared up at me. His leggings of fur smelled of fox.

What made the shooter's feat all the more supernatural was the strapping carcass of a human being flung over his shoulder, bouncing as he ran full tilt, as he poured gunpowder, as he turned and fired again.

The spirit of the dead man at my feet was tugging loose. Three hundred meters away in the clearing, this seeming demigod with the long rifle set down his carcass. No longer running and without burden to carry, he reloaded his rifle before the dead man's spirit could rise to join its brothers. Other fur-wearers were emerging from the trees. Another report of his rifle sent another spirit rising.

The tribe of chasers was now clearing the woods and howling at the scent of blood. The man loaded and shot twice more in quick succession before the long rifle must have balked in its burning. He shouldered the motionless body from the ground and took off running.

I followed.

From the treeline on the other side of the clearing, I stood and watched. The demigod loaded once more, his hands flicking against the sear of the rifle. After another pursuer was downed, he dropped the human carcass, pulled out his hunting knife, and prepared to meet them. While the vanguard sprang headlong, those in the rear stopped and positioned themselves, pulling arrows from their quivers.

One archer was quicker than all the others.

My blood quickened as his arrow was notched into sinew and drawn back. But the arrow sprang comically from the archer's bow, like a child's first attempt with his plaything. I was tempted to laugh at the ineptitude until I realized the man was clutching a shaft deep and golden in his chest.

My sister.

She had joined their midst, wide-eyed and laughing. She had revealed herself to them as we were warned never to do. The very man she was saving would now have to be sacrificed for beholding her.

She sent her glowing arrows into their hearts. To further her entertainment, she charged into the remaining throng with only her sword.

They swarmed upon her with fierce confidence. As quickly as the spin of a top they staggered in succession to the ground.

What have you done? I screamed at her.

I could hear my father's excuse-making in the background: Let Artemis be Artemis.

You wanted me to, she said. She sucked away a smile, but her face remained lit with happiness. I know you did.

We cannot interfere.

But he is worth saving.

He can be saved no longer, I told her.

We turned our gaze to the man dressed in hides. They were well-fitted hides that outlined an impressive form. A wife must have sewn the leathers for him. A woman who sustained the hearth. Even the passing image of his life away from me, away from us and our present moment together in this field, brought to me a visitation of disregard for his life. For an instant I understood my sister's constant jealousies and need to kill those whose daydreams were not singly populated with thoughts of her.

Carry it out, my sister said.

I could not bear to do it.

Show yourself to him first, she said.

I revealed myself to him, but it was for reasons other than to signal his execution. And when he saw me, the great Apollo, the god of sun, of music and poetry, the god of healing, light, and knowledge, he did not appear surprised. He had been seeing me all along.

Who is watching us? she asked. Here in the New World? Who is it that would care what we do in this meager place?

The man's gaze turned upon my sister, not in the wonder displayed by all her previous victims and then fear for what must come next. He watched her as he would watch a fawn, a beautiful sight but in the end a common one. More carefully and gently, he lifted the inert body from the ground and arranged it over his shoulder. The body, which had begun to stir, was clad as the shooter was, with a powder horn dangling from his belt. And big in the shoulder, as big as any human I had ever seen. This shooter, this mere man, had lofted him as if a half-sack of grain.

And who will know what we decide to do? asked my sister.

The man turned and disappeared into the woods, but not before sending me another of his smiles preceding another trick. I had found myself hopelessly enthralled. It was almost as if I had fallen in love.

It happened six months ago.
It happened on a February night.

In the morning

birdsong and a great uncertain heat.

Cinderblock steps, still cool from the night's rain.

Travis scratches his bare toes against the cinderblock. He has big feet, size 15 or sixteen depending on several factors, but they are not ugly feet. When you say huge feet you think ugly feet, but these are not ugly feet. They are smooth and muscular. He's proud of them. Beautiful actually. Beautiful feet. Will it be simply hot today or a deadly scorcher?

He has spent so much time this summer on the cinderblock steps, sitting and staring at his large feet, which each morning remind him how large life can be. The early sun comes to him as in a children's show, a happy lollipop rising to say hello. It welcomes everyone, even Travis, to its stage. And then every afternoon, almost on cue, the day cracks into something pointless. The sun dropping over the parking lot of Walmart just looks bad, the Speedway gas station looks bad, the For Sale sign in front of the mayor's office and Town Hall looks bad by definition—a mayor's place actually for sale looks bad because it is bad; the Taco Bell—well, Taco Bell doesn't look so bad—and night comes and the countryside goes black and the recent sounds he doesn't like commence.

He goes to bed lost.

He awakens.

Rises each summer morning feeling like a slob in a sweat pool, and he doesn't bother to dress before escaping the hot box of his grandmother's trailer to sit outside on the steps. Against the prickly cinderblock his feet scratch themselves back into happy. Large bare toes wiggle to life under the lollipop. The day looms large and cinematic again.

He is here again. Sitting here. He was just here the morning before.

But today is not like the other days. Today is a very large day. Not just the anniversary of his mother burning down their house, which is a large bad thing, but band practice begins today, which is a large good thing, a very cinematic event, and he'll see classmates for the first time all summer and then, if luck holds and the prime-time weather brings a scorcher, chances point to a tornado warning by sunset and if there is a tornado, he'll stand and greet it head-on, turning to take in his neighbor, the lovely Mrs. Keim, her panicked sprint to rope in the children. Mr. Keim nowhere to be seen. Somewhere with his goats. At the root cellar she will catch Travis's eye and thrash the air *Come come come!* And he will go. And that will be a major event. It is his seventeenth summer, after all, the summer when everything happens.

From the cinderblock steps Travis can watch Mrs. Keim's little boys. He rubs the hot sleep from his eyes. He wears colorless boxers, elastic gone, but the little boys next door are uniformly attired and already lugging sparkling milk canisters across the field to the barn—three boys tidily dressed in pants, suspenders, and tucked-in blue shirts. The milk canisters are as big as they are. Travis can detect stripes of a darker blue seeping from their suspenders. He didn't think little kids could sweat.

From inside the Keim barn comes a crazy barking. Mr. Keim sounds like an animal inside that barn. To paraphrase his English teacher Miss B, this kind of shouting displays a person going backward down the evolutionary chain. Mr. Keim has been losing it for months. Stepping inside the barn is one of his worst triggers. It sets him off, the way Travis, if he let himself, might be set off when he faces the aftermath of one of his mother's surprise visits. In Mr. Keim's case, maybe it's PTSD from losing his male goat when Jared Overholser spray-painted its balls orange. Mr. Keim has hated the world ever since. Travis has watched his abrupt oddities grow more abrupt, the way he turns away from any interaction even with his own kind.

Several months after the testicle spray-painting, another of Jared Overholser's pranks caused the car accident that has brought their town to this. It happened right in front of the Keim house. The accident came as a clap of ugly thunder, yet their house stayed dark. A car upended in a cornfield, the running footsteps, the heavy breathing. The Keim house: dark. Ambulances and lights strobing against the Keims' window. The house: dark. The police knocking on their door. The house: dark. The house: silent. Travis knows this because he stood on the wooden bridge. Saw some things he won't forget. Heard three guys in on the prank churning themselves into buzzsaws through bushes and knotty branches to hide under the tiny bridge where Travis stood above them, listening to their panic, their frightened whispers calling to Jared. He watched a car make its escape down the old Shawnee and Wyandot trail, sneaking along with only parking lights. The accident forced the town to take sides. Those who demanded punishment became the anti-Jareds, became a symbol of all things un-American because, after all, the high school football team would not stand a postseason chance without Jared Overholser as its quarterback.

So far Mr. Keim has not bothered to bring in another male goat, and everything smells so much better without a buck. It's been downright pleasant to sit outside and breathe deeply. Travis likes it out here, much more than the squalor of the tiny house in town he used to share with his mom, the neighbors keeping track of the human graffiti that scratched in and out, Travis thanking his lucky stars that his big size kept him safe from them. In one way his mom did him a favor by burning down the little house with the sinking roof. His grandmother let them move into this trailer on her property. Some guy was already living in it, free rent for clearing out his grandmother's two acres. The promised chore hadn't even got started but the guy avoided eviction by teaming up with his mom. Pretty soon his grandmother kicked them both out. For a while Travis could smell them in the woods somewhere, cooking meth. Sometimes he would hear her when she and that guy had a fight. And then they moved on.

This, too, shall pass. That's what Miss B likes to say. Meanwhile, do your homework.

The early-morning mugginess has already sent moisture down his neck and back, and he's sweating through his singlet. The heat has changed since July. This August heat is passionate, like the death of Romeo and Juliet, like him and Mrs. Keim saying good-bye forever because the bonfire of their love is too hot, too dangerous, and if Mr. Keim catches them he will rip out their throats with his teeth. For years afterward people will ask him for the story of his seventeenth summer except so far there is no story, this is how lies begin, small lies leading to big lies in service to the legend, the legend of that summer when Travis Hicks was seventeen. He doesn't want to turn into one of those people, he wants to get famous on the up-and-up, so things better hurry up, the summer is already almost ending, his final year of school will begin, and then that, too, will end. His seventeenth summer: gone. The book of his seventeenth summer: never written. The movie of his seventeenth summer: never made. The audio recording of his seventeenth summer: a long opera of human barking.

The three little boys dash out of the barn. They struggle to be quick, the canisters heavy with goat milk, their little blue shirts blackening with sweat. Now they will have to make it across the field without spilling the milk, but they are scared, Travis can feel it, and he can feel their inevitable clumsiness. It happens to him, too, when he gets scared. *One thing, Travis: Carry a drum in the marching band.* But sometimes he is so close to dropping it.

Something washes over Travis, the pressure of a hose being turned on inside his veins and arteries. It rocks his body. One day maybe he and Mr. Keim will come to blows.

Mr. Keim surely does not remember his seventeenth summer, which should be, as Miss B calls it, an object lesson to all seventeen-year-olds—carpe diem when you're seventeen or you might end up like this guy. Mr.

Keim probably remembers nothing beyond the crops he yanked out of the soil or the timber he axed. His kind of nostalgia is recalling the luster of a nice piece of wood forever hidden from view in its service as a stud. But that assessment of Mr. Keim is not totally fair. As Miss B told him, considerately escorting him to an empty hallway so no one would overhear, You're like a racist, Travis, except against adults. You mean I'm an adultist, he said, and Miss B said, No, I don't like the sound of that or the pictures it evokes for me—look, just because your parents trend toward asshole

(he had to set her straight that the passed-out guy in the photo was not his dad.

Who is his dad? No one knows, not even his mother),

you still have to give adults their due, Miss B said. Some adults, one out of three—start with that.

So he will give Mr. Keim his due. One, Mr. Keim is modest. Two, he is honest. Three, he works insanely hard but he only gets half credit because he works inhumanly hard and human beings by definition are not inhuman and shouldn't be insane or bark. Four, Mr. Keim is not egotistical. He does not think a movie should be made about the chores he did during his seventeenth summer

(Travis does, even keeps renaming his biopic)

and if Mr. Keim ever for a moment thought he was special enough for a movie he would have to drop to his knees and flagellate himself for the sin of vanity except Travis is probably getting his religions mixed up. Travis doesn't feel vain about imagining his own biopic but perhaps something is wrong with him that he doesn't notice any sting of vanity. In the town library where he conducts his business, he has already searched the ten characteristics of a sociopath, then toxic narcissist. No, he is neither of these people.

It's called being a normal seventeen-year-old, Miss B reassured him.

Maybe he tells her too many things, Miss B, that is. Miss B is older than his mother who is too young to be a responsible mom but looks older than Miss B and is way more immature. Way more immature than even snare drummer Kyle Jenkins who is so immature but good for a laugh. Travis's mother is not good for a laugh.

So a voiceover will start out the biopic. The camera will fly down like a hawk and follow Travis's gaze, which at this moment rests upon the three little boys delivering their canisters of splashing milk to the kitchen. Setting the scene. The lovely Mrs. Keim grabs the canisters one by one as savage roars erupt, a frightening man is tired of waiting! and she pushes her little boys back toward the barn. A push, a definite push, but a comforting push—get there quick and he won't be mad. I promise, he won't be mad, he won't be mad, just run a little bit faster. Closeup: her face, torn with emotion, strands of hair pulled loose. Cut to Travis staring at the camera. Voiceover: *The summer I turned seventeen, I saved a woman from a madman. I didn't save her because she was beautiful. I saved her because it was the right thing to do.*

Travis puts on his sneakers and light sweats, grabs the stainless steel thermos belonging to the Yoders, plucks a couple of dollars from the plastic Easter egg hidden inside the cinderblock, and scrapes down the path.

THE DOLLAR BILLS are damp. Last night's rain must have leaked into the plastic seams of the Easter egg. Travis tucks the thermos under his arm and flaps the bills in the air. A wind drift catches the dollar bills and off they fly as hawks. High in the air, green wings deliver the camera's aerial view:

Ribbons of tar blow freely from the insignificant town of Kattoga, Ohio, into green and velvet and lime squares of countryside.

Flat and low goes this landscape, no bell tower rising out of the flatness, no concrete parcels of a community college.

A few silos breaking up the rooftops.

A monster grain elevator beside the train tracks.

The train tracks. A favorite spot for people like his mom.

Along one of the black ribbons the camera drone catches a speedily moving dot: car. Then a jerky quickish dot: horse and buggy. And a slow dot: the drone follows it down. It's him, Travis Hicks, trudging down the Shawnee-Wyandot trail, a crumbling one-lane road to the Yoders'. Voiceover: *That summer, before everything changed, this was my daily routine, to buy milk and cheese and eggs from Yoder. Little did I know that my peaceful routine would be interrupted so violently and I would be called upon to save an entire town.*

Once over the small wooden bridge he can discern in the haze the powerful odor that rises from Yoder's fields. Their community telephone shack sits technically in Yoder's yard but in the far corner, as far from Yoder's barns and fields as possible, but the telephone shack still smells like a stable. Beyond that a hand-lettered sign is staked in the yard: EGGS NUTS CANDY BAKED GOOD QUILTS. The Yoders are the only ones of their kind who advertise, which is funny since their farm smells the worst. A perfect example of Irony —actually, the very example of Irony he used in Miss B's English class. In fact every example he used had to do with Yoder's manure—Pathetic Fallacy, Oxymoron, it was so easy to do with shit as the subject, and he looked forward to Miss B taking him back out to the hallway to explore his current wave of inappropriate feelings expressed inappropriately. Instead of telling him he was on the precipice of spiraling backward down the evolutionary chain, all she said was You're coasting, Travis. She paused. And then she said, But's that's okay, you deserve to coast for a while, let's say three weeks.

It was one of her less colorful comments, disappointing that way, not even doctored up with a *Why dost thou squinty at me?* and he assumed that she assumed like everyone else assumed that those mindfuck couple of months were due to the newspaper and internet and TV photo of his mother unconscious in a car in a fentanyl stupor. She looked dead but she wasn't dead, which allowed it to be hilarious. Nationwide it went, alive with funny tweets and GIFs. He wanted to say to Miss B, You are wrongly assuming it has to do with that photo, but the wrong assumption was the right assumption. Humiliating that his emotional makeup owned no complexity, that this simple explanation explained so simply the shitty pain in his being. Miss B didn't answer him directly. She seemed tired that day and her eyes were rimmed with a recent cry. He had a pretty good idea what that was about, given the news coming out of the trial that morning and how so many teachers and students had bypassed school legally or illegally to be there as character witnesses for star quarterback Jared Overholser and the tragedy he didn't mean to cause with a fake deer he accidentally planted in the middle of a dark country road after accidentally stealing it and accidentally painting it with obscenities. Miss B probably thought not mentioning the trial spared Travis since he had enough to deal with via the photo of his unconscious mother entertaining however briefly an ENTIRE NATION, but the accident already did involve him, if only she knew how much it did. If only she had asked him, right then.

No one is about at the Yoder farm. The house feels abandoned. The black buggies are here, untethered, their black traces bowed to the ground in doleful prayer. The laundry hangs on long lines. All of it is blue or gray or white. The look of it a depressing work of art from another century. A rogue sadness slides past, thankfully on a journey to somewhere else this time. Not meant for him. Not today with the crazy crazy crazy excitement ahead. Travis takes a deep breath. He looks down at his feet, these feet that will soon stand upon newly laid spongy thick blacktop, that will soon march on Cougar paw prints freshly painted in red and white. Today the day's promises are not an illusion. The afternoon looms large. The afternoon will be filled with 103 band members, plus Mr. Hurd and Miss Stacy and their assistants, plus the spirit squad, plus the cheerleaders, plus Kyle Jenkins, who always makes him laugh, and Kyle's sister Kassadee, who has renamed herself Elsa, who is the school's Letterette proudly holding aloft a giant K, plus the snackbar parents. Plus Hannah Kirkpatrick. Between all that and the football team starting its two-a-days, almost the whole school of 675 students will be involved. Anyone not there will feel left out, so even students not tasked with equipment, water, electrolyte powder, school newspaper, errands, mimeographing, photocopying, or schedule management will make sure to be there—there's something for everyone so everyone can be there. And onlookers. And retirees in their lawn chairs. And parents with little kids who will dream of getting to do this when they're in high school. Everyone will be there and it will be a large, amazing time. And Travis's role in this will be indispensable. The little kids will shout for joy each time he hands over the mallet and lets them take a whack on his drum. One thud bass in the whole band. One. The heaviest musical instrument given to the biggest man.

Yoder steps out of the feeding pen, sees Travis, ducks back inside. Travis walks up to the barn and waits until the old man has put together Travis's usual order: eggs and butter and yesterday's fresh farmer cheese. Yoder has thrown in four ears of corn and three ripe tomatoes as well. Travis returns an empty thermos and Yoder hands him another one readied with raw milk, cow milk, not the goat stuff. It's technically illegal to sell unpasteurized milk but Yoder does it anyway to certain customers and Travis stays healthy with all the undestroyed enzymes, the micro-organisms that sprout into sci-fi creatures under the microscope. He made slides of the bacteria in last year's biology class and labeled them creatively with monster names. Got a B+. Should have scored an A but he is Travis Hicks after all and teachers except for Miss B don't believe he can come up with such stuff on his own—as if Mr. Keim is his secret weapon cheat sheet. So far he's had three more years of schooling than Mr. Keim ever had and would ever want to have, three years beyond what is necessary according to Mr. Keim, three years when it is actually doing more harm than good according to Mr. Keim, and some mornings Travis leaves for school with Mr. Keim's disdainful shake of the head in his rearview mirror. Travis should go to college if only to cause Mr. Keim's fatal heart attack from disdain so that life with the young widow can take off like a bonfire and the three little boys will swing joyfully from the monkey bars of his strong big body and the mallet will whack the thud bass and not their little bodies.

Yoder strips the dollar bills from Travis's fingers without saying a word. He writes for a length of time in a ledger. He uses a clumsy-looking pencil also from another century, too stocky and strong for the fragile labor of script—it could almost be used as a pole for the laundry line. The farm is so quiet. The farm has no idea the excitement that is going to tear this town apart come afternoon. He wants to ask Yoder, Won't you be lonely hearing all the fun in the distance? But Yoder won't hear it because he is half deaf and too old to care and he is Amish and it's not his world and he doesn't care.

Travis is never sure how much he owes because Yoder never says, but he always seems to write up an elaborate accounting in his private book. He wonders if the ears of corn and tomatoes are a gift. He didn't order them. Does he have to pay for something he didn't order? And how much would it cost if he did have to pay? He doesn't want to ask because then it will seem as if he is expecting to pay but the truth is he doesn't want to pay for something he didn't order—and he also knows that corn at Walmart is 20 cents an ear right now. And tomatoes—tomatoes, wow, tomatoes, everywhere all at once, you can't give them away.

Travis thanks a silent Yoder and turns to leave. Someday he'd like to read the old man's ledger.

When out-of-towners pull up in their cars, intrigued by a place that sells quilts with its eggs and licorice, Travis has watched the disconcerting way Yoder gives inaudible replies and strands visitors while he disappears into a reeking barn to retrieve items they have asked for and items they haven't asked for that he intends for them to buy anyway. The customers are left sniffing the bad-smelling farm and then leaving too quickly. Yes, Travis knows that all the weirdness might make for an interesting cultural experience, but still, regular people in general don't like bad smells while they are buying food. Travis feels that he has expertise in how the people outside Yoder's world evaluate a shopping experience and maybe he could offer these insights to Yoder as a type of bartering. Yoder sounds a lot like Yoda and even though Yoder would never ever ever in this life watch *Star Wars* without having to fall on his knees and self-flagellate in a mash-up of religions, the point is that the queer disconcerting menacing and cinematic wisdom that envelops the

Star Wars creature Yoda, who is also cute and lovable, envelopes the creature Yoder. Yoder's bent figure is queer and disconcerting—and lovable on certain days. The way the haze rises from his field is cinematic. The barn he disappears into is a dark place of wisdom and fear.

When Travis lifts his head from these thoughts, he discovers that his designer sneaker treads have notched a hypotenuse straight through Yoder's garden. Travis stands in the very middle of the garden plot, stranded in no-man's-land. He spins uselessly, searching for a way out that won't further the destruction. He will take very large steps in order to halve the damage he is about to do. He closes his eyes as marigolds are sponged down, snap peas cracked, and coxcombs breached. The coxcombs create a line of defense to repel the deer so now the deer will probably come tonight and eat up the whole garden and it will be his fault but the Yoders won't say anything to him, they won't blame him, they won't say a word. He fluffs up the velvety posies, but the size sixteen treads have planted their geometric damage.

Hey Travis!

He takes off running.

Hey Travis, good luck at band practice today!

It's the good voice chasing him.

Hey Travis, don't know what we'd do without someone big and strong as you hoisting that drum!

He runs all the way to the small and useless wooden bridge. Below is a stream and culvert pipe and snarls of brush and weed trees. Through this stream once ran the Shawnees. Through these waters, the Wyandots.

Hey Travis Travis great to see you! Travis Travis you're the man! How much does that drum weigh! I can't even lift it!

"Oh fuck oh fuck oh fuck!"

"Are you there?"

The bad whispers.

Travis's chest thumps.

"Jared Jared oh fuck man"—

The voice is so scared. The voice is so clear.

Travis staggers back. Backing toward his trailer and his grandmother's small plot of land bought outright—bought outright, the deed's in her name, she won't ever hand it over to her daughter. "Jared Jared Jared JARED!

help me!

come on man HELP!"

This is his land and he's safe here. Get to his land and he is safe.

A horse clops from behind, a buggy overtakes him.

The driver, one of the Hochstetler boys, lifts a hand in greeting, indifferent to the weirdness of Travis's backward stepping.

The haze rises over the Yoder farm, not hearing, not caring.

A STRAND OF MUD edges the cinderblock rising to this trailer. It wasn't there before.

She's been here. And she has tracked in mud.

Travis dashes inside to the sink. The water glasses arranged on the dish rack to ward off curiosity haven't been upended. He lifts the rubber mat they dry upon. Twenties and tens still there. Huge sigh of relief.

But the refrigerator. It's been foraged. The four five-dollar bills inside the clipped frozen peas bag have been taken. He's upset to lose the twenty dollars, but they're his decoy. She would never believe he's got more than twenty dollars. He goes outside and checks the plastic Easter egg inside the cinderblock: still there, the chump change inside another decoy if it comes to that. Leaning down to the Easter egg, he smells it. The strand of scraped mud is not mud at all. She has stepped in the shit of her new fucking dog and brought it here as a gift. Like a new fucking dog is going to save her from her problems and lick her awake from an overdose. She has scraped off her shoes on his cinderblock. Her and her—a violent kick against the cinderblock to halt the nearly endless rush of words that fly out of his mouth *don't be like Mr. Keim!* He stomps to his car, kicks the tire. The words still tumble. Stomps back to the trailer, kicks it *don't be like Mr. Keim!* One more kick. A deep breath *don't be like him.*

He can't even believe her dog has enough inside its body to make any kind of pile. He can't believe the dog isn't dead from starvation. How can she provide it with food when she can't even feed her own fucking self? She can't possibly feed it, at least not enough, because it is a big dog, she needs a big one to protect her while she's passed out.

That's the lesson she learned from getting her passed-out fentanyl photo on web sites NATIONWIDE: it was a wake-up call to get a dog.

Inside he grabs a hunk of paper towel. His fists pound the sink. That is his cinderblock, that is his special place to sit. There's practically nothing left in the trailer. Now she has to come steal his money and shit on his cinderblock. She has to literally shit on his cinderblock. And if she thought his cinderblock was worth more than a dime, good-bye cinderblock. Which means he can't have a lawn chair worth more than a dime, he can't have a hammock, he can't have a grill, he can't have a picnic table. All of which will get stolen. All of which have been stolen. All he can have is a cinderblock. All he asks is for his cinderblock to stay clean so he can sit there and be happy.

A loud knock on the door. Travis jerks *don't be Mr. Keim*. Another knock and the flimsy door flies open *don't be Mr. Keim* and shoots against the wall. Travis holds in his screams of rage but he might strangle her.

The sun backlights her into the silhouette of a gunslinger.

He might rush her and push her backward down the cinderblock stairs. Her neck might break.

Coach McManus takes a step inside.

Travis is huffing, he's so out of breath. He has never met Coach McManus, officially that is. Everyone knows who he is of course. He runs the school. He is more important than the principal. He basically runs the town as well; he's more important than the mayor who is for sale anyway.

The Coach McManus in his doorway.

Coach McManus wears a fresh polo shirt, orange and ironed. He wears khakis that don't look like the boxy khakis Travis sees on other men.

These khakis look good and the way the polo shirt is tucked into his pants looks good. The polo shirt is the real deal with the Ralph Lauren horseman Travis prefers to think of as a Wyandot warrior. That means something. His hair is combed straight back. His tan has a glow to it.

Travis can't speak. Coach McManus is looking at him.

Sometimes Coach McManus stands in the school lunchroom, thumbs tucked into the belt of his khakis on either side of his nattily covered belly button. He poses motionless while the lunchroom carries on its chaos.

Travis says not a word to the silence between them. He is still huffing, almost hyperventilating.

Catch you at a bad time? Coach McManus asks. His eyes dart to the weights on the floor, two fifty-five-pound dumbbells and a loaded barbell, the only things too heavy for her to cart away.

My boys are still sleeping and you're pumping iron.

A ready excuse for the huffing and sweating. Travis settles.

Coach McManus steps to the sink, fingers the eggs and butter and cheese, lifts the thermos closer to his eyes, sets it down, fingers the ears of corn and the tomatoes. His back remains to Travis. He peers out the little almost plastic kitchen window.

Travis Hicks, the coach says.

Yes, sir. His first words aren't too bad to get out. Yes sirs and no sirs have gotten him over many a nervous hump to the tranquil meadow on the other side.

Hello, Travis.

Hello, sir.

Do you know who I am?

Yes, sir. You're Coach McManus. And now Travis has forgotten about his mother and sees only tranquil ironed orange before him. He has reached the meadow. And the stitched insignia on Coach's shirt is a horse with its rider swinging a war club. He will look up the prices later.

And then, because the coach hasn't acknowledged his identity, Travis bravely adds, Of the Kattoga High School football team, and the coach laughs.

The coach picks up the eggs and cheese. Already out farming today? He motions next door to the Keim farm.

I go to Yoder's farm.

Which is?

Up the Wyandot trail.

Coach lets out a whistle. The Wyandot trail. You keep impressing me, Travis.

The sweat drips down Travis's back. He picks up the fifty-five-pound dumbbells and arranges them against the wall.

Don't get along with your neighbor? The coach stands at the sink with his back to Travis. He stares out the blurry kitchen pane; his dirtied view is of land on the opposite side of the Keims'. If you can call it land. Tall weeds climb into ugly trees vined with daily metastasizing poison ivy. The side that his grandmother owns and will deed to him. It goes on for another couple of lesioned acres. The weeds could have been chopped with the parang machete he bought on the internet for just that purpose but the parang machete with its ethnic design went missing two days later and with it his plans for a driveway clearing. He was left to park on the impoverished grass in front of the trailer and one thing about impoverished grass, it makes a pretty good driveway.

Travis says, The neighbor has goats, sir. Everything tastes like goats.

Coach McManus laughs again. I hear you, he says. Country living, he says. Took me a couple of years to get used to it. He opens the carton of eggs, different sizes and different colors with even a big blue one and a small speckled one and holds it out to Travis. Check this out. How many chickens did it take to do this?

Travis tries to smile.

Look at this teamwork, all these different sizes and colors to make a unified dozen.

Travis tries to hold a smile that isn't there in the first place. The awareness of the creepy expression on his face is unbearable. The coach returns the eggs to the refrigerator. He lingers, fingering the empty refrigerator shelves. Maybe cooling himself. The open fridge functions as the only air conditioning in the trailer. Travis has heard the coach Botoxes his armpits so that no one ever sees him sweat. His own underarms have drained to his rib cage.

Travis could fill the silence by inviting him to sit down, but aside from the floor there is nowhere to sit. The orange polo shirt looks dry-cleaned almost, strange in some way Travis can't put his finger on. It's neatly tucked into those pants that look like khakis but fit better. Maybe it's the strong but slim body that make the pants look good, or maybe it's fashion. Fashion for himself is the next thing on Travis's list. But right now selling the Supreme clothing line is working so well for him, bland grey hoodies for hundreds of dollars in profit. No reason to expand just yet.

Travis edges toward the door in case the coach would like to step outside where it's cooler, but Coach McManus stays put.

What are you, Travis, about six foot five?

Yes, sir.

The coach smiles. I like you, Travis. You're my kind of guy. Most guys, they'd be so quick to correct me, tell me, No, sir! I'm six foot six!

Travis offers a shrug, the only thing he can think to do. Because he is not attempting to put another expression on his face.

Six foot seven or eight, I'd say.

Travis nods.

The coach chuckles again, a kind of secret to himself. He looks around, goes back to the sink. Is this where you live full-time? He fusses with the three water glasses in the dish rack. Mom and Dad here, too?

Here it comes, another joke about the overdose photo. What will it be this time, the way her mouth hung open, the sores on her face, the pulled-up shirt, the belly that flapped like a pancake over stretch shorts—or all of the above—not to mention the witchcraft hair or the best part of all, everyone's favorite, how she topped off her look with librarian eyeglasses? Professor O'Pioid, one of the posts called her.

Fashion tips for your job interview, said another tweet. It was pretty endless, the jokes that came out of that.

Six foot eight?

Travis nods.

Everything all right, Travis? The coach is staring at him.

Yes, it's true what they say about him: weird blue eyes that flash sparks. People say he hypnotizes you. Somewhere in the brain buzzing, Coach McManus asks his favorite course in school and the question arrives at his ears like an electrical underwater hypnotic murmur. And sinister, too. *What's your favorite course, Travis?* Travis says blue before his brain can correct him. English, he amends.

Blue is your favorite class? Or English?

Score one to the coach because a coach by definition would keep score.

I heard you play in the marching band, Coach McManus says.

Yes, sir.

I don't see your instrument here. The coach checks the kitchen again, as if it might be soaking in the sink.

I play the thud bass.

Which means what exactly?

It's that great big one. The big huge one.

The great big one. The big huge one. You mean drum? You play the drum? Coach McManus leans back to stick out his stomach, then beats his stomach. That one?

I'm the only one can lift it.

The coach gives a conspiratorial nod toward the dumbbells. That's a nice gig, he says. You never need to practice. Now the coach is just running up the score and Travis, though the foregone loser, is starting to gain optic points through the other's poor sportsmanship.

When Coach McManus moves to the curio in the living room and peers inside, Travis just wants him to go ahead and say it. Maybe he'll help him out. Yes, the shelves are empty because my mom is a drug addict. The cut-glass salt and pepper shakers paid for one overdose and my grandmother's sugar and cream sets paid for another and the

Hummel figurines belonging to my great-grandmother propelled her nationwide.

That's not a challenge, Coach McManus says.

True, stealing from a dead great-grandmother isn't much of a challenge, but Travis rewinds to the coach's last real remark, playing the drum and what an easy gig that is, something you can do without practicing.

You seem like the kind of guy who needs a challenge, the coach says. Who *likes* to challenge himself. Already up, already lifting weights, already walking down the road to the Yoders'.

What? Travis says.

Word has it the coach is someone trained in psychoanalysis. He likes to deduce and show off his deductions. The coach's eyes are inspecting the small, empty living room. He is stepping along the rectangle indented in the carpet, following it like a rope walker. He is deducing that a coffee table used to squat there.

During the lengthy deducing silence, another of Miss B's literary terms pops into his head: Foreshadowing. Yoder's manure fields were doing the work of Foreshadowing. Foreshadowing of the dog shit he'd find on his cinder block, which Foreshadowed the coach arriving at his door and stepping upon the cinderblock. Which means the coach has stepped in the shit and tracked it into his trailer.

Now the coach is treading all over the living room carpet. In a panic Travis checks for morsels of doo the coach might be depositing with every step, which has been Foreshadowed by Travis's own fouling steps through the Yoders' garden. He deserves it, he guesses. Karma.

Please please please don't take another step! he wants to scream at the coach.

The coach raises his head from the indentations where furniture once lived and gives him the famous stare. Travis knows that the coach knows what he is thinking. The coach knows exactly. He can spot Travis's panic, smell it. One more second and Travis will begin to shake.

Let's step outside, the coach says.

The front door still gapes wide open and as the coach steps through the doorway, Travis goes through several stages of joy. First, joyful relief at seeing that the dog poop remains a ruler-sharp trim on his cinderblock. The coach missed it coming in. Second, joyful satisfaction at seeing that the coach doesn't miss it going out; his canvas boat shoes take a satisfying plop. Third, future joy at imagining those shoes depositing dog poop on the logo car mat and brake pedal and accelerator of the convertible Mercedes parked next to Travis's thirteen-year-old Monte Carlo. The coach will need to use a toothbrush to clean off the Mercedes brake pedal. By the time he discovers it, he'll have no idea it came from Travis's.

They walk toward the parked cars. The Mercedes's tan finish shines against the Monte Carlo, which has no finish at all, just sodden primer. There is no shine to it, only a corroded debt-free dullness. At least it is paid for. Travis owes no money to anyone. And the coach? What does he pay each month for his Mercedes? He's obviously proud of it, the way he perches himself halfway atop the glowing driver's door because that's the kind of thing you can do when the top is down on your convertible. In fact that's probably why he bought a convertible. He can perch there and spread his groin, the glowing car and the glowing man, and pretend he is not groin-shoving $50,000 in Travis's face while ringing up touchdown after touchdown until he runs up the score too much and the glow becomes an unsportsmanlike glare and Travis, who would otherwise be shaking in fear of this man, is coming out a winner on the other side. He is a debt-free seventeen-year-old with his own car and no dog poop on his shoe. Three things the coach cannot claim.

The coach takes a big, satisfied breath and looks out upon the landscape. What do you like to do, Travis? I mean, besides the drum and English class? For fun, self-improvement?

The coach's hair glints yellow in the sunlight. He combs it straight back with gel. The gel darkens it and inside the dark trailer the hair looked brown. Now it's blond. Ghostly.

I like to draw some, Travis finally says.

The coach's blue eyes spark into lasers. This is probably something the coach practices in front of a mirror to get true answers when he asks his players stuff like *Were you drinking? Were you doing to that girl what they said you were doing?*

If Travis had such eyes, he would be practicing all the time.

You said you like to draw? Some?

Yes, sir.

Drawing, the coach repeats. *Like art.* He throws his head back and ruminates on the sky.

Coach McManus is one of those types, Travis can tell. Or else he's picked up on it and is faking it. For that's the only way of looking at things here. Men are this way or they aren't real men, women are this way or they aren't real women—that kind of thing. Yet the coach, even though his muscles are tight, isn't built rugged and he isn't hairy, even his forearms, and he doesn't have a military crewcut. He doesn't look the type. He looks kind of like a cinematographer. Once the thought crosses Travis's mind, he can't purge it despite not having a clue what a cinematographer looks like, even though he will be needing one at some point in his future. He knows this much though: the coach looks kind of artsy, kind of not like anything of this town. Coach McManus wouldn't pass for anything descended from these parts. He's from the outside, from Naziland and the pure races, and when he came to the small town of Kattoga he came to rule and everyone bowed down, the principal, the mayor, the hunters in camo. He had the blue sparks for eyes and it was rumored he had two master's degrees. He drove his expensive car as if he enjoyed outlandish bonuses whenever the high school team made the playoffs.

The coach surveys the landscape again. Mr. Keim is pulling the goats out into the field. The three stairsteps of boys are heading into the barn—with buckets this time.

Good work ethic.

Travis nods.

You friends with them?

They don't really want to be friends.

That other one, where you get your food. Yoder. Friends?

Yeah. He's eighty so we don't hang out much.

The coach stares hard at the Keim farm. He doesn't move his eyes from the goats when he says, Ever thought about playing for us, Travis?

Travis looks down, ashamed, and grateful the coach's eyes don't stray his way and afraid that if Coach does fix his gaze upon him, the laser look can make him do anything. He didn't get this offer his freshman year when he was seven inches shorter. Sophomore year his foot was in a growth-spurt cast, junior year his mother burned down the house. It's clear skies heading into senior year, but he did not expect this offer. It doesn't make sense, yet it does make sense, it makes perfect sense. The vaunted left tackle has graduated and gone to Ohio State, the new left tackle is Spalding Burker, a nice enough guy but a slow fat mess, everyone knows this but only the old guys at McDonald's will say it—every morning, they dissect the situation as if they have their own sports channel. The quarterback will need extra help this year, and if you want a big wall of protection around your quarterback, you've got to start with a big wall. Travis has seen the big men on the team and he's seen a whole lot of flesh and not too much muscle. He offers something the other linemen don't: several more inches and shoulders wider than a butt.

How far past three hundred do you push the needle?

About thirty, Travis says.

The team could use you, Travis. You could be a star. The coach pauses, glances about Travis's trailer, the weed trees, the poison ivy that has grown a couple inches during this conversation, the rotted-bark hue of his Monte Carlo. We're like family, you know, our team. All kinds of sizes, shapes, but we all fit into the same egg carton—colors, too— you know Winston Carter, don't you? We look out for each other. You wouldn't just make friends, you'd make brothers. You'd learn about loyalty. The rest of the school, you'd be a role model.

Be popular, the coach means, the way that kids like Travis are never meant to be. Be popular, be nominated for Homecoming King, be at the Taco Bell doing homework with his buddies, be the talk of McDonald's morning sports talk—all he would have to do is protect the quarterback.

Nobody has actually said the word *quarterback*, especially here at this spot, here where the accident happened, but Travis knows it and with it comes something else he knows: there is nothing he will ever do, ever, to protect Jared Overholser.

Travis forces down the heavy ragged breaths that would give him away. Clumsiness is seeping into his muscles. He dares not move. The lollipop sun braves higher in the sky. Travis can't see and he has no sunglasses. Lovely Mrs. Keim, the little boys wrestling the milk canisters, Yoder's farm, four ears of corn and three tomatoes—it all feels so long ago. The only thing before him is cinderblock.

"We'll see you this afternoon," the coach says, then hops into his convertible.

Five boys stole a deer decoy.

Judge Merle Herrick

read out loud the following on an April day:

Broken neck, crushed leg, splintered arm, four months in hospitals, twelve surgeries on leg, two surgeries on arm, steel plate in right forearm, steel pins in leg, skin grafts, medical bills $450,000.

He set down that sheet of paper, picked up another one, and read,

Collapsed lung, fractured skull, eight broken ribs, bruised heart, bruised brain, seven-day coma, five weeks in nursing home, memory loss, brain damage, medical bills $275,000.

Judge Herrick set down that sheet of paper. He looked out upon the packed courtroom. He said,

The court does not dispute that injuries took place. However, the court must call into doubt these hearsay accounts of injuries that have reached this desk without substantiation by official medical reports. Further, the assertion of four months in hospitals is an impossible assertion that stretches beyond the nine weeks that have passed since the accident occurred in late February. If such official reports exist that can corroborate this science fiction decoding of time, this court is not in possession of them. Nor is the court in possession of any statements from doctors or hospitals that would substantiate the sums of money involved. The lifelong consequences, if any, of these injuries fall under the category of speculation since one's life must be extenuated before lifelong consequences can be known.

Further, it has come to the court's attention that possible medical malfeasance at the site of the accident, on the part of the doctor or paramedics, or both, directly led to the exacerbation of injuries. So now, good people, we have uncertainty, and what amounts to an unprovable debate about the heat of the original flames and the dangerous heat of the flames enhanced by fuel. Burns caused by enhanced flames cannot be blamed on original flames or held liable thereof.

Judge Merle Herrick brought down his gavel and exited before the bailiff Brenda Mansfield could call All Rise.

The boys who crashed wore thin jackets.

Not Even The

dried mud of a single footprint spoils the road. The yearly asphalt was laid the beginning of August and a week later the school mascot was applied with stencils and bold utility paints. Cougar paw prints stealth along the jungle floor of fresh black tar. From the air it's a banner of giant red-and-white flowers.

Untouched. Police tape all around to keep it untouched.

The surface remains pristine partly thanks to the optional nature of the road's usefulness. It dead-ends into high cornfields where everyone knows are hidden cannabis plants. Its only destination traffic is to the high school; the police tape warns the cars to circle back to the parking lot so that Kattoga High can welcome the football season with the flawless brilliance of its frontage. All the alpha delinquents who would otherwise be quick to deface this fresh bouquet of school pride are themselves football players. Any beta vandals would have to answer to the football players. And so it remains: Cougar Country. Untouched. Proud.

It is the marching band director who takes the first tentative steps upon the fresh macadam. His name is Mr. Hurd and the slight curve in his back is from height and thinness. He lifts a shoe and checks the sole for cleanliness, swipes his hands clean—long white hands of a past-century undertaker. He retreats to the school sidewalk to park his shoes. Reenters the road in socks. How stupid he feels for these emotions overcoming him, the Gregorian chants he could swear he hears. It's early, the sun half risen. Out in the emerald cornfield floats a puff blanket of fog and chaff. When he steps upon the painted spongy blacktop, he does so as a religious acolyte entering a cathedral. His own smallness in the world clutches at him. He is thirty-seven years old. His own time and the way it ticks away is of such importance to him and of no concern at all to the world. He will come and go. Will anyone notice? Don't answer that, a girl he used to date liked to say. He didn't so much date her as speed date her. Their relationship lasted four minutes, nevertheless, the length of a memorable song that could keep replaying for years. Or like "Brown-Eyed Girl"—for decades! always on the radio as if it were yesterday. The next girl he speed dated didn't like music, not even the radio.

He is glad no one is here to watch him. They would be able to read his nerves, though he stands rock steady, just as he can read the nerves of his marching band. In a line of cadencing flutes he can detect in the unerring flair of fingers the one mistake about to happen. This is not something he can explain on dating sites, or why it matters,

why is sound so important to the ear? because the ear reacts to sound because the cochlea vibrates

or why insomnia has dogged him all summer, even to Vienna and the open-air operas. No one would believe that Beethoven spoke to him there, by his famous statue in Stadtpark. He revealed himself to Mr. Hurd, specifically addressing the rumors of a marching band protest. Upon hearing Ludwig, Mr. Hurd flopped back upon the lawn where he could no longer stay balanced because of the vibrations so strongly disrupting his inner ear and molars

Beethoven found a way to hear music through his jawbone by attaching a rod to his piano and clenching it in his teeth

as the answer was given to him and the answer was music. Music came home with him and music will not bow to the town's rupture no matter how loud. That night in Stadtpark sparked a frenzy of creativity. On the lawn during intermission he began his adaptation of "Midnight Train to Georgia" in the notebook he's become famous for among the students.

Mr. Hurd's burnt-orange Moleskine notebook: he likes that they have adopted this as his signature. Even while engaged in writing down his ideas, he imagined recounting this very moment to his students, drinking in the feigned boos (*Hurrrrrd*) when he mentions the Moleskine notebook. Upon return from the inspirations of Vienna, he and Miss Stacy brainstormed the song's drill formations on an iPad. The football team might get all the attention, but its stardom or its infamy will last a season and move on. Music: forever.

The Door On

the second floor of the courthouse says "Common Pleas Court Juvenile Division." On the wall is a painting of a young boy fishing. He is red-haired and freckled, his hand-me-down jeans baggy and rolled to his calves. He stands on the dock with a fishing pole while a fatherly figure leans down to help. Along the framing is written *One hundred years from now it won't matter what my bank account was, what type of house I lived in, or the kind of car I drove, but the world may be different because I was important in the life of a child.*

Judge Merle Herrick claimed authorship but was later called out as a plagiarist. Now the name Forest Witcraft is typewritten on an office address label and taped to the frame.

On the third floor the old courthouse has a drop for hanging prisoners. A wooden railing painted gold protects the spot.

Miss B waits here.

She stays sequestered from what she presumes will be a big, perhaps unruly crowd downstairs, not quite as big and unruly as in April since those three defendants were football players and the town was more invested. That's the word she prefers to use, "invested." She's trying hard to see everyone's point of view. The fourth and fifth boys don't play football and have been languishing in juvie since April and now it's August already—"already" for everyone not stuck in juvie, for whom summer vacation has passed too quickly. This kid today, Tyler is his name, he's a kid she barely remembers from study hall, which he infrequently attended for a couple of months, January, February, part of March, then disappeared. Once the writing on the wall became clear, that he would be taking the rap for the football players, he stayed at home to get in as much Xbox as possible before juvie began.

She slips off her high heels. They are blunt and short; still, they hurt. Her hosed feet slide on the marble and soak in its coolness. Around the corner glides a noiseless buffer. A young woman from the Plain community steers the machine in soft circles. She pauses, taking in Miss B with a sideways glance. Miss B's expression of greeting dies midway. The girl shows no sign of recognizing her.

She picks up her shoes and slides to the stairway. Cocks an ear. A little shuffling downstairs. Not much else. Her toes feel the depressions in the marble made by the feet that have passed before her. Tender gullies of humanity have been scoured into this hard, nearly eternal material. The noiseless buffer behind her unearths their silences. The souls call to her: two men from a hundred years ago standing right here, in topcoats, conferring with one another. There's a woman stepping alone, seeking the right office. She's very sad. Happy, though, are the young man and woman who work as a boilermaker and laundress as they arrive for their marriage license. Agrarian citizens file in like serfs, clothed in work overhauls. As soon as their business at the tax assessor's office is over, they will return to the fields.

Her students would listen to her reverie as if she were the smartest person on earth. They would ask her what a boilermaker is. A smart aleck would call out that it's a drink. They would ask her why the woman was sad (just widowed at age twenty-nine, searching for the probate office). They would want to hear most about the drop for executing prisoners. They would laugh if she told them that back then chewing gum and talking back to your teachers were hangable offenses.

She looks again at the Amish girl, who won't acknowledge her. Too young, too shy. Miss B tells herself, *Think nothing of it.* In a flash Miss B understands something she doesn't like about herself. She has power in this community, the power of being known. *There goes Miss B* are words that often trail behind her. *There goes my English teacher*. Without fail, she hears this every time she is out and about. And it keeps her from truly stepping out. It keeps her here.

Outside the window the angled parking spots of the town square stay mostly empty. She can see, two streets over, the giant crumbling hulk of Schmitt's buffet restaurant. The weed-pocked lot is huge to allow for the buses that no longer arrive. *Try Our Mudslides* says a towering sign, cracked enough to reveal the lightbulbs within. It would have been visible to the highway that bypassed them.

Anisha And Corbin

greet each other with reunion hugs as the marching band arrives at the school for its first August practice. They haven't seen each other for over two weeks. Corbin has just returned from drum major camp, Anisha from a bioinformatics camp where she learned about DNA sequencing. It was great it was great it was so great! they tell each other but almost immediately Anisha moans with worry. First cornet position in the band might be jeopardized by her decision not to take her instrument along to bioinformatics camp. Two weeks of no scale work and Mr. Hurd is wasting no time—chair challenges are set to begin the very first day.

Hey Hi Travis,

calls Hannah Kirkpatrick, easing by on her bike, tires fat enough for water tubing. She doesn't pedal, she glides, her bike like a docile St. Bernard. Everyone wants to pet it. She glides all the way inside the school. The cheerleaders and color guard get to practice in the gym. It's not air-conditioned but they have the hurricane fans going. Hannah also plays the xylophone whenever the band performs "Amazing Grace," usually during senior week. Hannah stands near Travis when she plays the xylophone and he helps her strap up. She's not just a varsity cheerleader, she's the head varsity cheerleader.

She was riding that St. Bernard last year when Travis ran into her and the new exchange student Chieko biking out on deserted country lanes. He showed them Yoder's farm. Chieko could say one English word: Okay? Okay? The rest were gusts of wonder as Travis trespassed with a confidence he didn't feel up Yoder's driveway and past the barns. They entered the woods backing the farm and parked their bikes and Travis showed them the trail where the Shawnee and Wyandot intersected and they came out on the other side, where Amos Goertz stepped out from nowhere and wasn't wearing a shirt. He was on the short side and hard-bodied and hairless. Another gust of wonder from Chieko. Amos was smoking a joint and he held it out to Chieko and that is how last year her year began, a Japanese girl and an Amish boy. Such a long year, it seemed, and now already over and Chieko as if she were never here.

No One, This

hot August day, sits in the courtroom with Tyler Newton except the four family members. Miss B came down from the hangman's drop on the third floor to find a mostly empty courtroom. It should not come as a surprise to Miss B. It comes as a surprise to her nonetheless. Invested— no one is invested in this sixteen-year-old boy except some immediate family whose last name has cut a wide procreating swath in Halstead County. Despite the dozens of Newtons running around, attendance to-day is limited to grandfather in hooded sweatshirt, dad in ponytail, dad's new wife, dad's ex-wife.

Miss B reminds herself that it is the first day of football practice, the first day of band practice. That pretty much covers the whole school and then all the parents and volunteers. Surely that is what is keeping every-one away. Surely all those dads and moms who supported Jared Over-holser would support this boy, too.

Completing the courtroom gallery, sitting in the first pew, are the mother and grandmother of one of the victims along with their victim advocate. The victim's mother will read the same statement Miss B has heard three times before. She doesn't want to hear it again. It is a sad statement and, saddest of all, it is the only time the victim's name is ever mentioned in the proceedings.

Sixteen-year-old Tyler sits with his lawyer at a table before the bench.

Maybe he's turned seventeen over the summer. He wears a patterned dress shirt, the cheaper version without a looped yoke in back. Bought at Walmart or Kohl's. His fingers pick blindly at something underneath the table. Miss B can barely recall Tyler Newton from his brief weeks in study hall. He's almost not recognizable. It might be the puzzling hair, an inch of awning across his pimpled forehead, the only length left from a severe buzzing. The food he's been eating has given him acne bad enough that he can't shave any of the teenage fuzz. He's the type of look and type of kid that at the beginning of each school year sends Miss B to her prayers. On her knees she reminds herself not to favor those she favors, Hannah and Anisha and poor Travis Hicks, beautiful Travis Hicks. She reminds herself that God does not play favorites, that no one is better and no one is worse. It is not a small part of God's magnificence that He is able to maintain this equality of love because Miss B has favorites and she plays favorites, and struggle as she might, she always will.

The judge walks in to a rustle of tension. It is not Honorable Merle Herrick, the man from these parts who understands these parts, who understands these good families that their essentially good boys come from.

So what's the fucking deal here? the grandfather in the hoodie whispers loudly enough for all to hear.

Shawna, the lone security officer today, bears down upon him with a glower.

The judge has black hair, a swarthy face. His first name is Javier. No, not Merle Herrick at all.

What the fuck, the dad says.

What the fuck, the grandfather in the hoodie says.

What the fuck, the dad says. Dad? says the dad. What the fuck, Dad?

What the fuck, says the grandfather to his son.

I would say please be seated, Judge Javier Tanguay says, but you have to be standing first. So the judge waits. He looks out upon his mostly seated courtroom. His eyes wander to Shawna, then to the bailiff, Brenda Mansfield. All of Brenda's weight has shifted forward since Miss B last saw her; her thin hair now hangs a little thicker in permed corkscrews. A coat rack quivers to the rear of Brenda, the stand-alone kind that might topple upon her. Shawna spots the problem at the same time as Miss B and rushes to save Brenda and push the coat rack into a corner. Shawna's fauxhawk from the April hearings has grown a tail feather in back.

Thank you, Officer, the judge says to Shawna.

Miss B remains standing. Those in the victim's pew remain standing, their higher torsos half hiding Tyler Newton's family squatting behind them. Miss B tries not to be the teacher in this situation, but the ringless fingers half hidden by her derriere have a life of their own and curl into a discreet *come on, come on*! Her pew finally takes the hint. They stand. They wait. The judge waits. Brenda waits. Shawna waits. Finally the grandfather unwinds himself with a crude sigh. This good enough? he says, not quite drawing himself up under the fake burden of sore joints.

Please be seated, the judge says.

Way to get him on our side, his ex-daughter-in-law sneers.

Who invited your fat ass? the grandfather says.

He's my son—

Oh my god, Miss B thinks, she's actually going to answer him and then he's going to answer her back and then she's going to answer him back and—

Let's have order in the court so that we can begin, the judge says mildly, attention on arranging his papers. He doesn't tap the gavel or look up toward the grandfather's emboldened glare. Judge Javier Tanguay has been brought in from Youngstown after Judge Merle Herrick recused himself over a reported conflict of interest, the fact that he had ruled in the custody battle of Jared Overholser's parents and was now overseeing Jared's disposition. Judge Herrick has been a double-chinned old bachelor for so long that those long-lived enough to be his contemporaries remember another conflict of interest, that he also once dated Jared's grandmother. Mostly they remember him as a mama's boy, an only child whose elfin features never quite hardened into adult malehood. No one really perceived it when Merle Herrick drifted past marrying age; he was still boyish and beardless and loyal to his mother. He went to Ohio Northern University Petit College of Law only twenty-eight miles away and continued living with his mother and listening to old Bobby Vee records until her death three years ago at age ninety-eight. As a young lawyer he was one of only twelve members of the Halstead County Bar Association and that made his mother proud and she liked the special status conferred upon her and her walker. Life was better with her walker because it turned every stroll into a queenly promenade down a row of well-wishers ready to help and flatter.

When confronted with the Jared Overholser connections, Judge Herrick said, Don't know what that has to do with anything—but he agreed to step down. He'd already in April ruled in three of the five cases anyway, Jared and his wide receiver and tight end, all of whom promised the judge to behave so that they could play football in the fall. The other two defendants, the non–football players, were sent to juvenile detention until arrangements for a new judge could be made. Enter Javier Tanguay four months later. On this very afternoon that Jared Overholser and Josh Greesley and Dustin Crosby have begun their first football practice, Tyler Newton has been released from juvie long enough to sit in the county courthouse.

Everyone knows everything about Judge Herrick. No one knows anything about this new judge bused in from Youngstown.

Does the court have the pleasure of speaking to Tyler Newton? Judge Tanguay asks.

Yes.

The lawyer whispers in Tyler's ear.

Yes, sir.

Do you know why you're here? the judge asks Tyler.

No, Tyler says. No, sir.

What?

No, sir.

You don't know why you're here?

No.

You and your friends placed a deer decoy on a road that caused a very bad accident back in February of this year. Does that ring a bell?

I already know about that, Tyler says.

So you know why you're here.

No.

The lawyer bends toward Tyler's ear.

No, sir.

I just reminded you.

Yeah, but Jared did that.

Let's stick to you. Agreed?

Okay.

Are we in agreement then that you know why you are appearing before me today?

No.

This doesn't get things off to a good start. But Tyler Newton has no idea about anything. Four months in juvie, he's a stranger in this world.

If The Protest

against the football team goes forward, the band will probably perform a silent march upon the field. Or else it will fail to fall in and take up formation. Or maybe Corbin as the drum major will hold the fermata a beat too long, many beats too long, until everyone gets it, this is it, this is our protest, let's do it. And then complete chaos and cacophony as their entrance march breaks down.

It's not exactly a well-kept secret that all these possibilities are on the table. The leaks are everywhere. The band moms talk it over in Burger King and they have loud voices. The moms are torn in their loyalty. The angel on one shoulder tells them it is wrong, perhaps even biblically wrong, to turn a blind eye to grave misdeeds such as the ones the football players committed. And playing music isn't even in the category of turning a blind eye. Music is actually a *celebration*. Their sons and daughters in the band are *celebrating* a football team whose members have destroyed lives. And gotten away with it.

True.

They are celebrating sin.

That's ... a way of putting it.

And they are also *celebrating* a system that locks up the other boys and lets the football stars go free.

Very true.

The more devilish angel on the other shoulder asks the moms, Why should the band have to suffer for the sins of the football team? Why should the town have to suffer? Everyone loves the band!

Also true.

So many people will be so disappointed if the band doesn't perform.

Yes.

Life isn't worth living without music.

And isn't that the truth.

The band kids—their kids—are innocent.

True.

But paying the price as if they're guilty if they go through with this.

Also true.

And the football players get to play regardless.

Yes.

And *all that fundraising* for the new uniforms!

True true and also true.

One time Mr. Hurd and Miss Stacy sat right there in a Burger King booth going over Mr. Hurd's new arrangement and formations for "Midnight Train to Georgia" while the moms held forth, sometimes lowering their voices conspiratorially when a secret was really secret.

—And then Mr. Hurd lifting his baton in front of the packed home crowd of four thousand. All 103 band members refusing to raise their instruments. This is his nightmare—

Mr. Hurd is counting on his senior class leaders to quash any signs of protest. First there is Anisha. Anisha has her life scheduled out for the next five or ten years; her mind right now is consumed by the SATs and ACTs and Advanced Placements, by staying first cornet so as not to mess up her résumé, by eating kale chips, by staying valedictorian, by feeding the homeless and saving the world. By staying perfect. Missing a game would not be perfect. What if the Ivy Leagues hear about it? Perfection has made her paranoid, and that works in his favor.

Second there is Corbin. Corbin has his heart set on being the drum major at Ohio State; he can't afford to miss one game, especially now that Mr. Hurd has put the bug in his ear that his dazzling routines are being scouted. Even more in Mr. Hurd's favor, Corbin's brother Josh is a wide receiver on the football team. Not just any wide receiver—the star wide receiver. And not just any star wide receiver—the star wide receiver who is one of the Diva Trio. Last April Josh walked into the courtroom, accepted Judge Herrick's reduced charge of vehicular vandalism, and walked back out. The unfairness has riled the band, but Mr. Hurd cannot imagine that Corbin will turn on his lookalike younger brother by agreeing to a protest.

He has rolled the dice on these two. Corbin and Anisha are the de facto leaders, the ones everyone looks up to. They are the rare kids he won't see again after this year. Maybe if they remember him he'll be invited to their college graduation parties. He'll be forty by then—no, forty-one! Already he projects his loneliness for their bright faces, but they are bound for glory beyond this town. Despite how the town at large is crossed when it comes to the girl cornet player and the girly drum major (*well-known as the two misfits*, the newspaper said), they still have the undivided love of their bandmates, of him, of Miss Stacy, of better people somewhere better in the world.

Some Had Taken

to sitting outside on the low stone perimeter, relishing the newborn warmth of April and enjoying to-go caffeine from the brand-new Java Jazzz (run by the ex-mayor's wife). People were caught mid-drinks and midmuffins when the lookout texted that Judge Merle Herrick was already set to deliver his final remarks concerning the fate of wide receiver Josh Greesley. They placed their half-full cups on a proprietary patch of cement, pastry as lid to coffee, napkin as cover to pastry. They balanced their half-smoked cigarettes along the edge of the stone wall. And ran in.

Corbin and Anisha looked at each other. They didn't know what to do. They were glad to be trapped out in the corridor, but then Officer Shawna made way and Corbin was plucked and squeezed into the family pew without Anisha. It was a beautiful spring day and no school because of Easter week and Corbin was stranded in his misery and already starting to cry.

It is my understanding, Judge Merle Herrick began, that this incident took place along a stretch of road populated by mostly Amish. It is well-known that the Amish do not rely on electricity for their lifestyle.

Rioting murmurs of assent. The crowd was still trying to force its way through the doorway, standing on tiptoe in the corridor. A second security officer had been detailed for crowd control—John Willis, mostly retired. Over the years his personal convictions had followed the seams of his uniform, easing into a type of surrender. He had come to realize that right and wrong didn't have much to do with justice. He moved slowly now with his potbelly—where was the hurry? The people pushing into the courtroom avoided Shawna and her frightening crewcut and appealed directly to John, for he was, in their minds, low-key and agreeable. He convinced Shawna to let a couple dozen spectators cram the reporters' benches. Blasphemy. But it kept the peace. John overheard the admiration from one of the reporters: Wish I had thought of that prank. The reporter was wearing a cheap black shirt with a Looney Tunes tie. He heard from a woman in a yellow jacket tight in the shoulders: Jesus Christ can change your spirit and that's a miracle.

Things were growing unruly, but Judge Herrick never brought the gavel down. Forty years in the judge's courtroom and John Willis had come to know the man. The man liked attention. Liked it more the older he got. He never hid this character trait from John. John was scenery and wouldn't perceive it. But John had learned a lot in forty years, some of it by osmosis, helpful lessons like what made a shirt look cheap versus what made it look expensive. Helpful lessons like maybe check your ego at the door, like facts are not the truth—like modesty does not thrive in public (a quote from John Adams himself, whose face in the mural he has stared at for two decades). Unhelpful lessons, too—like good and bad don't matter. Wished he hadn't had to learn that lesson. All of this made him think of his retirement cabin. Nine hours of driving tomorrow and he and Robin would be there. Of course the judge had a cabin in the U.P. as well, rather a chalet with a lakefront balcony. Didn't matter, he had to sit there alone.

These buggies are dangerous enough, Judge Herrick continued. A horse and buggy in the age of Tesla is doing nobody any favors, but mostly they are endangering themselves. When we bear down on the facts of this case, however, there is certainly a mitigating factor to be found in our separatist neighbors. The road in question is what I will call, for lack of a better characterization, an Amish road. If you travel down that road at night, as I have had to do on many occasions, it is an inferno of blackness. It is pitch black down that road.

Spectators voiced agreement. Even John Willis at this point raised his hand for quiet. Shawna—oh, Shawna—she put hand to gunbelt.

Judge Herrick said, Good luck seeing your hand in front of your face.

Laughter from the crowd, dying into the seriousness of the occasion.

The law allows the Amish to live without electricity. The law allows the Amish to make their own rules even when common sense tells us that it collides with public safety. It is common sense that when roads have streetlights upon them and lights emitting from yards and houses, public safety increases. Even those luminescent mailbox numbers—they help to light the way like Tinker Bell blinking us through a dark cave. For it is of the utmost importance for drivers to be able to see the thoroughfare and what is upon it. There is no reason for the Amish not to have lights and to endanger us other folks with their whims, because it is a whim, not a belief. It has had, in this case, unfortunate consequences.

It is also my understanding that the injured parties did not submit to this court the results of any blood tests that would determine if alcohol or other chemical substances played a factor in their decision to veer completely off the road rather than simply use the westbound lane to go around a deer decoy that had strayed into the eastbound lane. The lack of skid marks prevents us from determining how fast the injured parties' vehicle was traveling, but the very lack of skid marks suggests that no brakes were applied. Either the driver was impaired or going too fast or, in this inferno of blackness that is a corollary to the Amish lifestyle, could not see the impediment upon the road.

Now let me speak for a moment to this notion of impediments. Add this to the Amish lifestyle of darkness and we have a perfect storm on our hands. When we say impediments, we are talking all manner of tree branches, dogs, wildlife, deer, Amish buggies and their road apples, bicycles and fallen haystacks, buckets, Happy Meals, roadkill, and pizza boxes. All of these things can find their way upon a road. These impediments are a common and I daresay constant occurrence on country

roads. Everyone here knows of what I speak, and everyone knows—
we all know, don't we—whenever the city slickers come through our
town, oh yes we do. We instantly know them from the way they drive,
oblivious to the dangers of country driving, expecting stoplights to do the
work of keeping them safe. But we have no stoplights out on those roads.
We must do our own internal version of green Go, yellow Caution and
red Stop. This speaks to the heart of the issue of personal responsibility.
These young men who injured themselves were born and raised here.
They passed their driver's licenses here. They may not have more than
two years' driving experience, but they grew up riding the byways with
their families, negotiating at nearly every turn, if not an Amish horse
and buggy, then another impediment on the road—usually in the form
of a deer. These young men who experienced injuries were not new to
this world. They understood the terrain, they understood the frequent
obstacles put forth by a different culture.

They, and they alone, made the decision to go down that road at night
with full knowledge of the risks.

After The First

morning's rehearsal, the band breaks for lunch in the school cafeteria. The band members lounge in circles on the floor and eat the apples and baloney sandwiches the band moms have provided. Some stretch out their whole bodies against the coolness of the linoleum. They can see through to the gym where the cheerleaders and color guard still practice. Spirit! Spirit! We say Spirit! Some of the band members unconsciously mime the arm motions to each cheer.

From the rafters of the gym hang the school's triumphs. A banner home-sewn with Amish plainness announces the 1958 Division IV state basketball championship. A football state championship in 1968. And then the pièce de résistance, the state championship three years ago that moved their Division IV football team up to Division III, where, as two other banners proclaim, it has been regional champion the past two years.

We say Spirit! You say Got it! Spirit!

Got it! the band yells to the cheerleaders.

Spirit!

Got it!

Corbin jumps up and tosses his baton into the air, catches it easily behind his back.

Spirit!

Got it!

Spirit!

Got it!

The cheerleaders crowd out of the gym to watch. Now Corbin throws two batons into the air

   one

   two

   catches them both

   one

   two

behind his back. His T-shirt, scissored off midabdomen, shows off a rigid skinny six-pack.

   Spirit!

   Got it!

   Spirit!

   Got it!

And then Corbin debuts his new move, learned and perfected these past two weeks at drum major camp. He knife-throws the baton to the floor, where the rubber tip angles the baton right back into his hand. Wild cheers. Wild wild cheers. Corbin is fast, fast as his brother. Faster. He runs the 400 for the track team, has made it every year to the regionals where he falls to Columbus and Cleveland and their urban schools. That's code for certain beliefs, but Corbin doesn't believe them. He knows how fast he could run if he decided to actually train.

Kassadee, the sophomore Letterette who has changed her name to Elsa after a Disney movie, grabs her giant K and jumps up and down. Kyle Jenkins runs over to torment his little sister with his drumsticks. Stop, Kyle, stop stop stop! she screams. The school almost universally loves Kassadee/Elsa—more than Grace Lynn the other Down's kid—because Kassadee's mother doesn't stand guard over her with a police stare. She's got two sons to keep in line, Kyle and her puberty-crazed eighth grader, Kody. Kassadee is the easy one. All Kassadee wants to do is be the best Letterette in the universe, which means eating right, peanut-butter-and-marmalade sandwiches, grilled cheese sandwiches, mayonnaise sandwiches, peaches and apples and bananas, and doing the homework she can and going to bed early with headphones pumping her favorite *Frozen* song while she sings along with her favorite *Frozen* heroine Elsa, "No right, no wrong, rules for me! / I'm free! / Let it go! Let it go! / I am one with the wind and sky! / Let it go!"—*Shut the fuck up!*—but she is happily oblivious to Kody's screams and poundings against the bedroom wall.

Stop, Kyle, stop stop stop! Kassadee now squeals in the lunchroom, drowning out an announcement.

Quiet quiet! yell the sandwich moms.

Outside, an electronic megaphone is calling for the band members to line up. Everyone jumps up and runs outside. In mere seconds the lunchroom empties, and for a scary moment the sandwich moms see their future in the hollow echo of the tiles. Wish I had that energy, one of them quickly says.

Do You Know

the story of Simon Kenton?

It was in April that Judge Merle Herrick posed the question to the star quarterback of the high school football team. It was one of the first glorious days of spring and there wasn't an open parking space until you got to the abandoned asphalt of Schmitt's buffet restaurant and the falling signage glass from *Try Our Mudslides*.

Jared Overholser found Coach McManus in the crunched gallery of spectators. The coach's blond hair lit up the dark corner where he stood. Soon it would be the coach's turn to talk about his young quarterback's strength of character and depth of Christian belief. The coach had a way with words. It would bring many of the men to tears.

The coach gave Jared a reassuring head shake.

No, sir, said Jared to the judge's question about Simon Kenton.

Another vigorous head shake from Coach McManus.

But I would like to hear it, sir.

Coach McManus smiled.

Judge Herrick smiled.

Right answer, thought the semiretired security officer John Willis. How well he knew the judge's penchant for grandstanding teaching moments.

Jared had taken off school to attend his disposition. He had in his hand the school's permission slip to miss school for the entire day (folded by now into tiny squares), but the bailiff Brenda Mansfield hadn't collected it. She was distracted by her hair. Looking at it in the mirror that morning had almost made her late for work. Her hair was lank and getting lanker. Chemo three years earlier hadn't done it any favors. The judge's upcoming speechifying would give her time to mull over various hair remedies, including, she hated to think, Minoxidil for women. But so what, she decided.

At any rate, there was no need to collect Jared Overholser's permission slip. The courtroom was filled with people from Kattoga High—even the principal was there as a character witness. The superintendent as well. He'd known Jared all through elementary school and could testify he came from good stock. Everyone knew and respected the Overholsers, one of Kattoga's pioneering families.

No one knows who Simon Kenton is? Anyone? A pleased Judge Herrick looked over his courtroom. His smile grew. With all the high school teachers there, the Shawnee and Wyandot intersection just a stone's throw away, someone was bound to know of Simon Kenton. The hunters in the crowd likely were familiar with the name, and for god's sake there was a statue of Simon Kenton in the town square. But the courtroom stayed respectfully ignorant. The silence was long enough that Miss B took note of the Fruit of the Loom T-shirt under Shawna's uniform.

Do you know who this town is named after? the judge asked Jared.

No, sir, Jared said.

Care to take a guess?

There in the darkness Coach McManus's glowing head nodded yes.

That person you just said, Jared offered.

That's right, the judge said. Simon Kenton.

Coach McManus leaned back as if his boy had just won the lottery.

Simon Kenton was a contemporary of Daniel Boone, the judge told Jared Overholser. Every bit as much the frontiersman as Boone. In fact, Daniel Boone wouldn't have lived long enough to become so famous if it hadn't been for Simon Kenton.

Yes, sir.

Simon Kenton was famous for his skill with the Kentucky long rifle, .50 caliber, forty-six-inch barrel, with curly maple used for the stock.

The hunters in the gallery, some of them dressed in camo, murmured in accord. Jared noted them. Wow, sir, he said to the judge.

And weighed, well, I'd say eight to ten pounds, Judge Herrick said. Simon Kenton could shoot it, reload it with his horn of powder, and shoot again with deadly accuracy, all while on the dead run.

Jared Overholser stared up at the judge. Wow, sir, he said again.

Kind of like dodging defensive tackles, running headlong into the end zone, the judge said.

Coach McManus was nodding.

Yes, sir, said Jared.

And one day Daniel Boone and Simon Kenton were out scouting together and they were set upon by Shawnees. Oh, the Shawnees were always after Boone and Kenton. Their chief, Blackfish, had what amounted to an obsession with Boone and Kenton. He'd adopted them as his sons one year when they were captured and lived among the Indians, learned their ways. And then Blackfish felt betrayed when Boone and Kenton escaped and went back to normal living.

He's said the word, thought John Willis. Blackfish. That was the word. Shit, he'd said it.

Those in the gallery dressed in camo were bobbing along, mesmerized.

Judge Merle Herrick said, One could posit a connection of almost platonic eroticism between the Shawnee chief and his prisoner. At the same time that he wanted Simon Kenton's capture, Blackfish wanted his love.

Blackfish, thought John Willis. Just isn't ever a good thing to say that word.

So on this day in question, outnumbered by the Shawnee hunting party, Daniel Boone took the blunt end of a hatchet to his head and fell as if dead. Dead or not, Simon Kenton was not going to desert his friend. That sounds familiar, doesn't it? Judge Herrick paused to address Jared, who was checking out people he knew in the crowd.

The coach's head was jerking toward the judge.

Yes, sir, Jared said, swinging his attention back to the judge.

Loyalty to friends.

Yes, sir.

So Simon Kenton picked up Daniel Boone—Daniel Boone, who was a big man, a big big man as the song goes—and swung him right over his shoulder and took off running, loading his rifle and shooting as he went. Remind you of anything?

Jared looked over to Coach McManus.

Football, Jared said.

That's right, Judge Herrick said. Like carrying a tackler on your back and still making it into the end zone.

Yes, sir, Jared said.

Do me a favor, remember that name. Simon Kenton.

Yes, sir. I will.

You know why?

Because he was the best shooter.

Because, the judge told him, we get our town's name from Simon Kenton, from the Indian name Chief Blackfish gave him. Cuttahotha. In Indian language it means condemned to be burned at the stake.

Okay, thought John Willis. Let's end it there.

Which the Shawnees tried three times to do. Three times they tried to burn him at the stake, but they couldn't succeed.

Wow, sir.

Divine intervention maybe?

Jared looked to Coach McManus. Yes, sir.

And they made him run the gauntlet nine times. Do you know what a gauntlet is? Judge Herrick asked Jared.

John Willis was squirming now. He knew how much the judge liked the gory details of the gauntlet, the wild horse Simon Kenton was tied to, the quarter mile of Shawnee war club and axe taking turns at him, collarbone broken, hole in the skull ... Chief Blackfish's obsession with Simon Kenton had become the judge's own. Since the death of the judge's mother, John had noticed the judge getting lost in gruesome asides. Rumors swirled that in his house with a turret he'd become like Norman Bates in *Pyscho*, visiting his mummified mother in her locked tower room. People of curiosity drove by to check on this. Suspiciously, a light in the turret was always on, the shadow of her walker thrown against the wall. Of course the old mother was in her grave—but ... was she? Was she really? John knew the answer. The judge's mother was neither in grave nor turret. She was in the car. The judge sat in the car and talked long hours to her. The judge didn't care that John knew. John was wallpaper to him.

You think you could run a gauntlet? Judge Herrick asked Jared.

No, sir.

You sure about that?

No, sir.

You don't think you have the strength? The *will*?

Maybe.

In the gallery Coach McManus was nodding yes yes yes.

Yes, sir, I think I could.

Good. Because you're running a gauntlet now. You're running the gauntlet of public opinion. You're going to have to be strong and brave to get through this.

Yes, sir.

How are your grades? Judge Herrick asked.

Pretty good. Failing geometry, Jared said.

Gotta learn geometry if you want to be an engineer. Look up. You know why those holes are in the ceiling?

No, sir.

To make the ceiling lighter.

Shawna looked over to John with a helpless shrug.

Did that guy kill the Indian chief? Jared asked.

Did Simon Kenton kill Blackfish? Judge Herrick said.

Yes, sir.

Simon Kenton, that's a name you're going to remember now, isn't it?

Yes, sir.

His statue's right outside in case you forget.

For a moment Jared's expression went blank. He had spray-painted a courthouse statue in eighth grade.

To answer your question, the judge said, Blackfish was shot in the leg and the infection killed him. No one knows who killed Blackfish. Could have been me in another lifetime.

You killed him, sir? Jared asked.

Got my semantics wrong there, the judge said.

Leave it at that, John Willis thought.

It could have been me as Blackfish back then.

Now the judge would be forced to admit that in his previous life as an Indian chief he couldn't build a fire well enough to burn someone at the stake. A wave of pleasure rolled through John as he imagined the judge in front of his grand fireplace in his grand U.P. chalet, having to settle for a six-hour Duraflame log.

Shawna gave John another confused look. You don't know the half of it, he could tell her. The guy thinks his mother is a car engine. His own cabin in the U.P., he reminded himself. A long drive to shake it off. And Robin. And a sweet-smelling cord of wood.

Same Chair Formation

as last year? an ever-anxious Anisha asks.

First cornet here, Mr. Hurd says. That's you, Anisha.

Miss Stacy climbs a stepladder to give her special welcome to the band, to the parents, to the boosters, to friends and neighbors, to music lovers everywhere, to those who march to different drummers, to those who march to OUR DRUMMERS!

Cougars!

Cougars!

Cougars!

Cougars!

Cougars!

Travis Hicks smiles despite himself. The thud bass, locked safely away from his mother in the music closet all summer, is dusty and out of tune, but already he has provided fun for the little kids who want a whack at it.

The band moms celebrate Miss Stacy with a huge cheer—Miss Stacy, a one-woman antibullying force, has already made a difference in the lives of their geeky children. She has made geek great. She acknowledges the cheers with victory fist pumps that nearly plunge her off the stepladder.

Corbin and Anisha steal glances at each other: she never disappoints, Miss Stacy. All her gestures are wildly exaggerated and sold with excruciating facial contortions. Corbin and Anisha watch for that exact moment when everything tips over and becomes orgasmic. We won't have long to wait! their delighted glances telegraph each other.

Miss Stacy is wearing short shorts and a tank top and her breasts look bigger than last school year. It's the wondering about her breasts—rounder, harder—that makes Anisha glance again at Corbin, who mimics a sexy posture, more erect, chest out. They haven't seen Miss Stacy all summer. Clearly she's been busy at something or other. With her dark tan and bleached long hair, the stripper vibe is even more pronounced. Did she party on yachts all summer? On the Côte d'Azur, Anisha will suggest to Corbin later. He's the only one who won't require further geographic explanation. That's why they're best friends, all their private jokes, all their insider language. And tonight Anisha will tell him all about bioinformatics camp—DNA, RNA, protein!—and Corbin won't laugh. And Corbin won't laugh when she tells him she's getting close to it, her aha moment. She's getting close, she can feel it, she's getting close—a few more years. She's going to save the world, she just knows it.

What Miss Stacy does during off time is subject to constant speculation by everyone. But she's so good at her job and she stands as the line of protection between football and the band. The band members haven't been bullied since Miss Stacy came on board. The prospect of making a porno movie with Miss Stacy keeps the football players in line.

At parade rest in workout gear, the kids of the marching band don't look much like the precision machine they will become in a few weeks. The beating sun has driven some of the kids to wear goofy hats with hydrating straws or battery-powered propellers to fan themselves. Water bladders are tucked inside most upperclassmen's T-shirts—that's their style strut, no lowerclassmen dare to adopt it. When not being sucked upon, tube and mouth valves hang over collarbones in the casual sexiness of a seasoned pro.

The band moms have taken shade under a tent where they never stop selling brownies and cookies and slices of cold pizza that have actually grown warm in the heat. On this kind of day, the coolers of water and diluted Gatorade and lemonade are free.

Miss Stacy announces the new song they will be learning, "Midnight Train to Georgia." Whoo-whoo! calls a boy. Exactly! Miss Stacy enthuses. She does a whoo-whoo! herself, pulling down an imaginary train cord that again nearly sends her off the ladder. She is somewhere in her twenties, almost conceivably one of them but old enough to have a life outside the band, this greatly mysterious life full of orgasms that everyone wants to know about.

Another round of applause goes to Miss Stacy's introduction of Dick Tresor, white-haired and still full of youthful confidence—cockiness, Mr. Hurd would say (but to himself). Dick was a trombonist in the Ohio State marching band way back when Woody Hayes was coach. He spent several years in the alumni band, and now he volunteers to teach Script Ohio to Kattoga High. The Cougar band is one of the few high schools that can perform it. The freshmen peel off with Dick Tresor. They'll need a lot of preliminary work.

Mr. Hurd watches the freshmen follow Dick Tresor and wonders if any of the new band uniforms will fit them properly. The girls look too big and the boys look too small. Miss Stacy turns around and eyes him. She's thinking the same thing. All that fundraising work, the chocolate bars and flower bulbs, the bake sales, car washes, Christmas gift wrapping, which sounded stupid at first but there were so MANY MEN willing to pay, yard sales, baton-twirling lessons, and did we mention the car washes—all that work and they have an entering class way outside the standard deviations. Mr. Hurd doesn't even want to think about the extra money it cost just for one uniform the size of Travis Hicks. These freshmen sizes are not in the budget.

The Only Defendant

to smile was Dustin Crosby. As the most expendable talent of the Diva Trio, he was most in danger of being the sacrificial lamb to appease the other half of the town outraged by the preferential treatment given to the football players, yet he was the most at ease. The late April gallery of spectators and reporters was full, but not crammed as it had been with Josh and Jared.

A week earlier Josh Greesley's sharp cheeks had flamed red and his eyes watered throughout his time in the courtroom. Like his brother, who watched in misery from the pew, Josh was tightly muscled to the point of skinniness, and as for Corbin, a genuine tenderness continually threatened his composure. He swallowed hard before mustering yes, sir or no, sir. On the pew Corbin dripped tears.

Jared Overholser, on his day in court, had been a creature of nature without understanding of right or wrong, a lion sizing up the chances of survival or a possible feast of gazelle. A creature of nature who lived in a guiltless present. Also an easily bored creature of nature.

Dustin Crosby simply looked content. Content at the vagueness of his comprehension in all things, never itching for clarification. Content with a D grade in all classes. To all of Judge Merle Herrick's questions, Dustin Crosby said yes, sir and no, sir with a cheerful demeanor. If he wasn't sure, he waited for his lawyer to whisper the answer in his ear. He had forgotten his lawyer's name, but that was okay, he didn't need to know.

The judge asked Dustin to turn his attention to the mural behind the judicial bench. Dustin didn't know what a mural was, but the judge pointed.

That figure there might be Ben Franklin. What do you think?

Yes, sir.

A penny saved is a penny earned.

Yes, sir.

And next to him I believe is the second president of the United States, Judge Herrick said. Do you know who that is?

I've heard of him, sir.

That's John Adams.

Yes, sir.

And that judge fella sitting at the judicial bench? Looks familiar, doesn't he?

Yes, sir. Dustin Crosby was almost laughing now. At what, no one knew. He had no idea what the judge was talking about. Was just playing along, as Jared had told him to do. It was like when Jared told him to do a fade route or a zone slice. That's what he did. Jared had told him to say no, sir and yes, sir to anything the judge said and he'd walk out scot-free.

You know who it is, then?

No, sir.

That's yours truly, Judge Herrick said, gesturing to the judge in the mural. A little younger but a passable likeness.

Dustin's lawyer leaned in.

Dustin briefly wiped the smile from his face. Yes, sir. It's very nice.

The law is above no man, not even Benjamin Franklin or John Adams. If either one of them came to my court, I'd treat them the same way I treat you.

Thank you, sir.

Don't thank me. Thank the law. I like to apply what I call the telescope of truth to these matters. Do you know what I mean by that?

Yes, sir. We run a telescope play in one of our formations.

Strips the distance of its fantasies, doesn't it?

Yes, sir.

And brings life near in utter nakedness. Making cold reality too near.

Dustin grinned up at the judge, but the judge had turned fully in his seat to admire the mural behind him.

The judge said, When something is out there in the distance, how accurately you perceive it depends on how good your eyesight is, doesn't it?

Yes, sir.

If your eyes aren't twenty-twenty, you might be not be seeing things right. You might mistake a man in the distance for a woman. If your eyes are even worse than that, you might mistake a stone pillar for a human being.

Yes, sir.

So it all depends, doesn't it?

Yes, sir.

If the sun's in your face, can you see accurately in the distance?

No, sir.

If the black inferno of night envelops you, what do you see? What *can* you see?

Yes, sir.

We have here many reports of things being seen on the night of the accident, and each of those things is presented as accurate by the person who reported them. Who do we believe?

Dustin stared up at him with a smile.

Until we apply the telescope of truth, we just don't know. Which is where the court comes in.

Yes, sir, Dustin said.

I have in my possession reports of medical malfeasance at the site of the accident. One report claims the paramedics took one of the victims to the wrong hospital, our local hospital, which was not set up for thoracic arterial bleeds. You don't need to know what that means. That's for the court to understand.

Dustin nodded agreeably. Act interested no matter how bored you are, Jared had told him.

I have heard that the doctor on the scene was impaired, that the paramedics smelled alcohol on her. But do we call into question this account by the paramedics, who were themselves accused of a near fatal delay in life-flighting the victims?

Dustin stared in the judge's general direction, contentment on his face as he relived a touchdown catch.

Or do we blame the doctor, who is also accused of recklessly applying a tourniquet to one of the victims' legs so that we are already into the fifth iteration of surgery for that leg? Do we?

Yes, sir.

Do we believe the witnesses who saw other cars easily go around the deer decoy without incident?

Yes, sir.

Do we believe the accounts of speeding, that the victims were exceeding the posted limits? Of reckless driving? The reports of benzodiazepines and cannabinoids in their system? What do we believe, Mr. Crosby?

I don't know, sir, Dustin says.

Who will be the telescope of truth?

Yes, sir.

Me?

Yes, sir.

Do you believe that young people should have their life ahead of them?

Yes, sir.

And you, a tight end for Kattoga High School.

Yes, sir.

And I hear you're a good tight end, too.

Yes, sir.

Maybe something that will provide you with a college education.

Yes, sir.

Are you that good?

Yes, sir.

You're a big fella. You look strong. Your family is a farming family. I see farmer's hands on you.

Dustin grinned.

There's no room for a melancholy temperament down on the farm, is there?

No, sir.

The farm couldn't function. It takes an affirmative personality with positive momentum to get all the important things in this world done. The harvest doesn't wait for the bilious mood to pass.

The judge looked out upon the gallery of spectators. The reporters were scribbling down his words.

The court has no interest in shattering the future of especially talented young people. But there were victims as a result of this prank, and the court must acknowledge that. The court asks for $5,000 restitution from the defendant, to be paid in the following order: First, to Henry Zimmerman to compensate for the loss of his deer decoy; secondly, to the tow-truck driver, Hepsibah Miller, to cover his expenses for towing the Dodge Stratus out of the cornfield; thirdly, the remainder to the two victims of the crash.

Travis Lets Two

little boys tear the mallet from his hand and take a final whack on the thud bass. Then he picks it up, straps it over his shoulder, and belts it around his waist. The sun—Apollo's orb, as Miss B would say—is burning the road. It's almost mythological today in its toll upon humans. He hopes the treads of his new Nikes don't melt. They're untested rubber and they are soaking up the blacktop temperature to the point of blistering his feet, but he really wants to wear them. He wants to show them off. First thing everyone noticed, too. Not Hannah Kirkpatrick, she doesn't notice that type of thing, but the others. Yeah, they noticed. They noticed *with envy*. He's got a dozen more pairs in a U-Storage locker behind the Marathon station, and after practice he'll go to the town library computers and check his bot. With the money he's made from selling domain names, he's been able to upgrade to an even better bot that can bypass the security checkpoints for robots. It can answer the security questions and specify the letters hidden in a maze or look at photos and check off the ones featuring traffic lights or the ones with windows. It means he has added chances to grab the Supreme faux fur bomber jacket that sells out in less than half a second. It defies math and physics how it can sell out before time even begins. Only once has he ever scored it—last November, when Chieko then sent the jacket to Japan, where it sold for twice as much and they each made hundreds of dollars on it. Chieko, he's pretty sure, spent her money on weed. Amos wasn't even generous enough to give it to her for free, despite the nights she spent in his trailer. Travis knew all about it, but he kept his mouth shut. Chieko had stopped bursting into laughter at his size; from Halloween until her departure in August, she clung to him whenever she was fearful, which seemed to be often.

Anyway, he's got twelve pairs of his shoes to sell and he bets they will be sold in one day.

Good news: Mr. Hurd has suspended chair challenges until tomorrow. Not that anyone would challenge Travis for the thud bass, but he doesn't want to see the wrong person go down because they are about to faint from heat prostration. Travis sees Anisha Devajaran let out a cheer upon Mr. Hurd's announcement and jump into Corbin's arms.

The band members fall in and begin their march down the fresh asphalt. They follow the cougar paw prints to the stadium. They are stepped along by a military beat. Only the drummers, only the snare drummers in the silent march. Silent because the snare drums are loud and crisp but everyone else is hushed. The gathering crowd wants to cheer but they are too respectful. The retirees cannot extricate themselves from their old webbed aluminum chairs. They stand at attention, lawn chairs attached to their hips, as the band steps past.

When The Lawyer

for Tyler Newton stands to address the judge, his suit hangs like cardboard. The cold marble keeps August at bay, but there is perspiration on the lawyer's neck. Your Honor, he says, we were operating under the promise that—

Promise? Judge Javier Tanguay interrupts. What promise and who promised?

Maybe let him the fuck finish? the grandfather in the hoodie says under his breath.

Premise, Your Honor. We were operating under the premise that my client would plead no contest to two counts of possession of criminal tools in the form of a deer decoy, which I believe is a stretch of the imagination to call a criminal tool, and one count of petty theft. Tyler has agreed to no contest.

Judge Tanguay says, Frankly, a no-contest plea is something I seldom allow in my juvenile court, but I bow to this plea being allowed because of precedent in the cases of the three earlier defendants disposed by Judge Herrick before he recused himself.

Speak English, Pedro, mutters the grandfather in a hoodie.

Says the lawyer, I understand, Your Honor, and in return we were operating under the promise—

What promise?

Premise, Your Honor, operating under the premise—although I believe I can attest to it being relayed to us in the form of a promise—

You need to hurry to your point, Counselor, before this grave gets dug any deeper.

Fucker, the grandfather says. This time it is a whisper, but it's aimed in Miss B's ear and it reverberates in there like a tuba.

People can get arrested for whispering poetry, Miss B thinks. Somewhere. Russia during Stalin. Anywhere, at some point in time, beauty was against the law. But never ugliness.

Inside her ear more grandfatherly words rush in. She shifts away from the man as if her shoulders ache. Why pretend her shoulders ache? So his feelings won't get hurt? Why not let him know? This is her fourth trial. One more to go. Sometimes it's hard for Miss B to be Lady Justice with the blindfold on. These types of Tyler Newton kids and their families, they come and go, her classes might as well get turnstiles installed. They're forgettable until they do something wrong or get crippled in a crash. On the other hand,

on the other hand is Miss B's personal conjunctive adverb, tucked into her soul's pocket

look what the boy is up against. No, his family doesn't beat him. No, they don't starve him. Sometimes they laugh with him. Sometimes they compliment. But Tyler Newton is up against something eroding and he doesn't know it and if he felt it he couldn't spell it out. So many hours she's thought about this. It's a life without beauty, that's the best conclusion she can reach. Where is the beauty in wearing a hooded sweatshirt to court to honor your grandson. It's not wrong, but it isn't beautiful.

And where is the beauty in the mural behind the judge's bench, an exercise in self-satisfied ugliness commissioned by Judge Herrick himself. An eagle of justice—a ribbon of Old Glory in its beak and the golden words "Halstead County" between its upraised wings—divides the mural in half. The scenes on the left side picture domesticity. A mother in a shirtwaist dress drops off her children at a one-room schoolhouse while a smiling teacher rings her handbell. On the right side of the mural are painted manly scenes of commerce and business and law. At the forefront, out-of-proportion figures dressed as the Founding Fathers stand before a judge who looks distinctly more modern, who in fact resembles Judge Herrick with a better jawline. It looks very much as if Benjamin Franklin and John Adams are posed in deferential awe before Judge Herrick—it might be Benjamin Franklin but the artwork is bad, as if the Rebekahs and Odd Fellows were set loose upon it and the senior center helped color it in.

On the other hand

it represents a democracy in its very democratic embrace of art as wretched masses yearning to draw.

On the other hand

it offends by its lack of beauty.

And what is Miss B to do about it? Offer a critique that will sound snobby to teenage ears? Expose her students to more Michelangelo, more Rembrandt, so that they can see Monet as better, not blurrier, and Judge Herrick's self-portrait for what it is? Sometimes it's so hard. You'd think that beauty would be such a noncontroversial thing. But there was the poet Anna Akhmatova keeping her beautiful words inside her until there came the reprieve of noise and she could whisper them into another's ear. Her son and husband in the gulag. Still finding beauty in the ugliness, a hangable offense.

Tyler's lawyer is saying, We were under the expectation that the felonious assault charge would be reduced to vehicular vandalism. My client is fully prepared to write the five-hundred-word essay adjured to the previous defendants.

What essay is this? Judge Tanguay asks.

An essay on why I should think before I act.

The judge says nothing.

Prompts the lawyer, sweat on his brow now: Its mandatory length requires a level of commitment that is both punitive and instructive.

What mandatory length?

The mandatory length of the essay, Your Honor. The court believed it was of sufficiently punitive length.

What court?

This court.

Counselor, you are speaking to this court.

Asshole, mutters the grandfather to Miss B, whose aching shoulders pitch her down the pew.

Understood, Your Honor.

This court hopes so. Judge Tanguay leans back. His shift is enough for the mural's eagle of justice to find a perch upon his head. Ha ha ha, laughs the grandfather. Miss B scoots farther. A five-hundred-word essay, Your Honor, is a lot for a young man to handle. But Tyler is anxious to do it. He is very repentant.

That may be, Counselor, but in the court's conversation with him it has become evident that the young man doesn't have a clear idea of why he is even here.

To that point, Your Honor, the language of the court confuses him and no one has bothered to explain it to him or the differences between hearings and dispositions and trials and the like.

Wasn't that your job, Counselor?

The lawyer takes time to sip from his glass of water. I take your point, Your Honor, but again I want to return to this—PREMISE—of felonious assault being reduced to vehicular vandalism.

The court does not retreat from its position.

Respectfully, based on what, Your Honor?

Based on the fact that felonious assault and vehicular vandalism are two completely different things, Judge Tanguay says. Causing irreparable bodily harm to a human being is not the same as harming a vehicle.

If I may, Your Honor, vehicular vandalism led directly and without intent to the bodily injuries. The defendant had nothing to do with it.

Explain how that works, Counselor.

The vehicular vandalism, Your Honor?

Which vehicle are we talking about?

The lawyer shuffles his paper. The only one vehicle that I'm aware of is the Dodge Stratus.

Which is the vehicle the two injured parties rode in.

Correct, Your Honor. The lawyer stands as if finished. As if his point is made.

A Dodge Stratus, the judge prompts.

Correct, Your Honor. Again the lawyer sips from his glass of water.

The judge says, The Dodge Stratus flipped off the road to avoid hitting the deer decoy placed in the driver's lane by your client and others.

I would rather say VEERED off the road, Your Honor. Veering is a quite common and necessary occurrence on these country roads. In veering to miss the deer decoy, the driver lost control of the car and spun off the road, thereby damaging the vehicle, which in turn caused his injuries and his passenger's injuries.

So the driver caused his own injuries?

In a manner of speaking, yes, Your Honor.

That's a manner of speaking the court hasn't heard before.

Listen and learn, the grandfather says. He has stopped bothering to use any type of whisper voice.

Shut. Up. A hiss from his ex-daughter-in-law.

Fat. Ass.

Shawna's cold stare.

I believe it was used as an effective defense for the other three defendants, the lawyer says. We are simply operating under the same premise.

But you are in a different courtroom—

It's actually the same—

The judge's hand stops him. Metaphorically you are in a different courtroom. And may the court remind you, you are quite literally standing before a different judge. Are you intending to speak to the court about jurisdiction? The court won't take kindly to having to explain the law to you on this particular point.

Of course not, Your Honor.

This is my courtroom, Judge Tanguay says, and this is not a reduced plea I accept in my courtroom.

Respectfully, Your Honor, very respectfully, this is a small town out in the country—

I come from Youngstown, Counselor. I don't need a lecture on small towns out in the country.

This is a small town of eight thousand, Your Honor. I believe Youngstown is about ten times that size. This is a small town where everybody knows and looks out for each other,

Damn straight, says the grandfather

but small towns can have their downside, too, like the lack of a movie theater, which can lead to boredom on a Saturday night.

Let me get try to understand this, Counselor. If there had been a Cineplex in this town, the accident wouldn't have happened.

It stands to reason, Your Honor, that you can't be in two places at the same time. A simple law of physics.

The court is afraid it cannot take this simple law of physics into account as a mitigating factor.

Your Honor, a young man is basically being punished for living a wholesome country life. He is being severely punished for a prank that actually proved harmless to the several cars that, just minutes earlier, successfully avoided the deer decoy and veered around it using the westbound lane. A prank that would not have happened if there had been a movie theater—or Cineplex, to use the court's words—in town. A prank that was harmless except for the reckless driving that escalated it.

Counselor, let the court give you its understanding of a prank. A prank is throwing water balloons. A prank is someone jumping out of a wedding cake. A prank is stuffing a birthday card with annoying confetti that sprays all over. When a prank is committed, at least one of the parties tends to laugh at the prank's effect. I see no laughter here. I do not see the victim's family laughing. I do not see the defendant's family laughing.

Hey, I can laugh, you want me to laugh? The grandfather shoves himself upright and pulls the hoodie over his head.

Shawna lunges forward. The new feather tail at the nape of her crewcut turns her into a falcon. The judge raises his hand. He doesn't use the gavel. In his gaze expression fights expressionlessness. He waits for the grandfather to sit. The grandfather sits. He's quiet. Everyone's quiet. There is profound silence. There is ugliness everywhere. Miss B tries not to cry. Her left eye always drips first so she pulls it open wide as if adjusting a contact lens.

This was not a prank, Counselor. This was a crime. A crime that resulted not in property damage but human damage. Permanent human damage.

Before She Leaves

Miss B checks in with Roxanne Burker at the clerk of court's office. A friend of sorts and she hasn't seen her all summer. The visit will also allow her to avoid Tyler Newton's family, and especially the grandfather in the hoodie.

No one is in the main office. On the counter sits an eight-by-ten placard: Rules of the Office in gold leaf.

1 Whatever goes upon two legs is an enemy
2 Whatever goes upon four legs, or has wings, is a friend
3 No animal shall wear clothes
4 No animal shall sleep in a bed
5 No animal shall drink alcohol
6 No animal shall kill any other animal
7 All animals are equal

It's directly cribbed from George Orwell's *Animal Farm* but signed with Judge Merle Herrick as the author.

Roxanne steps out from an inner office with an angry face. Oh hi, she says. Here for the show? Her face relaxes. Not quite a smile. Smiles aren't something she bothers with.

How are you? Miss B asks. You look thinner.

Forty-seven more pounds to go.

You can do it, Miss B says.

Outside in the corridor come angry voices. She recognizes the grandfather in the hoodie and his ex-daughter-in-law, each of them blaming the other for Tyler's sentence of felonious assault with enhancement and a continued stint in juvie for another five months. Miss B can't help but slice through all the other airwaves to their primitive laryngeal cave babel—words, sentences, the tempo of vulgarity, the way they hack their throats, the way they burp themselves into exclamations. They are seared into her like long-lost lovers, not that she would know about that.

It's so hot out, Roxanne is saying. Is it still so hot out? I'm worried for Spalding. She shakes her head. Just sat on his bum all summer. How do you think he's going to do today? Not good I can tell you. He'll collapse. I'm sitting in there waiting for the call to come from the hospital. He's not too young to die from a heart attack.

He's a little young, Miss B says.

Don't check your newsfeed then, Roxanne says. Some high school in Texas, first day of practice, 100 degrees. One of those tackle guys? Dead. There goes their season.

They take it easy the first day, Miss B assures her. They'll probably lift weights inside.

That sounds like a treat. Brain aneurism.

Are you doing okay? Miss B asks.

Did you hear about John?

Miss B raises her brows.

John Willis. The security guard. He died. End of July. Heart attack.

Oh my god, Miss B says. Nice man.

So I'm just a little ...

Miss B does something she is careful never ever to do with her students. Almost never. She takes Roxanne's hand and holds it in both of hers. Breathe, she says. She waits for Roxanne to calm herself.

So I'm not friends with the football parents, Roxanne tells her after several deep breaths. Funny, considering I am a football parent.

That must hurt, Miss B says.

It is what it is.

It still hurts.

Yeah it hurts. And now BY PROCLAMATION! I can't be friends with the band parents either. The mad mommies of the marching band, that's what I call them. They're on the warpath.

I heard, says Miss B.

Everyone knows the mad mommies go to Burger King and the happy football mommies go to McDonald's. So where does that leave me? Taco Bell.

Roxanne lets that sink in for a minute.

Taco Bell where guess what all the students go. So if I go, which I don't anymore because of my diet except once a week, I have to use the drive-thru and guess who's doing drive-thru ... Roxanne closes her eyes in pain, pulls away from Miss B's comforting hand cave, and leaves the room. She returns with a box of tissues.

Who works the drive-thru? Miss B asks.

I don't know her name, Roxanne says, but it's one of those people from the school. And if it's not her it's someone else. And it's embarrassing. And I can't sit in the parking lot and eat because the students will see me. So I have to go home, where Freddy is, and the whole point was to get away from him. Half the time I have to go back and get him tacos, which defeats the purpose. Besides, he makes me go to Burger King, where the drive-thru doesn't work, so I'm standing inside at the counter afraid of being attacked by an angry mob of band mommies.

I'm sorry, Miss B says. She hands Roxanne another tissue.

I don't even want to be friends with the football moms. I'm sorry that it makes me such a weirdo that my goal in life is not to be a MILF who goes around seducing her son's friends. And there's a scandal for you to uncover, Miss Teacher of the Year Miss B. Believe me, when I lose forty-seven more pounds, the last person I'm going to seduce is a sophomore.

You look great. Whether or not you lose any more weight. You look great the way you are.

Roxanne blows her nose into the second tissue. Pulls out a third. Piling up, she says about the snot wad in her hand.

That's all right. That's why God made tissues.

Jesus, I hope that was a joke.

It was.

Freddy, he wants to be up there with them during the games. He wants to be friends with the football dads.

That's a positive step for Freddy. Socializing is positive forward momentum.

Except he sits up there and brags. All during the game. About crazy stuff, you know, these outlandish accomplishments. Like he's on drugs or something.

Are you sure he's not?

Yes, I'm sure. He's a walking drug himself. He is his own drug. You know him. A Class B felony drug all unto himself. Thinking about himself actually makes him high. Everyone knows what Freddy's saying isn't true and they just want to get away from him. I'm like, Don't send him down to my row! I want to get away from him, too.

Miss B pats the hand she is holding.

If Spalding weren't on the team, he'd be one of the bullied ones. That's the sad thing. I've known Jared since kindergarten.

We've all known Jared, Miss B says. For a while now.

And not a single, excuse my language, effing—a single effing person shows up for this poor kid today, whatever the hell his name is.

Tyler Newton.

I mean not poor kid, he's a jerk I'm sure and two kids maimed for life, so … But compared to—excuse my language, but the F-bomb effing courthouse was so jammed for our F-bomb quarterback when he had to appear. Violated the fire code, so many people came out to support him. Barricading the stairway. A giant macramé of human …

Roxanne stares into the tissues.

Rubberneckers? Miss B suggests.

No. And I don't mean human filth. There were nice people there. I mean complicated human people who let themselves get completely uncomplicated when it came to a winning football season. Freddy doesn't see it my way.

Miss B is reminded of why she likes Roxanne despite the anger and her stuck life that she stays stuck in. She gets a glimpse of what Roxanne could have become.

Had to clear them off the stairway. Shawna was going berserk but holding it in. You know how Shawna is. But I could tell. She was one trigger away from gun time. Reporters were here. TV cameras.

I know, Miss B says.

Yeah, you were here, that's right. But you came back, Roxanne says. The only one. Nobody cares. Football! Yay! I hate that kid, Roxanne says.

It's complicated, Miss B says.

Not for me. I hate that kid, but I love my son more. There it is right there. The simple equation of parenthood. He's happy in his football uniform. Part of the team, yay. You know, kids commit suicide from being bullied. It's a national epidemic. So if he's happy in that fucking uniform, I'm happy. I just pray every game I don't overhear the shit people feel free to say about him. It's not ALWAYS Spalding's fault when Jared gets sacked.

He's improved a lot, Miss B says. It might be a different story this year.

Well, he's uncoordinated. And he hasn't improved that. And he's slow. And playing video games all summer hasn't made him any faster. You're lucky not to have kids.

Oh, but I do, Miss B thinks. I have so many kids.

Hannah Kirkpatrick's Grandmother

has parked her RV on the edge of the visitor's lot of the football stadium. She and her picnicking friends enjoy their front-row seats as the marching band drums into the lot and lines up in parade-rest formation. Hannah's grandmother is young enough to go through boyfriends. Nobody has a fondness for her current companion, so he stays inside with the air conditioning and reads a book. He's weird like that, the grandmother says to her friends.

Permission to speak, Mr. Hurd. This comes from Zachary Bartel, who draws to attention. He's a tiny sophomore cornet player awaiting his growth spurt. Mr. Hurd has fitted him with a uniform that's too big, but he's seen those thick wrists and he's not taking any chances.

Mr. Hurd says, Speak, young man, or forever hold your peace—but Zachary is also in ROTC so there's no point kidding around.

I have a dentist appointment tomorrow morning. They're going to tighten my braces, so I won't be able to ...

Tomorrow we're going through the new formations for "Midnight Train to Georgia,"

a whoo-whoo! train-cord pull by Miss Stacy

so a minimum of playing, Mr. Hurd assures Zachary. Just do what you can.

Mr. Hurd doesn't like wasting time like this on a personal issue, especially when it's so hot. Zachary could have told him this after dismissal.

No, it's not that, Mr. Hurd, it's that if we do chair challenges tomorrow, I can't do it.

Anisha's happy but worn-out face drains.

Mr. Hurd looks to Miss Stacy.

Zachary? Miss Stacy asks, stepping forward.

Could I challenge today? he says.

This has been an exhausting first day, Mr. Hurd says.

And it's not up to us, Miss Stacy says. We've already said no chair challenges.

Everyone looks to Anisha.

It's okay, Anisha says.

Are you sure? Mr. Hurd asks.

She said it was okay, Zachary said. Those are the rules.

What rules? Miss Stacy asks.

It's fine, Anisha says. Really.

Corbin steps over to hug Anisha.

Mr. Hurd says, We'll do last year's centerpiece, "My Generation" by the Who.

By WHO? Miss Stacy asks.

WHO? yells the band.

Mr. Hurd says, Do the first half, eight to five step with a minstrel turn.

Could I get a couple people to turn with me? Anisha says.

Three volunteers? Mr. Hurd asks.

The trombone row jump to line themselves behind Anisha. God's gift to man white-haired Dick Tresor scoots over there, raising his own trombone in triumph.

Thanks, Dick, but three's enough, Mr. Hurd says. Is three enough, Anisha?

Nice try, Dick! yells Hannah's grandmother.

Nonstop attention-getter, Mr. Hurd thinks. He's going to have to physically brush him aside now.

Trombones are not playing, just marching, Dick.

That's okay, Dick says, big grin to the band.

Anisha removes the water bladder tucked inside her T-shirt and hands it to Corbin, who whispers to her before stepping back. She gathers herself,

Dick, please, says Mr. Hurd, swiping him away

counts it out, raises her cornet. The notes stay pure, even during her turns, even with Dick too much in the way. Except for the air time, when she yanks into the minstrel turn, her long black braid hangs motionless down her back.

Well, I don't believe what they say about her! comes the voice of Hannah Kirkpatrick's grandmother as the cornet's last note fades. Maybe it's the beer in her hand that makes her speak so loudly.

Zachary takes his turn without any trombone players. He marches solo, quickly and confidently and loudly. His overbite makes his gums bleed whenever he applies force. He starches the turns. Anisha gives a silent whoa of appreciation. His instrument thrusts are precise and military. His marching practice with the ROTC has paid off.

Miss Stacy and Mr. Hurd walk away from the band as they confer. They reach the gates where beyond come the cracks and thuds of football practice, the sizzle of whistles. It's music to Mr. Hurd. Everything is music to him until it's turned into something else.

As they walk back to the band, Hannah's grandmother calls over to them, I thought the boy was better!

No, he wasn't, says her friend. You just think a girl shouldn't play trumpet.

It's an E-flat cornet, Miss Stacy explains.

Whatever you say, honey.

You're too kind, Mr. Hurd whispers, pulling Miss Stacy away.

Converts, she whispers with a fist pump.

Anisha and Zachary line up before Mr. Hurd and Miss Stacy. Dick Tresor joins their judging unit. One word, Mr. Hurd thinks. One word and Dick is gone. Period.

Anisha, please step forward, Miss Stacy says.

Anisha takes a step forward. By now her sunburned cheeks have blanched.

Anisha, you were gracious enough to put first chair up for a challenge when you didn't have to. It was not the best day for you. We felt you struggling against the heat and the unexpected impromptu performance you did not expect to give. But your eight to five steps were sharp and organic. Your flow was unconscious, as all attention was on your instrument. Although you worried about the minstrel turn, you performed it well. The pitch of your instrument was perfect, a clarion call to your bandmates. Your long braid led your line like a mace.

Anisha nods her head in a bow and steps back.

Zachary, please step forward, says Miss Stacy.

Zachary advances. His tongue wipes at a spot of blood.

Zachary, you wowed us with the passion you felt for this song. You made all of us feel that we were hearing it for the first time. You sustained the notes without any wobble even during the most abrupt turns. Your lines were sharp. You might have been a little self-conscious in your eight to five steps, which led to ending on your right foot instead of left.

Zachary's face clenches.

But, Miss Stacy continues, we can certainly imagine you leading the line as first chair.

Zachary bows, then steps back beside Anisha.

Anisha and Zachary, begins Miss Stacy. Congratulations on a job well done. Each of you is supremely qualified to lead the cornet section. But as you know, there can be only one first chair.

Miss Stacy looks to each one. Anisha is pale and sweating; Zachary is bleeding at the mouth.

Anisha, Zachary. First chair goes to ... Miss Stacy again looks to each one.

Long pause.

Cut for commercial, thinks Travis. That's what he'd do in his movie.

Anisha.

Anisha quietly shakes hands with Zachary, then runs to Corbin and collapses against his shoulder. She wipes her tears with Corbin's T-shirt.

Miss Stacy shakes Zachary's hand. Good luck tomorrow at the dentist! she says with tearful fervor.

Kyle Jenkins, never not the fun-loving snare drummer, starts a paradiddle to break the ice.

Okay, guys, Mr. Hurd announces through the electronic megaphone. His words exit the megaphone as an autotuned song. Tomorrow then. We've got a big year this year.

No response.

Right? A big year this year. We're all going to do our best no matter what. Right?

No response.

The protest rumors start a seed of panic in him.

Miss Stacy takes the megaphone from Mr. Hurd. Good luck! she calls out. She looks directly at Corbin and Anisha. Good luck!

Don't suck! Corbin and Anisha call back.

Good luck!

Don't suck! Corbin and Anisha shout.

Don't suck! the band yells.

Good luck!

Don't suck!

Good luck!

Don't suck!

Good luck!

Don't suck!

Why?

We're the band!

Why?

We're the band!

WHY?

WE'RE THE BAND!

Good luck!

Don't suck!

GOOD-BYE!

Eight a.m. tomorrow morning! Mr. Hurd reminds them through the megaphone as everyone disperses back to the school. Miss Stacy turns to Mr. Hurd and gives him the thumbs-up. Dick Tresor peels off toward the picnicking RV. Got a beer with my name on it? he asks Hannah's grandmother. Mr. Hurd is almost sorry Dick didn't interfere with the judging so he'd have an excuse to sack him. Volunteers can be the worst, certain types. Every annoying thing they do they think is a big gift.

Miss Stacy falls in step with Travis as they walk back.

The boy was better! calls Hannah's grandmother to Miss Stacy. Even though I like that girl and I don't believe what they say about her! And I don't have nothing against girls playing trumpets!

E-flat cornet, says her friend and they lose themselves in laughter.

We're the band, Miss Stacy says to Travis. We're the band! We're the band, Travis!

It Is Afternoon

in Ohio but the day has come and gone in northern Japan, where Chieko has returned home after many tears in the airport. Already the present is past. Already the language she has not heard for a year has reshuffled her. Already the earthquake has come and gone.

Five boys on a winter night.

It Came In

with a yawn to the rural community of Nishigun, where Chieko had returned home, a minor celebrity with her newfound American-sounding English that was more slurs and mumbles than fluency. It proved useless back in the Japanese school system she hated so much, where the English they studied remained as incomprehensible as ever. A year in America and not a whit of improvement in the tests they forced her to take. She was no closer to deciphering cruel paragraphs written by Charles Dickens and Edgar Allan Poe. Upon her return from Ohio, her celebrity status had surged, then quickly flattened; she was close to being outed as the same old dim Chieko. She rode her bike home from ronin study, head lost in dark dreams. She rode with the other girls who for now were silent. She probably had another week before their laughter and taunts began. Kimi-chan would stand by her, she was a friend, but she missed her American friends. She missed Hannah to the point that her chest ached, her heart.

She wasn't thinking much about the earthquake on the bike ride home. The major damage had already occurred farther north on the island boot of Hokkaido. All eyes were evaluating the earthquake's infrastructure damage to its capital city. Gas leaks had forced fuel outposts to be shut down, the Sapporo airport was closed, there was no electricity to soothe the August oppression. In the one piece of good news, the epicenter was far out in the Pacific where the tidal waves gamboled remotely and harmlessly like ancient forgotten gods.

When the aftermath of one of the tidal waves traveled south and intruded into the countryside of her own village of Nishigun, she barely noticed. The seawater lazed ashore without intention. It came across as a briny profusion more trapped than predatory. The ocean's ebbing rhythms washed it backward. For a moment the water retreated, before it righted itself and calmly advanced.

Chieko watched it from atop a hill. It was soothing.

The surf lapped forward toward the bridge. The water level remained low. The cars on the bridge had jammed and now celebrating guests returning from a wedding had gathered at the railing. There appeared to be no danger of the water lurching upward to sweep them away. The earthquake was over. The aftershocks were over. And this little tidal wave had turned into a sightseeing opportunity.

Chieko observed with confused wonder. Finally to see a tidal wave, this legendary creature their country was taught to fear, finally to see it in person. It was not at all what she imagined. Not at all like Hokusai's woodblocks that they studied in school. His blue ukiyo-e waves rose with hungry white froths like tiger claws. Not at all the mountainous water, the poems they had had to memorize, not at all Kawabata's roiling clouds. The reality below her was a wandering pool, an infinite bath. It had been set in motion by a mother ocean far away but had become in its journey a lost child floundering about in sluggish gulps.

There seemed no chance of Hokusai's tiger pounce with these modest swells, yet a hidden power simmered within. The undercurrent began to weaken the stanchions of the bridge. The bridge began to sway. One end tilted. As the bridge surrendered into a slide, the shocked wedding guests were poured into their newly created inland sea. The bridge pitched slowly enough that most were able to run away; an old woman in a black kimono was grabbed by a rescuing hand before slipping off. The last lucky one was not so lucky and she fell into the water just as escape was within another step's reach, another step she could have made had it not been for the pinched gait forced by her chrysanthemum-painted kimono; she slipped in gently, and gently she was carried along. Chieko watched her. The woman did not appear to struggle; she bobbed lightly in the water, a flower. A good strategy, Chieko thought, until she realized the body was lifeless.

Still she felt calm and protected. Months earlier she had experienced the same feeling of protection when the high school quarterback had tricked her and pulled her into an Amish barn and before she knew it he was at her clothes and she could do nothing but let him, frightened, then knowing she was protected by Amos and the other Amish who came wreathed in a blinding gold. Jared—that was the name of the high school quarterback—and she hated him, and everyone always asked her to say his name and then they laughed at her pronunciation.

She stood with her bicycle, watching the scene as it transpired below. At first the path directly downward had been her shortest route to refuge. After a quick descent into the valley that the bridge arched over, the path tunneled inland and then straight up to safety. But safety was out of reach now. It was already too late for Chieko. She had delayed too long in her dark dreams. Her friend Kimi-chan, on the other hand—Kimi-chan had not hesitated. She had powered the bicycle downhill, under the bridge, and with a head of steam frantically pedaled upward—her soccer legs shooting her higher into the secure hills. Chieko heard screaming as the other girls on their bicycles could not keep up with Kimi-chan. Their ankles were tickled by watery fingers; then the sea's hand wrapped around their legs and they were pulled into the water's embrace. The bicycles bobbed one way, their bodies another.

The wedding party escaping the bridge made loud clackings with their decorative sandals. Chieko could hear them. She thought of Amos and the clopping of horses, the rides he had given her on his wagon. And other things, all of them done for the first time with Amos.

Cars came quietly, she thought. A speedy bicycle was soundless. The louder the running, the slower the clacking wedding guests must be going. How loud they were on the bridge. How unlucky for them to schedule joy for this day.

The people on the bridge were waving as they ran. They were waving to Chieko. They were screaming at her to get on her bicycle. They are waving at me, she heard herself say, Watanabe Chieko, third child and only daughter. Everybody loves Chieko. Everybody wants Chieko to live. Chieko's been to America. And she thought, I look nice in my school outfit. For a moment she was not so sad. A sadness had been drowning her. She had been living in the very water she was staring at. She had not realized it until now. Finally it had come to take her home. She bowed to those she had harmed. She asked Hannah for forgiveness; she cried it out loud. She loved Hannah and wished Hannah loved her. Hannah protected her but wouldn't say that word. Chieko loved that English word love, she said it all the time and drew hearts for Hannah that said love! love! love! She couldn't say love to Amos though what they did must have been love. She called to Amos to remember her. She touched at the spot that had not yet grown, the child inside her, but she could not find its life along the flatness of her stomach. There was no heart on her stomach that said love! love! love! It was better this way. Her family would never have to know.

Fly! someone screamed.

In a leisurely undulation the bridge completed its tilt into the sea. Chieko was, for the moment, still perched above the water. The only path forward stayed at this height but no higher, and it ran parallel to the coast. Riding further inland meant the scribble of hills and all its ups and downs. Already the trough of her first descent was filling with water. The water was not yet dirty, Chieko noticed, so new was it to this green land. It had not had time to find the dirt underneath.

Fly! someone screamed again.

It was a real voice. Was it Hannah's voice?

In the puddle of a descent flared something golden. The same golden she had seen before in the barn. She jumped on her bike and rode toward the glowing beacon. Fly! screamed the voice again.

They broke into an old man's barn.

It Was Friday

in late February, and Henry Zimmerman and his wife sat in front of the fireplace. Ginny had the TV on. She was watching one of those afternoon shows. He never looked up unless there was singing. That caught his attention. He liked singing, any kind. The chatting stuff was white noise to him. He could do without the TV on.

He'd carried in all the firewood he was going to carry, and now he sat. His big country body snugged into the easy chair. He was in his seventies and earlier and earlier in the day that empty easy chair started looking like a teddy bear whose soft furry arms were calling for him to keep it company. So he kept it company, plopped right down in the teddy bear's lap. There was a time for sitting. And it was Friday afternoon and it was four o'clock. He was going to sit. Maybe a song would come on that talk show. If it was a new song, he'd write it down in his book. Ginny didn't even make a move to start dinner. They were both tired. Long week.

Their farmhouse had two bedrooms upstairs; the sewing room downstairs could serve as a third, which it did when Henry's mother was dying. For two years they didn't build a fire because of her oxygen. Their heating bill shot up even though their home was a compact space, cozy and well shored. The main barn was bigger than the house of course, but even the service barn rivaled it in square footage. There was also a sizable play hut Henry had built and shingle-sided. When Danny moved out, he turned it into a maple syrup still. His own father had had the foresight to plant a field of maples, two hundred of them on their property. So there was Zimmerman land that stretched back, something that wouldn't have been obvious to anyone seeing a small house crammed close to the road. Too close. Thankfully very little traffic. At night any car headlights lit the bedroom. Even from far away, the headlights threw stripes high on the wall; closer, they grew brighter and crazier amid the road bumps, and then the high beams full-out attacked their poster bed like hurtling spaceships.

It could drive him crazy if he let it.

Even the lantern on a buggy could send a glow into their home. The clopping of the horse was soothing, though; it took him out of time. He could be young or old when he heard that sound at night.

You want dinner?

I don't know, Ginny said.

Something crazy but maybe, Henry said.

What's that? Ginny asked.

I could go get us a pizza.

You have to drive a long ways for that.

Just to town.

I don't know, Ginny said.

Would you eat it if I got it?

Ginny didn't answer. That meant her guilty conscience wouldn't let her say yes.

People as old as us eating pizza, she finally said.

If I'm going into town, I could rent us a movie. It's Friday night.

Yes, Ginny said. It is.

There a movie you want to see?

What do you want to see?

She wasn't going to say, Henry knew. Guilty conscience again.

What about the weather? Ginny asked.

There's no weather. It's a nice day out, Ginny. You want to drive with me?

All right.

It's Friday. We could paint the town.

Pizza Hut has salad, she said.

Look at you over there. You're getting excited.

She was laughing. It wasn't that she didn't laugh. She did laugh. With the way things were, she laughed as much as possible.

Henry rose from his easy chair, which took longer now and was more embarrassing. He'd broken his hip thirty years back in a quirky otherwise innocent fall from a hay wagon, and the doctor had laughed about what his old age was going to look like.

It's not for sissies, Ginny said, watching him struggle.

It still ticks me off, him laughing at me like that.

It's funny the little things you never forget.

I didn't believe him.

Neither did I.

Henry was glad when the doctor retired. Glad he wasn't going to be around to watch old age arrive for Henry along with all those other medical predictions the doctor was so fond of chuckling over. Henry much preferred this new doctor in town, well, new like ten or fifteen years now wasn't it. She never laughed at him. She actually seemed to admire him, he could see it in her eyes, and that made him feel good. He made sure to get flu shots and the Hep A shot and the follow-up Hep A shot and the shingles shot and the new-generation shingles shot and anything else he could think of, just so he could talk to her and see her smile at him. One time she had on different-sounding music in a foreign language, Indian he guessed, which she turned off as soon as he walked in, but he told her to turn it back on—it was that very song that got him started on his book. Her hand when he shook it was tiny and fragile. So few times he had shaken a woman's hand. He felt a thousand bones in there but wouldn't have described the hand as bony. Different maybe. Different from any hand he'd ever touched.

Outside came the clopping of a horse. A wagon turned into their drive. Henry went out the back door. He shrugged on a jacket as he headed toward the storage barn. Most times his wool shirt would do, but he'd been sitting in front of the fire getting too warm, and now he was too cold.

One of the Goertz sons was standing by a wagon of fertilizer. Henry eyed it with a brief inspection.

This is daggone horseshit, Amos. It's Amos, ain't it?

Yah, sure it is.

Well, it's daggone horseshit.

It's good fertilizer, Mr. Zimmerman.

Not in the winter it ain't. It's frozen turds.

You throw it in the garden, Amos suggested.

Throw what in the garden? Ginny had joined them. She had quickly wrapped herself in a green-and-gold shawl her sister had knitted. It wasn't enough for the cold.

Frozen turds, Henry told her.

Ginny craned her neck but stepped no closer to the fertilizer. It was a dainty gesture, one that confused Henry and brought back memories.

You don't have anything better than this? Henry asked the question but his mind was suddenly on other things. How he had once fixed up the bathroom for Ginny with wallpaper he despised. Yellow, with pictures of flowers and straw baskets. Little Danny had sat on the potty trainer and watched.

It's good fertilizer, Mr. Zimmerman.

I'm surprised at your father, Henry told him, his own vehemence a wonder. Surprised your father would send this over.

Ginny gave a tight smile. I think Amos is selling this on his own, she said.

Your father know about this?

Henry, Ginny said. She spoke in a gentle undertone, the words something he could nonetheless perceive because he was used to her voice. You know, she prompted. Her head nodded toward Amos, the young clean face and the bowl haircut no longer a bowl, but Henry waited, clueless. It's Rumspringa, Henry. Amos needs to make do on his own.

So it was also Amos himself who had decided to rent out the Zimmerman trees to make syrup, not the whole family Goertz. Beyond the barn stood the bodies of maples. They stood tall and armless before the bare branches started, the thinnish trunks a surprise. And on each trunk hung a white plastic bag thickening with sap. The sky was dimming and the fat bags were shining. The white bags hung ghostly in the darkening crowd of maple figures.

Ginny wrapped herself tighter in the shawl. Henry wrapped his arm around her. Amos looked down and away as if to give this immodesty some privacy. A flush had overtaken Ginny's neck and the tips of her cheeks. Her lips had begun to quiver from the cold. Henry remembered them taking Danny to the zoo one autumn day. It was a long drive and Danny, who was always such an overheated baby, had begun to shiver when they pulled him out of the warm car and sat him in the stroller. His jaw trembled wildly. Henry opened his own jacket and held him inside.

You do drugs on your free year? Henry asked Amos.

Yah, no, Mr. Zimmerman.

I heard you do. Heard there's lots of drugs.

Amos shook his head. He still wore the handmade blue shirt, although his new work jacket said Dickies and so did the new trousers. His cheeks were red and delicate as if two poppies had landed on them, but his neck and hands were muscular. Henry could see strong thighs pressing against the Dickies.

Only on that condition, then, Henry said.

From the trees they watched.

Down The Road

churns Travis Hicks's Monte Carlo, windows rolled down, air conditioning via the wind. Freedom. Speed. Travis plays a beat on the roof, fingertips fiddle with scabs of the primer paint. He is wearing his new band uniform. Off to join the Revolutionary War. Marching a full head above the other soldiers, a hefty target for the enemy, a hero for all to see.

Despite his great height and muscular wide build, he was not afraid to lead the frontline and brave the musket fire. All of the enemy took aim at him. The cannonball that landed harmlessly at his feet spurred his troops into a victorious charge. He thought of Mary waiting for him in her garden as he rushed toward Death. She would never again know happiness if he were to fall. The rest of her life would be spent grieving and holding between her breasts the medal of honor he had been posthumously awarded.

First stop, the post office. He has limited-edition Nikes to mail, the payment for them in escrow. In the ditch up ahead is the roadkill of a dog. Travis shoots by. No collar on the dog's thick neck.

Opening game tonight.

Band meets at five thirty.

Entrance march six thirty.

Game at seven.

Halftime show.

His heart starts up.

Pounding heart.

Breathless lungs.

He had sped home from school and changed into his uniform. Before leaving he lingered outside the trailer. He shone like a god and he wanted the Keims to see him. Come! Mr. Keim barked to the three little boys, who stopped and staggered and stared. Travis marched to the edge of their property, never overstepping, before parade turning and marching back. He could feel Mr. Keim knuckled by his pacifist fury. He was a strange combo. Travis hoped she was looking out the window. Of course she was, she had to be. She looked out that window all day long, so lonely during the day when the trailer was empty and he was at school.

A second dead dog in a ditch. Travis hits the accelerator and the muffler roars. When the ditch offers up a third dog, Travis slows. The dog is big and sleeping peacefully on its side. At a barely-there crossroad, an instinct tells him to turn. A high cornfield darkens to jade where the treeline beyond throws shadow over it. In the sunlit swaths, the stalks picked of their ears are already bottomed in gold.

Another dog. Number four. Peaceful and uninjured but dead.

He stops the car. Question: should he get out? If he gets out he might not have time for the post office, which means he might not get money until Tuesday. Question: Should he leave the thirteen-year-old Monte Carlo running and use up gasoline, or should he turn it off, save gas, and risk not getting it started again?

It's the opening game. Cannot miss the opening game no matter how much money it costs him in gasoline. He keeps the car running, yanks tight on the emergency brake, and steps out. Removes his uniform jacket. Red and white and gold are its resplendent colors; custom-darted with brass buttons, shoulder caps, ceremonial cord. He hangs it from the backseat loop, then begins to walk along the cornfield, scouting the shallow ditches.

Closer, a man steps out from the trees.

Travis jerks. The only reason he doesn't jump sky high is that the man looks familiar. Travis knows him from somewhere. He has a memory of him, the clouds refusing to part, some kind of memory.

Already the man has vanished.

Something oozes through Travis, his chest goes heavy and cold. Fear maybe. But he has known fear, sleeping alone in that trailer. He has been afraid. This man is familiar. Familiar is safe.

The ancient asphalt under his feet has long deteriorated. He follows fingers of cement that crumble into gravel and dirt. He walks in partnership with the cornfield until it terminates in a row as sharp as the band lined up on the fifty-yard line. In the scraggly clearing between woods and cornfield are parked a pair of junkers—one of them his mother's car, he is almost certain. She and that guy used to live in an abandoned barn back when Amos Goertz lived there, too, but his year is over and the Amish have probably kicked his mother out by now.

A line of hackberry weed trees tracks a boundary fence that has rotted into the ground. The little forest doesn't look like much, but it hums with its own forbiddenness.

He steps over the rotted fence into the woods.

Mom? he calls.

His T-shirt is snagged by branches. There is no worn path inside the woods, nothing that says people have come here, yet each of his steps finds things manmade. Squashed tin cans and two-liter soda bottles and beer bottles. Snippets of wire, barbed wire as well, and a mattress. And old tires, and scrap metal.

Mom? Hey?

A woman. Among the trees. She darts behind a trunk and disappears.

Alone in his trailer at night, sometimes he is so afraid. He is so big, no one could knock him down. He is so afraid and he doesn't know what to do. Doesn't even know where to sit. There are no chairs. He stands. Until it is time to sleep. Sleep makes him stop shaking.

He follows after the woman he saw, but finds nothing. He crashes through bushes and fallen branches. His band pants and his T-shirt are snagged with brambles. Hey? he asks the woods. Hey? There is no one, and he has reached the end of the little forest. He is back on the road, his car no longer in sight, but he hears the Monte Carlo, its snarling anger. It's leaving him. He steps out to chase it down, then steps back in. Back into the treeline.

A white Ram pickup rumbles into view, slows as it nears Travis. Stops. Its macho engine idles loudly. A man gets out. His hair grabs Travis's attention: unusually thick and wetly ridged with the curls he has tried to comb out. That's the main thing about his face because the man wears a surgical mask. His torso—not fat but all marshmallow. A cowboy shirt is tucked softly into a big Texas cowboy belt. The man drops the tailgate in the manner of a Ram-tough rodeo rider but his weak muscles meet their match against the tonnage of his cargo. He is not strong. He dresses like he is strong, but he is not strong. He yanks and yanks. A growl leaves his throat and vibrates through the woods. The leaves shake in warning and the boughs above Travis begin to crack. The woods whisper for him to move, but Travis dares not move.

Finally the man yanks the cargo far enough over the pickup bed for its own weight to tip it over. It drops it to the ground. A dog. A big one. The man drags the dead dog to a ditch. The effort takes everything out of him. He leans over, heaving, hands on knees. When the man straightens, his eyes above the surgical mask land on Travis standing in the treeline. He gets in the pickup and drives away.

Five boys painted Hit Me! on a deer decoy.

Henry Zimmerman Waited

until morning to call the police. They had come home happy from the pizza and salad. Ginny had been almost giddy to get unlimited greens and he liked teasing her as she listed the pieces of nutrition in her bowl: lettuce, broccoli, cucumber, defrosted zucchini. Chives even—they were green. Just pour on the ranch dressing and give me whatever, he told Ginny as she fixed up something healthy from the salad bar.

I know you think I'm an old backwater, he said to her.

Just want to keep you nearby a few more years.

Don't go superstitious on me, Henry said. In January he'd had a birthday and now he and his dad matched ages. His dad had died at seventy-four. Heart attack. Too much red meat weighed him down. That was the cause of death. Someone without any knowledge named Ginny's sister had declared herself coroner and the diagnosis had stuck all these years. But when it came to pizza you had to have pepperoni. They made one side of it mushroom and olive, but Henry didn't touch it.

Oh, God, this is raw. Henry picked up the broccoli floret and set it aside.

Dip it in here, Ginny said, sliding over the extra bowl of ranch dressing. George Bush didn't like broccoli either.

Rest in peace, said Henry.

When they got home and pulled into the drive, their car headlights lit up the house and Henry saw it. *Pussy* was painted on the side window. *Fuck* on another. Ginny had her eyes closed, dozing as if it were midnight. It was a little before seven. He quickly killed the headlights just as her eyes fluttered wide. By the time the motion beams flicked on, he had angled her past the obscene glass. Inside, Ginny got a second wind and made them coffee and they watched a movie from Redbox, something British they were both surprised they liked so much. They had turned on the subtitles and that had made all the difference. I think we're on to something, Henry said.

Let's get Netflix! Ginny suggested, her eyes almost a wild shine.

The coffee gave Ginny fits. He stirred briefly awake at three to find her just then crawling into bed. Car lights were hurtling toward them. It's okay, he said, pulling her close. We're safe. She'd be asleep for a while.

At sunrise he got up and dressed and made hobo coffee in a tin can the way his father had taught him. It was something he did every once in a while to bring enjoyment to a morning spent alone. He didn't know what he would find outside, but for the moment he was doing this. He stared out the window. Some of the birds were back. He could hear them.

He finished the hobo coffee. The sediment at the bottom of his cup brought him a wave of sad pleasure. Dad, he said out loud. He went outside and checked around. Nothing was painted on the house itself. That was good. Maybe he shouldn't bother reporting it. Then he saw what was left of the lock to the storage barn. The crowbar or whatever tool they had used to break it had also damaged the wood around the lock. Yes, a crowbar, judging from the initial cut. He took a peek inside, couldn't see in the mess if anything was gone. From a mound of paint supplies he picked up a razor-bladed scraper, then made the call.

It was early Saturday morning. The town was quiet and sleeping off winter. The calendar wouldn't leave February. But the birds were back. Soon now. It didn't take too long for a cruiser to appear. Henry stood as if waiting for it this whole time even though he had just now finished a look-round atop his acres.

The cruiser turned on its flashing lights as it pulled into the drive.

That was stupid. Erly Johnson stepped out. Well, this problem just met a dead end, Henry thought when he saw who it was.

Please turn your flashers off, Henry said.

Erly flipped open his notepad after he took a preliminary stroll around the crime scene. He wrote down the words "Amos Goertz" when Henry backstepped through the previous night. Amos didn't do it, Henry said.

How do you know?

I just do.

Until he's cleared, he's a suspect.

Henry sighed.

You know, Erly explained to him, flipping his notepad shut and tucking it into his back pocket, a lot of the ways of our world are attractive to them, and they might not be above stealing to get a piece of the American pie.

Okay, Erly, Henry said. Put Amos down as suspect number one on your crime evidence board. (There had been an elaborate board for a string of murders on the British show the night before, index cards, thumbtacks, photos, and string.)

With your permission I will, Erly said, snatching back his notepad.

And then explain to me why he'd shoot his own sap grabbers.

Henry pointed to the woods and the Zimmerman maples. The plastic bags that had hung bulbous and heavy the day before blew empty in the wind. The birds had stopped singing. A ghostly winter hole sent a chill through him.

Looks like they took a little target practice, Erly said.

Guess Amos went to all the trouble to tap them trees and collect the sap only to shoot it all out of the bags.

Erly squinted at the distant trees. Henry knew what he was considering, whether it was worth it to walk over there and take a closer look. Climb that mild incline to the trees. There was nothing more pitiful than an out-of-shape country boy.

BBs, Henry said. Case you're wondering.

Okay, Erly said. That narrows it down.

We're looking at teenagers.

We might be. Erly took a step inside the storage barn. I'll need a list of the items stolen, he said.

I really can't tell, Henry said.

Looks like they used your own paint to paint the windows.

That came as a good observation on Erly's part. I guess there are some cans missing, Henry agreed.

I presume brushes, too.

I presume, Henry said. I had some stuff over here. He swirled his hand toward a mound covered by an old rug. Heavy dust took a hop when he lifted the rug. Nope. Thought I kept my deer decoy here.

It's missing?

I don't know. Might be at the back wall, Henry said. He and his dad had taken Danny out hunting a few times but even as a bloodthirsty little boy, he had never taken to it. Didn't like sitting around and staying hidden. Now that was all he did, he had stayed hidden from them for years; somewhere he was sitting around, and the target he was waiting for was himself.

You want to take a look? Erly asked him.

Everything stored against the back wall was hidden by a barrier of stacked chairs and the spiderwebs connecting them.

Erly, I can't get back there.

Why don't you go to some of these antique places next week, see if any possessions show up. You'd recognize if you saw your stuff, right?

This most of it belonged to my dad and mom. I'm not going to forget it.

I think that's a good plan then. People sell it, you know. People on drugs. Erly once again flipped open the notepad. We got a big problem here. Good people, they start doing the wrong thing. Erly's pen was poised.

Don't write down that name, Henry said.

I'd be remiss in my duties.

Don't write down that name.

Erly pocketed the notepad.

It wasn't Danny, Henry said.

How do you know?

Because maybe your sister did it.

Yeah, maybe she did, Henry. Maybe she drove all the way up from Columbus after working late as a distribution engineer at AEP and painted your windows because she knew you were going to be gone for an hour to have pizza.

Just take some photos of the windows, Erly. I gotta get them scraped off before Ginny comes down.

You're good at photos, Henry decided to add.

Just doing my job, Erly said.

Of course you were. The world needed to see that photo, didn't it?

A bit ago Erly had found Danny and a woman looking dead in their car. He'd given himself enough leisurely time to take a photo before administering the Narcan. The photo was posted online and it went viral and Ginny's sister told him she saw it on the national news with one of those warnings that it was a disturbing image. She was telling Henry all this because he would want to know it.

Henry started with the uglier word first. He charged the scraper through all the letters at once. Made *Pussy* look like it was written twice. A thought came to him: perhaps he didn't eat right because then he might live longer. He might live longer than his own son.

He was hard at work scraping and ignoring Erly when Erly mentioned something about catching the perpetrator and Henry didn't turn around but wiggled a weak little thanks with his scraper. Whenever that word came up, "perpetrator," that was a signal that nothing was going to get solved. It just made him so mad, that word. He turned toward Erly stepping into the cruiser and said, I'm sorry your sister has nothing better to do on a Friday night than drive up here and paint my windows. I guess she's not dating anyone.

We're not in touch so I wouldn't know. We don't agree with her lifestyle, Erly said.

Be nice if she could meet a nice girl and settle down.

Erly pushed into his seat.

And I was the first one spotted it, too. Knew it from the time she was twelve years old. Shoulda took a photo! Don't slam the door on me, asshole, he muttered. He turned back to his window, shaking with anger.

He'd scratched the F off the second window when Ginny stepped out in one of Henry's barn jackets. The long sleeves covered her hands. Well, what's this? she said.

I've reported it. Erly Johnson was here.

That's what we get.

Oh, now, don't say that.

We can't go out now.

Oh, Ginny, come on, now. And it wasn't Danny, he said, scraping hard, not turning around.

Who then?

Erly thinks it was Amos Goertz.

Oh, for god's sake, Ginny said and went back inside. Then she popped her head out. Need some help?

Almost done, he said.

It happened on a Saturday night. Five boys
put a deer decoy on the road. From the trees they watched.

It Was True

what I suspected of Artemis. I had been tracking her without pause since she had lost her little mortal to the tidal waves. On that afternoon, any loose shards of my sister's better judgment had been washed away. A giant swell of sentimentality had surged up and engulfed her. Oh, sister! Whenever I saw those mawkish tears, I knew she was at her most dangerous.

I kept her close. I followed her here, where it had all begun. Where one evening she had saved her little pet's innocence. Where another evening she had watched her lose it.

We were back.

At first we frolicked with a lad we'd come to recognize, young but of impressive godlike mass. We teased him in the woods but my sister's attention quickly ebbed. She was focused on something bigger, else we would not have been here. I left my sister to have my own brief moment. I traveled to the epicenter of heaved stone and wood where the townsfolk sat in their powered vehicles. Here in miniature was all that I despised. How strongly it sparked in me the urge to toss the sun and bring eternal darkness to their lives, to the ruined topos they must take blame for. Yet I cleaved to my duties, as I must. A slap at the head coverings of the few plebeians who exited their vehicles was the trifle of entertainment I allowed myself.

Why did I come to a place I hated?

It was only at this place I could offer tribute.

There he was. I stood alone before his statue. A flawed human had cast the bronze into such an inferior likeness that Hephaestus himself would have been motivated to exact personal punishment from the artist. Solely recognizable in the statue was the long rifle. Who among these indifferent mortals passing by his memorial had known him in the flesh? Only I was left as witness. When I had first come to this land and spied him, I should have claimed my spoils and called myself happy. How many times had I saved his life? How many times afterward had I let the forest win back his heart? Believing he was a god, I had let him grow old. Seeing him old, I had let him die.

In mere moments the New World had changed to this. I wanted it no more. A skyless residence with Hades offered more cure than chasing my sister in the sunshine, she who still held to our mythos. And to our sacred covenant of revenge.

I will slay them all, she said.

Now we stood together in the town's coliseum, where all were gathered for the night's sporting competition. The populace had reacted with mad proletarian joy when the musicians had entered the field. My sister and I laughed to see the drummer we had tormented in the woods bringing up their rear line. He was easy to spot even disguised so ridiculously in his uniform. His head rose a full moon above the others and on his face was a smile. My sister wanted to slay him then and there for daring to grin, for she preferred her humans pathetic.

The musicians cleared the field in a stiff trot that seemed as fiercely entertaining to the spectators as the melodies they had so miserably attempted to play. Music of the gods it was not. But off they trotted to savage roars. Truly I feared for the human race.

One musician resisted the urge to flee and was quickly deserted by her comrades. She stood alone in the middle of the field. This girl. A tiny pillar enveloped by the deserted plain upon whose exact center she stood, for it was marked with the numbers and stripes of the forthcoming competition. The plain was richly green. The arena bristled with

silence. The spectators, so bloodthirsty minutes before, had fallen unnaturally still. The sun was dipping toward the horizon yet shone still.
How quickly I could make it plummet and cause a panic.

The face of the lone musician was all but hidden by the tower of a
headpiece that wobbled atop her skull, but below the headpiece and
down her back snaked a long black braid. The girl raised a horn to her
lips. I was prepared for my ears to flare in outrage, but the notes that
poured forth were bearable.

I will start with her, said my sister. Her arm cast backward to her quiver of arrows.

She had nothing to do with your dear pet crossing over.

She looks like a slave girl. Look at that braid. A slave braid. She is a
good one to start with.

Have you cleared this with Father?

For how long has he been reduced to a burden of lard and indolence?
Artemis scoffed. And the others as well. All of them. I hate them all.
Even Aphrodite has no sway except in the places where old mortals go
to die. She gives them one last thrill before the throat rattle.

Stop, I ordered her.

And our own uncle. More blubbery than his whales. Too slow and
indifferent. He could have saved her! I called for his aid.

It is his time no longer, Sister. For how many centuries has this been
the lesson you will not learn? The moonstruck waves do what they do
without Poseidon's intervention.

Me! she protested. Artemis herself calling for his aid. How dare our
own uncle ignore me?

You showed her a path to escape. You did what you could.

I should have pulled her from the waves myself.

You have no power in Uncle's world. Be happy that she crossed over
swathed in your golden comfort.

You and I are the only ones left, she said. Here came the tears. Here
came the wet dripping signals of danger.

Then we must honor our duties, I told her. I went so far as to grab her shoulders and shake her. We must stay strong. We cannot make our own rules and throw the world back to the Titans.

I could slay all the Titans with one hand.

No, I said. No, you could not. You do not want to go back there to that time.

You do not know your own twin if you believe in my surrender, she said. An arrow was already threaded in her bow. I can start with that one.

The arrowhead indicated a boy dressed in sun-touched yellow. He was suited differently from the other musicians, who could play no tune and fight no war, who were more stretcher bearers than gladiators, feeble Ottomans who would lose a clash against an olive twig, who could not even play the cacophony of warfare without sounding defeat by the second note.

He is another who was there, she said. The boy in yellow. See him? He was there. I remember him.

Leave him. He is innocent.

I will drop them all and be content. Agreed?

The boy decorated in yellow held a long mace that had been silver-smithed. He had led his musicians onto the field and he had led them off. I had watched him minutes earlier hasten across the field, fed by the arena's hungry ovation. He was swift as a deer even in the contort-ed position that defined his charge. His spine curled back and his head watched the sky, perhaps trying to find me hidden among the clouds. He claimed a superior indifference to the erratic fury of the spectators, to whether their thumbs would go up or down as he finished his backbend and posed immobile, his eyes steady and faraway and yes, for that mo-ment, godlike.

No, I said. You will not start with him.

She began laughing. You desire him, she taunted.

Stop, I warned.

He is a tender sapling, she said. How much your fine-leathered dearest would enjoy knowing your true tastes.

The boy is swift, I said.

She drew back the arrow. I stayed her hand.

History has forgotten us, Sister. We can no longer do this.

Him, she said, pointing suddenly to the arena stands. I dislike him.

A man stood immovable, a stiff salute at his brow, until the horn music from the slave girl died out.

He is no different from the others. They are all standing, I said.

And they will all die.

No, they will not.

I will start with him.

I knew why the man's salute had vexed her. He stood in full thrall to something besides the goddess Artemis. She was nothing if not transparent in her petty jealousies.

Come, I said, leading her to the stands, where spectators had renewed their rabid cadences of hurrahs. Two new guilds of gladiators ran onto the field and lined up to face each other. For what purpose was impossible to divine until a ball emerged and was gently placed, like a newborn, upon its cradle. The heads of the gladiators were full helmeted and their shoulders widened by colorful armor, but their legs were unprotected and it would be an easy matter to hobble them. They dug in like bulls and snorted and pawed. My sister was momentarily distracted. A smile played on her face as she watched them hare aimlessly about the plain, stop start dart left dart right, rabbits all. The plain's rich green already being torn by their lamentably prosaic chaos.

And yet the distraction worked. My sister chuckled as a ball was thrown long and high and a mound of gladiators threw themselves to the stained ground like locusts fooled by an empty husk and we listened to someone's voice descend from the clouds and call out numbers that incited chants by the spectators and foot stomps like battle drums. She began to laugh. Her ripple swelled into a storm. She laughed so hard she could not stop. So thunderously did she mock and hoot that our presence was nearly felt. Nearby spectators turned confused in their seats. They squinted at the bristling air where we stood full next to them, our golden skin touching theirs.

Before I could stop her, she had drawn her bow. An arrow flew to the airborne ball kicked by a gladiator and knocked it off its course. The arena's bloodcurdling cries of woe ignited more delight on her face.

All of them should die, she said.

Over here, I called to her. I was standing next to a girl who sat with other girls who looked the same, none of them as comely as their aspirations for immortality dreamt them to be. All of them had dyed their cheeks with numbers. One girl wore number 9 upon her cheek. Another number 11. There were 12 and 7 and 31. There were many numbers.

More slave girls, said my sister.

Here is a girl you can slay, I said. Number 23. My finger buzzed golden down her marked cheek and tingled across her lips.

Thank you, said my sister, drawing her sword. I will slay number 23. Move.

Before you claim her, witness this, I said. My arm outstretched and my fingers tapped along the fascia of the sky until I found the crack and dug in. Or do you not want me to? I asked.

Artemis was sniffing the air. Suspicion and her ancient calling to protect the forest alerted her posture. I smell dead animal upon someone, she warned. A killer is among us.

She turned to follow the scent. Him! she called, pointing to a lone man at the top row. Quickly I pulled back the fascia and quickly her glance at the scene therein rooted her in place. She forgot about the dead animal and the man and the forests she protected, for she was also the protector of young girls, and this oath still tugged most deeply at the conscience she had nigh abandoned. She froze. She stared. A childish wonder opened her jaded features.

So many times my sister had begged me to do this, to shear open the past, but I had never indulged her.

It is not a wise idea, I said, dropping my hands.

No!

You wish to see?

Yes!

I pulled the sky full open to the past. Your dear pet, I said.

To draw back the scrim of time was a power entrusted solely to our father and me. I unveiled the scene to her. Now stood before us this same girl, number 23, in the same spot, one year earlier. And on number 23's lap sat the dear pet, the one she had lost to the waves.

When my sister gazed upon her little mortal returned to the flesh, the tears fell. Theatrical tears, of course. And so abundant they could have drowned an audience left bereft by a tragedy of Sophocles, something she had once effected when she felt the audience was swayed too deeply by its loyalty to Athena. But those were different days. We ran the world as we pleased or displeased.

As staged as the torrent of weeping might have been, there were genuine tears involved at seeing the little mortal she had loved, now sitting among the cheering girls. The dear pet was as I remembered her, mute and unresisting. She was, as most humans had become to me, mortally wounded by her own colorless drears. In time past I had directed no attention to this submissive creature, so forgettable was she, until it was too late and my sister too advanced in her passion.

Girl number 23 caressed the shiny black hair of the dear pet. First she ironed it out with the flat of her palm, then gathered it into a tail and held it, then let it spring loose and ironed it anew. Now and again she hugged the dear pet with impetuous squeezes.

My sister reached through time's veil and laid her hand upon her little mortal, but even she with all her power could not feel the flesh.

Would you kill number 23? I asked. Would you kill the one who first showed her kindness? I made to close the scrim until my sister stayed me.

Show me further, she said.

I must have your word.

My word. For tonight.

I drew back the scrim.

We love you, Cougars!

We love you, Cougars!

The cheers mingled past with present, for nothing had really changed. The screams came from both sides of the scrim. Her dear pet shivered into translucence as both time spans played out in unison.

We say Spirit!

Spirit, spirit!

Say it, Chieko!

Spirit, said the dear pet.

Chieko speaks English!

Chieko speaks English!

They further caressed the dear pet's hair. They hugged her. They fought over whose lap she was favored to sit upon. The substantial mist that was the dear pet floated from numbered girl to numbered girl.

We love you, Cougars! They jumped up to cheer.

We love you, Cougars! Just as they jumped up to cheer in the present moment.

They stomped their feet then. Just as they stomped their feet now.

We love you, Chieko! Stand up, Chieko! Stomp stomp stomp your feet!

Sit down, cunt.

What?

The line of numbered girls turned as one. There was a woman behind them.

Sit down, cunt, the woman said.

Where did that come from? they asked the woman behind them.

This woman had many more decades of life left in her, that is to say, she was not yet half along her mortal accounting, but vibrant living had already died. She had advanced to an age that was uninteresting and that she cloaked with a shapelesss garb that left her heavy forearms to swing free.

None of us can see, the woman said. The woman's shapeless garb had words written upon the chest, but I was not interested in her words.

You don't use that language, the numbered girls said.

If the shoe fits, the woman said.

Hey b, you can't talk to us like that.

You're a cunt and you need to sit down.

You're the cunt, cunt. The number 9 girl dared this.

No, Elsa! No no Elsa! Don't do that! the other numbered girls warned. They grabbed the number 9 girl and hugged her down to the bench. That's Hailie Atkins's mom! Why don't you go over to the other side, Mrs. Atkins? You're the one who decided to move out of town, not us.

I can sit where I want.

You can't come over to our side and tell us what to do. It's not right to root against our side.

It's morally wrong, added number 23, hugging the dear pet close.

I'll get security if you don't sit down, the woman said. I'll sue you for harassment.

I'm calling security! the number 9 girl said. Security!

You're scaring Chieko! girl number 23 yelled.

Chieko is scared!

She's our guest in this country! You can't sue her, b! It's morally wrong! She's a guest in our country!

I pulled the scrim closed. I turned to my sister. Is this what you miss? I demanded. Their witless incessant tedium? Is this what you miss about your little mortal?

Yes, she answered. Yes!

This is what human life has become, I told her. It is no longer worth the effort to exterminate them. Let them live and kill each other.

It happened on a February night.
The boys who crashed wore thin jackets.

At The Bony

etching of the crossroad, Travis makes the turn and parks. This time he cuts the engine. The one-lane road before him ... deprived of life and asphalt, bleeding into the forest's canopy. The creepy little woods ... inhabited perhaps ... filled with disturbingness.

His decision is to wait in the car.

Even the cornfield spooks him now. His imagination? Or has the tick of twenty-four hours already aged the stalks ... the airwaves from last night's band performance maybe, the shock of decibels bleaching the green right out of the cornhusks? He'd never felt anything so loud and so exciting as when the band marched *under* the stadium then *out* of the stadium then *onto* the field in their new uniforms. Obliterating the football team. MAKING THEM IRRELEVANT! as Miss Stacy screamed. Even Yoder—Yoder stopped outside the barn to listen—probably he did, yeah he must have, of course he did ... the countryside reeling and rocking and cocking its ear, wondering, Hey what the hell is going on? wondering, Why can't we be part of it? Does Yoder know he plays the drum? He did last night. Euphoria throbbed in Travis's throat as they finished the halftime show. His bandmates took flying leaps to high five him. "Midnight Train to Georgia." The flutes danced out of the pack and just like the Pips to Miss Stacy's Gladys Knight did a whoo! whoo! train whistle … in the stands shocked delight, everyone screaming. And then when Miss Stacy stepped back in as Gladys Knight and the trombones came out as the Pips for their whoo! whoo! …

Jesus fucking Christ! screamed Kyle Jenkins, beating the elated hell out of his snare drum.

Mr. Hurd is a genius and it's also already too hot on a Saturday morning and Travis is sweating. He gets out of the car. Turns his back on the woods. Walks to the crossroads and rocks leg to leg. Keeps eyes averted from ditches … face forward. He's in a good mood still … such a good mood … good mood dancing through him. He'd like to run as fast as possible. Just go.

The car coming down route 418 is Miss B's sporty SUV. A blueberry-colored RAV4. So perfect for her. He's going to get a Hyundai Santa Fe, he's decided. Or a Chevy Tahoe. Twelve hundred in the bank so far, but that's reserved for higher education. He's got $250 coming in this week from the domain name. He buys domain names whenever he sees lists of military. Kattoga puts up banners of local heroes, active and vets and national guard and army. He didn't mean for any of them to die, just figured they'd want their own website at some point and he'd sell it back to them at a profit. When Anisha played "Taps" last night he felt so guilty, and then that military guy riveted at attention in the stands, that brought tears to his eyes. The dead soldier's family had already contacted him to buy back the name. They had no idea the seller was in the same state, the same town, the same football stadium as they were.

The blueberry car shoots toward him, suddenly brakes. He can guess. The first one starts about there. The RAV4 slows to rubbernecking speed. At the crossroads Miss B turns and parks behind the Monte Carlo.

I saw, she is already saying as she gets out. I saw.

Travis is so charged from last night he doesn't have to do the countdown he usually does before speaking: five, four, three, two, one, speak. He can speak, and he is in a talkative mood. All the words partying inside him.

The one down there has a collar, he says. He points near the woods. Looks like a chocolate Labrador, he adds.

You didn't touch it!

No.

Miss B is wearing pants today. She never wears pants to school. The pants make her look more feminine. He has never thought *those things* when it comes to Miss B. Maybe that's the point of the skirt, a style that doesn't suit Miss B at all, so you don't think those things, so no teenage hormones get hurt during the making of her lessons. Skirt (sissy) times Miss B (not sissy) equals zero. Teacher love, the sex canceled out.

Did you continue farther down? Miss B asks. She shoots an invisible basketball beyond the woods.

No. Not yet.

Come on. Miss B gets in her RAV4 and signals Travis. After a struggle to slide back the passenger seat, they course down the lane on a lookout.

There's one, she says.

That's the one with the collar, Travis says. The brown Lab.

Miss B takes her foot off the accelerator. The RAV4 crawls on its own. The overhanging trees weave a tunnel. The sunny day fights through branches to spill puddles of deceptive shadows. Shadows in the shape of dogs. Shadows ready to pounce. Everywhere is an optical illusion of dog, a shivering border collie draped over a log, an obedient beagle sitting among shivering leaves, a furrowed bulldog carved into furrowed bark.

Until a real one appears, permanently napping in a ditch. Unmistakably not shadow.

They don't look harmed, Miss B says.

She gets out of the SUV to inspect. Travis gets out and stands beside her. He would not be doing this if he were alone. He steels himself. He wishes every moment could be Friday night marching onto the field. No one strong enough but him to swing that thud bass around like it's nothing more than a tambourine. That moment then has become this moment now, the very moment when there is a brown dog in a ditch that looks like a brown deer. But this moment will also pass, he tells himself, so don't worry. He is safe here, death at his feet. This moment will pass, the death will leave. He didn't understand why yesterday he felt compelled to make the turn even though it almost made him late for the post office. Now he knows why he turned. *Hit Me. Hit Me.* He is looking down at the dog, but what he sees is the deer decoy. The deer decoy landed in the ditch at Travis's feet. Just like that. It flew through the air. It was already flying before he heard the sounds of the crash. In the pitch dark he could still see it plain as day. The deer's eyes stared open. Flirtatious eyelashes. *Pussy. Hit Me.* The letters shimmered on its flank. A golden dead deer shining at his feet except it wasn't a real deer. Somehow even worse.

Country ditches.

Nothing good to be found in country ditches except sometimes they save you from tornadoes. He is safe here. If a tornado comes they will flatten themselves in the ditch on the other side. He is safe with Miss B. Nothing will happen. Miss B is invincible. They look down at the dog. Maybe someday it will be his mom lying in a ditch. Nothing good about country ditches.

Travis clears his throat. He calls himself back to a happier time, just last night, mere hours earlier. Kyle Jenkins going crazy on the snare drum, to the point that the whole drum line started laughing. Travis started laughing, too. And this is just their first game. More to follow, and craziness on the buses to away games.

I can't believe him, Miss B says.

What's the man's job? Travis asks.

I can't believe he'd do it.

But his job, maybe it has something to do with dogs?

Graphics and shipping.

Pictures of dogs?

Not that kind of graphics. Why? she asks.

Just wondering.

No. No, Travis. Miss B smothers him with those classroom wide eyes that mean think about it now, take all the time you need, but think about it and explore your reasoning and then speak clearly and forcefully and enlighten us all. Miss B's wide eyes are not ones like the Bambi decoy. Hers are cow eyes, the straight lashes thick and aimed downward.

Because maybe they're mercy killings, Travis says. Maybe he's an angel of mercy.

Yes, Miss B says. One would like to think. He's not an angel, God help me. He's not an angel at all. But I didn't think he was this. But you know what I like, Travis? she asks.

Travis, she repeats. Do you know what I like?

What?

I like how you're looking at this. It's very mature. It's very empathetic.

Okay.

Don't okay me, Travis.

Sorry, I'm afraid I don't know the answer to your question, he blurts. Random and makes no sense but it doesn't matter. It's what Miss B instructs them to say instead of *Um*.

Oh, lord, Miss B moans. These beautiful creatures. Oh, lord. "When sorrows come, they come not as single spies, but in battalions." What would our William say about this most ghastly scene, Travis?

It might be a lame question, a fake teaching moment meant to disguise the distress on her face that says I'm going to throw up and allow her to shore herself back up to bulletproof teacher of Kattoga High, but if any moment deserves Shakespeare a dead dog in a ditch does and he wants to answer it anyway and he wants to get the answer right, especially since he screwed up with Miss B's other question. Last night's adrenaline is still feeding his brain though the main partying has drained and a funeral guest has entered. Friday night is draining away, he needs to grab at it, one last moment of magic. He practices the words in his head, some are more CNN than Bard of Avon, goes through words like deceased, murdered, massacred, et tu, searching for something poetic. Stabbed through innocent heart, eternal sleep, killing field, brutal assassination, thus with a kiss I die.

Fair dead dogs landing in ditches foul, he says.

Miss B covers her mouth with both hands and appears to rest her head against the heavy air. My lovely Shakespearean boy, she sniffles. What are we going to do with you?

She hugs Travis. Her arms struggle to go all the way around his torso. He can feel her fingertips fighting to grasp each other. Suddenly she is crying against his chest, more like his upper abdomen. She pulls away. I'm sorry, she says. Oh, god, don't start, she says. Because I had dogs growing up. Don't start, don't start. Did you have dogs?

My mom has a dog. She doesn't love him.

I loved all my dogs, Miss B says. So much. Don't start, don't start. I'm going to cry again.

Travis steps back to the car. Miss B remains at the ditch, looking down, shoulders shaking. The pants give her a different figure altogether than the skirt. They shape her bottom into an apple. She leans over further and the high elastic waistband of her jeans comes into view.

Don't get any closer in case he used gas, Travis warns, remembering the man's surgical mask. This is something he has over Miss B because he takes science class and she only does English.

First one was Boy, Miss B says. Boy was a mutt but with a lot of Lab in him. He was big like these dogs. If I'd ever found Boy like this in a ditch ... my god. She wipes at her eyes. Boy had a son, Buddy. We liked Buddy, not as much as Boy. Boy was special. Then Yuri and Rupert came along—they were Doberman Pinschers but very very nice. Boy went off into the woods to die, that was a sad day. He knew we'd be sad so he limped off into the woods to die alone so we wouldn't have to watch. He could barely walk by then. His black fur was turning white and hung down old and dry. He waited until Buddy and Rupert and Yuri were taking naps and then he went off. He wasn't going to let us see him die. Not Boy. He wasn't going to do that to us. Then we got Robert H. Boston bull terrier. Oh, my god, could Robert H catch a rubber ball. At any angle off the wall. Hunter and Rascal came next. Hobo, a cocker spaniel, inaptly named, very much a prima donna, so we changed her name to Bedazzled and she was never the same, got very confused. Then Spot. Then Bubba, Zoey, Winnie, and Rex. Bubba was a rescue dog but he ended up rescuing us. Then Clarence, whom we adored because he was so so charmingly stupid and tried to replace with Calvin, who was also very stupid but lacked Clarence's charm. I couldn't look at Calvin without being reminded that he wasn't Clarence, and I couldn't look at Clarence without being reminded that he wasn't Boy.

Miss B returns to the car and they turn around to head back to the crossroads and route 418, where, in perfect timing, the car driven by Dr. Devajaran is slowing for reconnaissance. Miss B honks the horn.

Poppin, Dottie, and Ronnie, Miss B finishes up. Poppin was another Boston bull terrier, Dottie was a golden retriever mix, Ronnie was a mutt with some Irish wolfhound in him. Regret that name Ronnie because it didn't fit him, but I didn't dare change the name after seeing what it did to Hobo slash Bedazzled.

Dr. Devajaran slides out of the car and walks toward them.

Are Clarence and Calvin famous people in books? Travis asks.

No. Why?

You don't have any literature names, Travis says.

They're dogs, Travis. They're not characters in books. They're real people. Although we did have an incredibly annoying Chihuahua we named Tiny Tim. Hi, hello! Good morning! Miss B calls to Dr. Devajaran. Thanks so much for coming!

Seldom does Travis feel awkward about his size. That's who he is. He suffered through a stress-fractured foot the summer before sophomore year to make it to this size, so he needs to appreciate the torture his body went through to get him here, up high and wide. And he does. His size is Travis size and he's Travis. However—however, when Dr. Devajaran shakes his hand and pats him on the forearm, he feels shame. He feels like a freak. She is so tiny. He is so big. Her hand wraps babylike around a couple of his fingers. Her hand can barely cup his elbow. His roiling insides heat up and send flames out of his mouth. Temperature rises. Meltdown. How large are his large intestines? They must be monstrous.

How long are his small intestines? Must be miles long. There's so much square footage inside him. How long are Dr. Devajaran's intestines? Not very long, how could they be? Her intestines laid out next to his? His would trail past the cornfield all the way to the woods, he bets. Hers would barely wiggle to the first line of stalks.

Are you with us, Travis? Miss B asks.

Yes, he says. These are all compliments, he wants to explain to them. These thoughts about intestines. It's because she's a doctor. More than a doctor. And plus he suspects she's his benefactor, the one footing his dry-cleaning bill. All the marching band members are responsible for dry cleaning their uniforms every week, especially now with the new ones. Even factoring in their courtesy discount, that comes to $7.50 right there. Every week. Which comes out to $30 a month. Some of the band members win merit scholarships that cover dry cleaning. No one knows where the merit scholarships come from, all Mr. Hurd will say is that they come from the land of merit, but it was a little bit odd when Anisha was the one to tell Travis he had just won a full-ride dry-cleaning scholarship. He knew right then her mom had something to do with it. Probably Dr. Devajaran feels guilty she can't be a regular band mom and do more. She's never at the brownie sales, but once she sent over sweet milk balls and a little sign spelling out the dessert's foreign name and the ingredients she used so they wouldn't be scared off and once people tasted them they sold out quick. Anisha gave him a doggie bag of them, freebies because of his merit scholarship. *Travis* was scripted on a brown paper bag that looked store-bought and branded for the purpose of being a doggie bag, and the handwriting of his name didn't look American and made him rethink how to do his signature, and he sat outside the trailer on the cinderblock steps, barefoot, looking at his feet and eating free gulab jaman and air-writing his new signature. So sweet were the balls that the top of his head blew off. It was warm and the sun took so long to set. As his head was exploding, the god Apollo strode up to his trailer and said, I'm keeping the sun up a little while longer—this one's for you, Travis. This is one of his happiest memories, the sun paused in the sky and on his lap the food they made for him, with thoughts of him, with love. He knows now what Miss B thinks about when she needs to go to her happy place. She thinks about Boy. He thinks about the time sitting on his cinderblock as if Anisha and Dr. Devajaran were there beside him keeping him company, their renewed delight at each bite he took, the pleasure of each ambrosial nugget the two of them had labored over.

Dr. Devajaran and Miss B stand at the ditch where the swollen Labrador rests.

This seems to be the only one of them with an ID attached, Dr. Devajaran says. She snaps on latex gloves and a surgical mask. Travis watches her hands maneuver the mask strings swiftly and expertly around her hairstyle ... the long hair she wears in a loose tail instead of a braid like Anisha.

You don't need to do that just to look at its collar, Miss B says. I can tell you who it is. That's Licorice.

You know this dog? Dr. Devajaran asks.

Not very well. But yes I know him. Knew him. Licorice belongs to the Atkins family.

Hailie Atkins?

Hailie Atkins.

A wordless communication passes between the two of them, one of those things that wouldn't be wordless if Travis weren't standing there.

They moved out of town after—Dr. Devajaran stops herself. They moved out of town, she says, sending a bright smile to Travis.

But they were at the game last night, Miss B says.

She was, Travis confirms. Just the mom. I saw her.

He shouldn't feel so elated simply because Dr. Devajaran beams a supportive smile to him and Miss B nods at him like he's a normal adult contributing to their normal adult three-way conversation, but he does. He feels so happy standing there with two other people on a mostly dirt road.

Mrs. Atkins was rooting against our team, Travis adds.

Seriously? In Miss B's voice erupts outrage. Last year's fight wasn't enough? She has to come back and do it again?

Yeah, Travis says. And Erika got involved.

Oh dear, says Miss B. As if the c-word wasn't enough. I hope this doesn't lead where I hope it doesn't lead.

Erika's mom and dad stepped in.

Lovely people, Miss B says. I hope Hailie can get her mom to stop doing this.

Hailie wasn't there, Travis says.

Miss B and Dr. Devajaran again exchange that look. As if Travis isn't going to be able to deduct it out to its obvious conclusion. He's not innocent to the ways of the world. No one's ever accused him of that except his mother, who was pregnant with him by his age now. Sexual intercourse is her great accomplishment that she lords over him. He'll never be able to accomplish what she accomplished by age seventeen. More than once she's made fun of him because he hasn't had sex. He doesn't bother to tell people what she's said because he knows they'll find it too hard to believe, a mother saying that as well as the actual content of her words because everyone has noticed that whenever the marching band plays, it's like Travis is the lead in a rock band—the girls flock. They are ready to throw themselves at him. When the band travels to away games and rides the buses home in the pitch dark, it's a nonstop makeout session or it would be if Mr. Hurd and the band parents didn't roam the aisles and prevent it. He really likes Mr. Hurd, admires him, but no thanks to him, he still awaits his first kiss. So he might be innocent technically speaking, but he's not stupid. Something happened to Hailie Atkins where a teacher had to get involved and a doctor had to get involved. It's possible her dad beat her up or Licorice attacked her, but that's a stretch. You know it's not that, you know it had to do with sex. Hailie went to Miss B to tell her she was pregnant, Miss B went to Dr. Devajaran, and Hailie either had an abortion or gave the baby away (probably made a lot of money if she took that route) and then she had to move out of town because of the shame. Except nobody really cares about that stuff anymore so why would she feel ashamed?

Because ... think, he tells himself. Think! Because! Because because because! He replays last night's third quarter in his head. Third quarter is when the band gets to take a break and sit in the stands and he can see everything that's going on. Third quarter is when the band members get to unbutton the top of their jackets and let their collars fly free like wild rebels riding the wind. The sweet spot on their throats glistens with sweat. Everybody's face beats red from the heat and their hot heavy uniforms. Their hairlines are wet from the effort of the halftime show. Third quarter they can get something to eat, the snack-bar parents have food lined up to go because there are 103 of them and their time is short. They can sit wherever they want in the stands, usually with friends and family members still excited by their performance. Anisha and Corbin always sit together and eat a barbecue pork sandwich and a footlong hot dog. Anisha puts the pickles on her side of the sandwich, and six inches of the hot dog is covered with relish—that's her half. Corbin is all mustard all the way. Travis has always picked a spot to sit near the girls of the Spirit Squad with their colored faces, despite the dismal sight of too many red cheeks painted with a white number 9, Jared's number. Sometimes Kyle Jenkins sits behind him and plays his drumsticks on Travis's shoulders. Also during third quarter Hannah and Erika and the other varsity cheerleaders come up for a few minutes to let the JV squad get their chance. They squeeze in with the Spirit Squad girls. That's what they did last night when Mrs. Atkins started up again, just like last year when she called their new Japanese exchange student the c-word and then again last night when she called Erika the n-word, which Travis hasn't told Miss B because it'll upset her too much. All of it starts the usual way, with Mrs. Atkins sitting directly behind the Spirit Squad and then telling them to sit down because she can't see. Travis has seen Mrs. Atkins come early to the games when most of the rows are still empty and she could have any primo seat she wants, but still she chooses to sit directly behind them. So then postgame Mrs. Atkins was filing out and Travis was watching her, watching her because he didn't know why but watching her. He could see Spalding Burker heading his way, Spalding who was so happy he had not completely failed in protecting Jared, their hero who had thrown a touchdown on the second play of the game and it was full speed ahead after that, he had a big fucking heroic game which was so depressing to witness although Travis did notice one inspiring thing: only one Spirit Squad girl had painted number 9 on her cheek this year and that was Kyle Jenkins's sister Kassadee, who stays innocent with her Down syndrome and has changed her name to Elsa after a movie the name of which he keeps forgetting. So that part was okay, painting her cheek with number 9, but the trouble with Kassadee or Elsa is that she has no filter so she repeats all those words back to Mrs. Atkins and the rest of the Spirit Squad has to stand up for her, which leads to a fight. Travis was loitering after the game, in no hurry to leave, a god in his new uniform, drinking in the departing tossed compliments, when Spalding charged up to him. He was embarrassed for Spalding with his fat love handles and misshapen pudgy frame. His position as offensive left tackle is the very spot Coach McManus wanted Travis to take over, something Travis will never reveal to Spalding. He was almost tearfully happy for Spalding and for any back pats that came his way as they stood like the hungry homeless near the exits, waiting for scraps of flattery, and he was watching Mrs. Atkins, something weird about her in her loud loud loneliness, the way she came to the games all alone and was so loud about it, not embarrassed by it. Mrs. Atkins's angry face turned and Travis turned in the same direction. He followed her eye daggers to a sight that jolted his heart when it sprang full-figured right in front of him, the man with the soft body and thick wavy hair and cowboy shirt: Spalding's dad. He didn't know it was Spalding's dad at first, but he guessed it when he kept interrupting Miss B and Spalding's mother as they tried to chat. Travis could see by their body language that Miss B and Spalding's mom were friends and he could see how much it bothered the dad and how he had to keep interrupting and how he would turn to shout something grating and friendly to the other dads who pushed into their strides to rush past. One guy even shoved his shoulder against him in his hurry to get away but didn't turn back to excuse himself. Travis remembered the contemptuous eye roll Spalding's mother gave him at each interruption. He carried that eye roll home and forgot about Mrs. Atkins and the obvious connection between her and Spalding's dad. Until now.

I think Spalding's dad is the father of Hailie's baby, he blurts out.

What? Miss B says.

Why would he go all the way out of town to get their dog?

Hailie doesn't have a baby, Travis, Miss B tells him.

Yeah. But.

But what? And why would he take their dog because she's given birth? Miss B asks.

Revenge, Travis says.

Miss B turns to Dr. Devajaran. See, this is what I try to teach my students all the time to no avail. Life doesn't operate like a TV series. But all their critical logic follows Netflix logic.

Miss B, I'm sorry but you're the one said he wasn't an angel.

Which does not mean he's the devil, Travis.

Definite possibility, Travis thinks.

Are we certain about the identity of the perpetrator? The way Dr. Devajaran offers a gentle correction in her lilting accent makes it sound so much better than the way Miss B corrects him.

Travis tries to explain it to them, last night's adrenaline slow dancing enough to feed his logic: the other dogs with no collars are like nameless prostitutes and bag ladies who are murdered to hide the suburban soccer mom who is the real target. Get it? Travis waits for their lightbulbs to go off.

You've been binge-watching something, Miss B says.

You told me to stick up for my beliefs, Travis says. He forgets he's not in class and raises his hand.

Why would he want revenge against Hailie Atkins? Miss B asks Travis. Wouldn't it be the other way around, her wanting revenge against him for getting her pregnant?

This is a theoretical conversation, correct? Dr. Devajaran says. Correct, Miss B tells her—

Travis explains that it's revenge against the *mother*, who took the object of his obsession, daughter Hailie, away from him, and now it's the *mother* who returns each Friday night to root against Spalding Burker, the devil's own spawn!

And we're absolutely certain about the identity of the perpetrator? I'm not doubting you, Travis, but we need to make sure.

That was so beautiful, the way Dr. Devajaran said that to him.

There's no doubt about that part of the story, says Miss B. Freddy Burker did this. I saw the look on Travis's face myself when he spotted Freddy. I was talking to Roxanne after the game and Spalding was talking to Travis—Spalding really admires you, by the way—

Really?

Yes. And then Freddy came down from the stands and I saw Travis's expression with my own eyes.

My jaw dropped, Travis tells Dr. Devajaran. He smiles proudly. He's on fire. He's never felt so alive. Dr. Devajaran smiles at him encouragingly and he just goes, My jaw literally dropped. He says it again and again she smiles and it's like he's shouting out a list of symptoms he's had for years and never told anyone until now and then he can't stop, symptoms and more symptoms to the doctor listening to him so intently that he wishes he could be sick forever. He says, First I remembered his hair because it goes up and down in waves. Then I remembered his cowboy shirt with metal tips on the collar and he had on a big cowboy belt, and then I remembered he drives a white Ram pickup, a 1500.

Oh, my goodness, she says. She touches his elbow. Are you always so observant? She turns to Miss B. Is he always so observant?

For the rest of his life, Travis knows that he will replay this moment over and over.

Always, Miss B says proudly.

All right, Dr. Devajaran says. She turns away and steps in delicate treads down the road, leaving them stranded.

Did I make her mad? Travis asks.

She's thinking, Miss B says.

Dr. Devajaran strolls back to them. Her feet are feathers too light to mark the dirt. She grasps a bitsy section of Travis's forearm as she says to him, a doctor's reassurance, Putting aside all your theoretical theories, let's put that aside, all right for a minute, Travis? You are still a witness to a crime nevertheless. And so the question for us is this one.

Yes? he and Miss B ask in sync, leaning in, both of them mesmerized by her fragile and lovely omnipotence.

What do we do now? That's our question, Dr. Devajaran says.

Travis and Miss B exchange glances. Each politely defers to the other.

I don't know, Miss B says.

I don't know either, Travis says.

Should we report the crime?

What's the crime exactly? Travis asks.

Kidnapping, murder, abuse of a corpse, Miss B says. Her voice trembles with heat. Why don't you let me handle this. Oh god I wish Rupert and Yuri were here! They'd take care of him.

Who are Rupert and Yuri? Miss Devajaran asks.

My Doberman Pinschers. They'd rip his throat out. Long passed away and I haven't had a Doberman since. They're really the only dog I'd trust for this kind of job.

Whoa, Travis thinks. A new Miss B emerges and she has a dark-side superpower.

Miss Devajaran observes Miss B with a long, kind, studious expression of doctorly concern. We have some decision to make, she finally says. Whether or not we should involve the police and who should initiate that involvement.

Which means, Travis knows, that Dr. Devajaran does not want to interact with the police. Who would after what happened?

Let me talk to Roxanne first, Miss B says. Before we do the police. Freddy's been having some mental health issues and things are hard enough for Roxanne without adding this. And Freddy isn't the father of Hailie Atkins's nonexistent baby, Travis.

Travis isn't listening. A horrible but utterly rational thought has landed a new blow.

It's not only Dr. Devajaran who will stand to lose if they go to the police. Once the police are involved, this man Freddy will know right away who reported him and he will find out Travis's name, which he probably already knows since his son, Spalding, really admires him according to Miss B and probably talks all the time about this cool dude at school named Travis Hicks.

Travis does not have a dog, so the man cannot take revenge on Travis via his dog. He will have to take revenge on Travis himself.

Police or not, it's over for Travis. He's very much the innocent guy who witnessed a mob murder. Now the mob will have to get rid of him, too. Running into the killer a few hours later at the game, where he was still in that rodeo shirt, so seized up Travis that he hasn't realized until now that the killer also saw him … also recognized him … watched him interact with his son … stared at him … began his plan to eradicate him.

Five boys. It was a Saturday night.
Two boys. Thin jackets.

Clay Rhinehart Was

a passable trombonist on the Kattoga High marching band. Barely passable, but passable. But barely.

You couldn't lay all the blame on Clay Rhinehart, however. Every
marching band instructor, Mr. Hurd included, viewed the trombone section as a rocky coastline: visually impressive, uneven, and treacherous.
The trombone gave you licks and rips unable to be produced by other
low brass instruments, but it came with pitch and tuning problems. And
no keys meant each player varied the slide positions so that precision of
movement became a celebration of disarray.

Always there were problems with trombones.

Clay Rhinehart played eleventh chair, another way of saying dead last.
He often did them the favor of not playing at all when they marched.
That helped, especially because Clay could then match his slide to Taylor's next to him. Better visuals—Clay and Taylor were also the same
height—but that didn't solve the bigger issue—

whether to have trombones at all.

The bones gave Mr. Hurd fits. He had been weighing switching them
out with a mixture of baritones, euphoniums and tenor horns and just be
done with them. A lot of high school marching bands did that. Throw
the bones to the boneyard. In fact, this very topic drew one of the most
crowded sessions at the marching band conference he had attended in

Phoenix: *76 Trombone Problems in the Marching Band!* He thought what a great little vacation in the bargain, but it was June in Phoenix and an absolute death trap, anyway beside the point.

Then Dick Tresor showed up, former trombonist from TBDBITL. A senior citizen by now but with legitimate bragging rights. The Ohio State marching band really was The Best Damn Band In The Land. He introduced himself to Mr. Hurd as Dick Tresor, National Treasure. He might have been half joking, but the other half was definitely not.

Dick immediately went about teaching the trombones the suicide choreography. Its main benefit was that the trombones didn't actually play during it, which was why Mr. Hurd allowed it. It was all visuals. The trombones stepped out from back of the band and lined up in front. The snare drums stepped out from their rear positions and lined up behind the trombones. The drums kept the cadence as the trombonists shoulder to shoulder took alternating turns bending down then swinging to the right then bending down then swinging to the left. Faster as the drums got faster. Bend swing, bend swing.

If somebody mistimed it, swinging when they should have been bending —trouble. The wielding of a trombone by a thrill-seeking, hormone-laden teenager into what should have been his partner's empty head-space resulted in a bloody nose, broken teeth, or worse. Dick called the drill "headchoppers" with a little too much glee. Mr. Hurd made them practice well apart to avoid hospital trips during the learning curve. Last year when they debuted the choreography during the senior week halftime show, Ego Dick came out to take a bow during the huge roar. Trouble, Mr. Hurd thought about his grandstanding volunteer. Trouble right here in River City.

The trombone suicide wasted time, but it was a crowd pleaser. And it gave the trombonists something extra they had to practice because trombonists were the mischief-makers of a band and time on a trombonist's hands was an invitation to trouble.

What Clay Rhinehart got into went beyond mischief even though the February accident was five months in the future on the last day Mr.

Hurd saw him. By then Dick Tresor had come to annoy Mr. Hurd so much he had begun meditation strategies whenever Dick took to the megaphone. When mentally flipping hot spots on his body to cold spots on his body stopped working, when simply noticing and honoring his stress did nothing to make it float away, he simply allowed himself to get lost in whatever maze of feeling overtook him. He didn't care what kind of feelings they were as long as they weren't Dick Tresor feelings. He found himself reviving boyhood memories. He reexperienced them step by step. Threshing days with his dad, for example. With his undertaker's body Mr. Hurd looked like someone who had grown up in an urban apartment without access to daylight, yet he was actually a farmer's boy. He needed the sun on the back of his neck although Phoenix, Arizona, in June had been too much for him, anyway beside the point. Dick Tresor, National Treasure, had begun to raise his blood pressure. Mr. Hurd completely blew a Match-dot-com date because he was too busy obsessing over Dick's egotism, which sounded so trivial when he voiced it over the restaurant table to a kindergarten teacher from Berrysville. He wasn't jealous of the cool flair to their halftime show that Dick had added, but he kept feeling that persistent encroachment, Dick too close at his shoulder so that the band's sightline to its leader was a sightline to Dick. Dick too quick to give a nonbones directive before Mr. Hurd did. Dick too eager to take a bow on the field.

Thank god for Miss Stacy, who despite being new quickly sized up the situation and took over. Took completely over without somehow ever taking over Mr. Hurd's power. All of her power in deference to his power. She stood apart from Mr. Hurd and well behind whenever Mr. Hurd spoke to the band. When Dick Tresor spoke, Miss Stacy jumped beside him so that the sightline to Dick became a sightline to her. And she captured all eyes. There was no way Dick Tresor could compete with Miss Stacy's untamed show-stopper frenzy just as there was no way Mr. Hurd could compete with Dick's ego, his bragging rights, his Big Ten adventures, his trouble-making (like a good trombonist). In the end, though, Dick didn't have youth and he didn't have beauty, and repetitive old-man narcissism began to work against him as the season wore on. With Miss Stacy, everyone had a crush on her, the boys and the girls. Despite the tight clothes, the plunging necklines, the flying hair, the lipstick like a police siren, the rumors by the football team about her past as porn star, Miss Stacy *enacted* Mr. Hurd's genius while Dick Tresor competed with it. And Miss Stacy would never have jumped back on the field for a bow, even after debuting as Gladys Knight during last week's "Midnight Train to Georgia." Even after every single person in the stadium went crazy. Even after the football team came out to watch. And best, he and Miss Stacy had inserted the trombones as the Pips' whoo-whoo! without any help from Dick.

On the day last year when the bones lost their eleventh chair, the September afternoon was glorious and sunny. They had entered the driest month of the year, which didn't mean drought in Ohio, just meant they didn't have to worry about splatting mud from last night's rain. Meant they could practice on the field instead of the road.

At Dick's insistence they were practicing "Dick's Headchoppers," the new amended name he had given to the trombone suicide. Mr. Hurd's arms were protectively crossed against his chest. Croakied sunglasses on. This was his typical attitude of listening and it fooled the band. He was dealing with Dick during practice today by being busy on the thresher with his dad. His dad had reached the end of a row. His dad was saying something about how much longer he could keep the farm going. His dad had bought him a piano even though he was only ten years old, and that night his dad made a request for a song: "Liebestraum" by Franz Liszt. Mr. Hurd as a boy thought nothing of it. He played it. His mother in her chair smiled and went back to her knitting. So many times he's looked back on that and thought, What an extraordinary request. He wishes he'd gotten to know that side of his dad better. His dad gave him this musical essence and now he's not there to be thanked. Mr. Hurd was twelve years old when he died, or eleven. It was a vague time and he has trouble clearing a space to ponder it.

Mr. Hurd jerked from his memories when a shout went up. He uncrossed his arms. Pushed sunglasses to forehead.

Two policemen were striding quickly toward the marching band.

Without pause, without a second's hesitation, Clay Rhinehart broke from the trombone line and took off running across the football field. He wasn't stopping and he wasn't looking back. Kyle Jenkins laid into a snare drum roll faster and faster as Clay Rhinehart sprinted across the field, trombone flying out to his side. It was like something out of a movie, a black comedy. Clay raced smack into the nine-foot-high chainlink fence. No exit on that side. He climbed, still holding his trombone. Adolescent magic and maladroit panic rolled him over the fence.

Only then, having completed his slapstick cameo, did he bother to look back. What he saw was a band on the far side standing in place, watching him. And the two policemen also standing in place, watching him.

When Clay disappeared from sight, Travis Hicks gave a final boom on the thud bass, possibly the only time he came in on the beat, and then one of the policemen handed Miss Stacy a meal bag for third cornet Chase Walton, the cop's nephew, because his mother was working late and wouldn't be able to cook dinner, plus five dollars in case he wanted to go to Taco Bell instead.

Mr. Hurd never saw Clay Rhinehart again, not until today. Clay turned sixteen a week or two later and dropped out of school altogether.

The Lawyer Reminds

the judge that they don't have the brain development they get at nine-
teen or twenty years of age that would allow them biologically to understand the ramifications of experience.

Who is they? Judge Javier Tanguay asks.

Juveniles, the lawyer says. She is a no-nonsense woman who thirty
minutes earlier dropped anchor at the lawyers' table in the nick of time,
right before the twenty-one inches of files in her arms bowled her across
the slick marble floor.

Miss B sits in the gallery. She came early to the courthouse, searched in
vain for Roxanne Burker. Though she doesn't know how she will break
the dead-dog news about Freddy, the news will have to be broken. She
will go into teacher mode and the news will be broken. Even if she has
to write it on a whiteboard with smelly erasable marker, the news will
be broken.

But no Roxanne.

She chatted with Shawna, was glad that predatory feather tail she had
grown had been snipped off though she didn't say so. She told Brenda
Mansfield she liked the relaxed perm and how thick her hair looked,
asked about the latest scan (clear), took a seat with homework to correct,
then watched Clay Rhinehart's lawyer arrive with her mountain of files,
this woman in a brown puffed-sleeve jacket and pink shirt with sewn-in

striped tie who talked nonstop and unsmiling to her assistant, a mini-me in the same kind of outfit who also carried twenty-one inches of files and kept her mouth set. Miss B wondered if the lawyer lived in Kattoga or another small town. Had to be a small town. She could tell the lawyer was country cooked from her choice of businesswear. A sewn-in striped acrylic tie? Not that Miss B is any great shakes when it comes to fashion but when she sees someone in a good outfit, she asks where they shop. She takes advice from the people who look good, Corbin and Josh's mom, Dr. Devajaran, the ex-mayor's wife who runs the coffee shop. That's how you get it done. And if Miss B happens to not look stunning all dressed up, which seems to happen every time she dresses up, it's certainly not the clothes' fault. Surely the image the mirror plays back cannot fully account for the love that has bypassed her. She is still young. She is forty-two years old.

In these minutes before the court was brought to order, Miss B watched the lawyer and her mini-me fuss with the laying out of folders, binders, loose documents, many pens, several yellow legal pads, a notebook. It was the kind of theater her students might go through to eat up vital minutes in their ten-minute reports—that is, if they cared enough to fake it with a flurry of fake work, which after all required a bit of work in and of itself just to be fake. Those students who would care enough to mount a fake production would also care enough to do the real work. The others would happily take their D grade and go back to juvie, English class, whatever.

The tornado of files the lawyer and her assistant flew across the longish table trumpeted its warning: this defense was going to be a disaster.

Moments before the proceedings were set to begin, there was still hardly anyone in the gallery. Mr. Hurd sat quietly at the other end of a pew, the only other representative from K-High. He was wearing sunglasses and reading sheet music when Miss B looked over at him. He sat in the only place where a stream of sunlight could catch him in its bright shaft. Shawna went over and asked if he wanted her to pull the blinds but he shook his head and Shawna shrugged her shoulders at Miss B as she walked back to her spot against the wall.

The lawyer talked rapidly to Clay Rhinehart. She offered him a legal pad, which Clay took and held in the air like coffee. She handed him a pen, which he held like a baby spoon.

By now Miss B recognized the juvie acne that blared on Clay's face. Juvie food had also tipped the weight scales against him. He looked too old, too young, denuded yet peppered with blotches.

Then Judge Javier Tanguay walked in and Brenda Mansfield said All rise and Shawna sent Miss B a tight smile and off they went.

Last time in court, Miss B pep-talks herself. What she initially thought of as a good deed all those months ago has put her at risk of becoming uncharitable, a person who has lost her fondness for mankind. Humankind. Girlkind. Mankind. Whatever!

Soon she might begin snark attacks in the comments section of any internet news. She'll join the Russian bots and tell readers that the father who drowned saving his children had it coming. The bicyclist biking in the bike lane thought she owned the fucking road and had it coming. The DIY man climbing the ladder to clear his gutters had it coming. She has even found herself wondering if this pink-shirted lawyer with the sewn-in acrylic tie is on drugs. She has it coming, too. All her nonstop talking: that's drugs. All those files—storm warning of drugs. And now she's wiping her face. She's sweating! Drugs!

If Miss B has to go to another one of these proceedings, no telling what she will do.

But this is it. Last one. It's over. Number five coming up. Last one. All boys accounted for. Football players: good boys. Study hall boys: bad boys.

It's proven by scientists, the lawyer is now insisting, as if she's on drugs.

What is? the judge asks.

The biology of the juvenile brain, the lawyer responds. Mentally they're not adults so they can't be tried as adults.

Counselor, we are not trying him as an adult, the judge reminds her. The young man is being tried as a juvenile.

The lawyer briefly looks stunned before diving to her table and the storm of files. Final proof: drugs!

When Miss B looks at Clay Rhinehart all alone up there, she thinks of Travis Hicks. No member of Clay's family appears to be in attendance, just as no member of Travis's family would bother to come to court for him. Miss B has lately entertained the idea of doing an ancestry test for Travis. No one knows who Travis's father is, not even Travis's mother. Perhaps a DNA kit would reveal enough paternal ethnicity to make him appealing to colleges—real colleges looking for diversity students and willing to pay for them, good colleges, not the for-profit centers he's been looking into that take up the bottom two floors of a building in an office park. He's told her about his Wonderlic score at one such for-profit, part-virtual university. Wonderlic, he explained to her with visible excitement, is the same test taken by football players at the combine

What's a combine?

football players going into the NFL draft. Travis was rushing forward. The test took twenty minutes and the university didn't charge to take it and they told him he scored really high, exceptionally high, high enough to get into any of their programs though they recommended their top programs for someone like him, criminal justice or electrical engineering

Do you become an electrician or an engineer?

and he also qualified for a loan they would help set up for him

electrician, Miss B told him

easy, they'd do all the work because he qualified for their top program

electrician—not engineer—*electrician*

The ACT and SAT take hours

scamming you

Hours! Travis complained. And the SAT costs $64.50 and the ACT costs $50.50—$67 with the writing portion, something he would be good at but he didn't want to pay the extra $17. Plus he heard you have to take the tests two or three times to work up to a decent score. That's hundreds of dollars!

She didn't bother to tell him that it was another $94 to take an AP subject test, something no one at K-High did anyway except Anisha. Instead she kept saying I understand, Travis, I understand—I understand BUT. She tried to explain to him that it's about the future, seeing beyond the present-day stumbling blocks. She showed him the FAFSA online, where he could begin the procedure to get legitimate financial aid, not the kind of shark loans those other places were eager to arrange for him because federal funding covered the loan, not them, so go ahead, full steam on loans without a care for defaulting. She's in an ongoing email with the community college in Columbus. It's a huge program, twenty thousand people, and it might be perfect for him. The school is geared toward the culture shock experienced by first-in-family college-goers. She found out about its "college credit plus" program for students at risk, the test-prep services, and a seminar covering the skills needed to succeed in college. Travis could go to that seminar for free and even get one academic credit if he ends up attending there. And he could transfer to Ohio State after sophomore year if he maintains a 3.5 average. The community college's emails were helpful and friendly and encouraged Miss B's student to schedule time in its computer lab where people could help him work on his application, show him how to do research, or set him up for practice ACTs.

Of course, attending a seminar or going to a computer lab also means over an hour's drive in a car that might not make it that far if its paint job is any indication, so now Miss B is looking at her weekends being eaten up by chauffeuring. She wishes she saw dawning hope on Travis's face rather than mute panic when she went through all these opportunities. She's feeling a desperation when it comes to him and his senior year and what lies beyond, and his college application essay is about playing the thud bass in the marching band when it should be about all the hardships he's overcome and his possible minority status via the dad he's never known. How about this: living alone in a trailer while his drug-addicted mom lives at the railroad tracks? How many other kids can say that? What if he learns he is part African American when the DNA tests come back? How about this: trying to scrape together enough money for his next meal? Even being friends with Yoder and learning about another culture is a much better essay than playing the thud bass.

And she's also realizing it's a full-time job to save a single life. Better to be teacher of the year and a beacon to many.

Just looking into getting test fees waived (including the writing portion) and college application fees waived meant a week of lunch hours gone. On Friday, with fifteen minutes left of her break, she dumped her Hot Pocket in the microwave and googled whether there were any scholarships for overly tall people. Turns out there are. So now she's been emailing Tall League International.

The judge's gavel rains down. Why, she doesn't know. There is no one here. Shawna sends her a shrug. Shawna told her Roxanne hadn't been into work for two days. Bruise here, Shawna said, bruise there. Probably now moved to the facial area where she couldn't hide it.

In the gallery sits one of the victims' mothers along with her victim advocate. It's their fifth time, too. The other mother dropped out after the second disposition. Not this one. This one hasn't given up. She will read her victim's statement for the fifth time. Miss B will listen to it for the fifth time. This mother will live a long life, Miss B is sure. She will have to live a long life. Every day, all the hours of her day will be devoted to her son. And no one will know and she won't get an award and no one from Congress will visit her during an election campaign because no one will know about her, she stays inside mostly and she's too busy with her son. Once her son gets older and his friends leave him, he will still have his mother and they will sit together in front of the TV for a long, long time. A single life saved and a single life lost.

Hannah Kirkpatrick Sits

in third-period class. Inside her it's black. Black and cold. She doesn't even try to listen to the substitute. She knows the name of the substitute, Mrs. Stine, but that doesn't require listening. The name is written on the blackboard.

Hello, I am
Mrs. Stine
You may call me
Mrs. Stine

Kyle Jenkins asks Mrs. Stine to repeat her name so they can learn how to pronounce it. She writes it again in giant letters.

MRS. STINE

Yeah, but could you pronounce it out loud? Kyle Jenkins says.

Stop, Kyle. Hannah turns in her chair and mouths the words.

Are you talking? Mrs. Stine asks Hannah. She uses a very incredulous tone.

On the sidewall whiteboard is a note from Miss B, who is not here today because of court duty. Her perfect cursive script lights up the board in thick neon. Whenever Hannah or anybody else writes on the board, the letters are so faint as to be invisible. Even Travis Hicks can't seem to press his three hundred–plus pounds into the dry-erase marker held warily between his thumb and two fingers. He stops after two or three letters and checks the marker tip. Holds it right up to his nose. It confuses everyone, writing on the board. Doing it properly on the board is a skill only teachers have. Teachers Only. That's a sign Hannah sees on doors throughout their school. What does that make you want to do except open that door? Last year they got Chieko to open one of those doors on the pretext that Chieko didn't understand and when she opened it, Hannah and Erika behind her, Mr. Golder, the practical arts teacher, was making out with Hailie Atkins. There was a souvenir for Chieko to take back to Japan. Mr. Golder almost lost his job, almost went to jail. Hannah's mom said that kind of stuff happened all the time when she was in school—what was the big deal? I think texts, Hannah told her. So what, her mother said. Photos, Mom, she said. Her grandmother said all they were doing was making out

Not in the photos, Grandma!

in my day the teachers had sex with you, every girl knew the men teachers accidentally slipped you a peek at the taped condom inside their grade book to see your reaction and when they did that to me

Shut up, Grandma!

has a happy ending

Shut up, Grandma!

but we didn't talk nasty like you kids today. Some of you kids are really nasty.

Hannah drops her head on the desk. Where is Chieko? Why won't she answer her?

Head up! Mrs. Stine yells.

How do you say your name again? Kyle Jenkins asks.

Head back up!

Hannah raises her head.

Here is Miss B's assignment on the blackboard:

Hello, Class! What a beautiful splendiferous day! How *ironic* that today's assignment takes you out of the sunshine and into the darkness. Your name is Hades and your job is to assign the punishment in Tartarus a.k.a. Down There that fits the crime. What is the crime and what is the punishment? Use classical mythology for your inspiration. Have serious fun!

Usually Hannah likes Miss B, but this morning she hates her. The note on the board turns her stomach. How dare she be so happy? She just hates Miss B. She hangs her head.

I hate you, Miss B.

Head up! Pen on paper!

It has become clear that Mrs. Stine is not one of those substitute teachers content to sit with her stack of magazines or the thank-you cards she needs to write or the scrapbooking she's working on—such are the September and October preferred activities. After Halloween the substitutes get more focused. Substitutes in November knit scarves and woolly mittens so thick and shapeless no one would want to wear them. Substitutes in December write Christmas cards. Substitutes in January sometimes pretend they left their car running and bolt from the school and never come back and there goes their New Year's resolution to get a job. Once in a while there's a substitute who is so proud of being Ph.D.-level smart they think they'll just chat and let the confetti of their intelligence float down upon your head. Judge Herrick's mother did that. She was ninety-seven years old and sat there and chatted with them. Hannah was a freshman and didn't want to be mean because she is not a mean person and tries to be kind, but it was insane and the elderly lady made no sense. Usually Hannah says senior citizen to be respectful but this lady was way beyond senior citizen. She was obviously about to die, not to be mean, but it was obvious. She got up with their help and shuffled down the hall on her walker and then the famous judge was finished with his presentation to the upperclassmen and he found her in the corridor and drove her home. Maybe she wasn't a substitute after all, just someone who had wandered into their classroom on her way to finding her son.

The smart Ph.D. substitutes are all the same. They like to read to them from *The Stranger* by Albert Camus.

Maman died today. Or maybe yesterday. I don't know.

I got a telegram from the house. "Mother deceased. Funeral tomorrow. Faithfully yours." That doesn't mean anything.

Maybe it was yesterday.

TRANSLATED FROM THE French!

They all do it.

Hannah is not a mean person and tries to be kind. Every morning she tries to be kind and every morning it is getting harder and harder and she's only seventeen. What will happen when she's twenty-five? What will happen when she's thirty-five? She doesn't want to end up mean like her grandmother, no offense, she loves her Nan but she is mean and hides it under trying to be funny. People who laugh too much with their smoker's hacks—watch out. Not to be mean. She loves her grandmother, but she is afraid of being like her. Laughing too loudly and too often with her smoker's hack, being mean underneath. Why keep on living like that? What's it worth?

Afraid of being like her mother, too. Her mother, who gives too many rides to underclass boys without their driver's licenses. That's her excuse—no driver's license. Her mother who was named MILF of the year by whoever does that.

Hannah is pretty, she has long hair, she is head cheerleader, she is a straight-A student, everyone likes her, she is pretty and nice. She has long thick hair and a lot of it is still naturally blond. She wants to die. Almost every morning she wants to do it. One time she actually told someone (as you're supposed to do!) and all they said was But you have such nice hair.

She should have gone back to Japan with Chieko. She took Chieko under her wing. She tried to be kind. She took Chieko everywhere. She tried to teach her English. Chieko had problems with that. She sounded so silly most of the time. Where is she? She has heard terrible things going on over there, the tidal waves and earthquake. Nobody has mentioned it. Nobody seems to care.

Assignment! orders Miss Stine. Pens! Paper!

Hannah looks over at Travis Hicks, who sits beside her. *Hello Friend Welcome to Hell* reads the title of his paper. He cracks his knuckles.

Stretches out his arms. She starts her own story under Miss Stine's watchful ominous squint.

Neptune looked out on the sunny day. Neptune watched a girl being mean to another girl. What Neptune didn't know was that the other girl was a bully and the first girl was just standing up for herself. She had to be mean back because that was the only language the bully understood. Neptune rose out of the ocean and called to them "Hi-ho! You disrespect the great Neptune." The other girl said "So what go drown yourself." Neptune was so surprised. Only then did he realize the second girl was mean too so he decided to punish them both and raked the water with his trident until it rose up in a giant ocean wave that aimed right toward them. Neptune's hands came out of the waves and grabbed the girls who screamed "We are sorry we are so sorry we will never be mean again!"

MRS. STINE STANDS beside her. Hannah's pen moves faster and faster to stay ahead of the nasal eruptions of displeasure. Mrs. Stine removes her eyeglasses after reading. This has no detail whatsoever, she says to Hannah.

The whole thing is detail, Hannah says.

Objection. Detail would be telling us what the girls look like.

They're Japanese. They look Japanese.

I guess all Japanese look alike?

I have enough detail, Hannah says. I need to rest. She puts her head on the desk and closes her eyes.

I guess we're supposed to know who Neptune is?

Yes, Hannah mumbles into her arm.

You need a comma before dialogue begins.

Hannah raises up and quickly puts commas where Mrs. Stine points.

And you have to start a new paragraph with each new speaker.

I can't do that. It's already the way it is.

Your teacher has your name down in her lesson plan. Apparently you're the student I'm supposed to rely upon.

Hannah lifts her head. I'm sorry, I don't feel well.

Do you want to go to the nurse?

Yes! says Kyle Jenkins.

No, Hannah says. I have existential malaise.

My, those are big words, Mrs. Stine says.

My teacher gave them to me.

She doesn't always have emotional malaise, Kyle Jenkins says.

Shut up, Kyle. Hannah puts her head down for good this time. Her arms wrap around her head and shut out the light. She gives herself up to the darkness. She feels the warmth and heavy air beside her as Mrs. Stine lingers. Then the body moves on.

A folded-up note is pushed under her forearm. She raises slightly to let in the light and reads it.

Something weird going on with Hailie Atkins. She left town because of something weird. Ask me how I know.

Hannah drops her head in exhaustion against the desk and turns toward Travis, one eye peeking over her arm. Under the title of his story, *Hello Friend Welcome to Hell* is a big blank. She writes back,

she has syphyliss spelling

and shoves her arm across the aisle and drops the note.

Travis rears back as he reads. Hannah waves the note back. She writes,

a bunch of people thanks to her

Travis stares down at Hannah's words. He writes,

Spalding Burker's dad has been killing dogs and throwing them in ditches. Ask me how I know.

Hannah reaches over to retrieve the note without lifting her head. She scrawls, with the greatest fatigue stiffening her lettering,

he's weird prob kills peep 2

She closes her eyes and feels the note snatched from her fist.

Head up! orders Mrs. Stine.

Hannah raises her head.

You know what happens to note passers, don't you?

They go back to seventh grade? Kyle Jenkins says.

A very good guess. They go back to seventh grade after I read their note out loud. Mrs. Stine clears her throat. "Something weird going on with Hailie Atkins. She left town because of something weird. Ask me how I know. She has sinfulness spel—. She has syphilis. A bunch of people thanks to her. Spalding Burker's dad has been killing dogs and throwing them in ditches. He's weird prob—He's weird. Probably kills people, too."

The room is dead quiet.

You want to add something to that? Mrs. Stine addresses Kyle Jenkins. Kyle Jenkins shakes his head.

At least you know you don't know how to spell syphilis, Mrs. Stine says rather weakly. She sits down at Miss B's desk and no one says anything.

To You Five

boys who did this, to you Jared and to you Josh and to you Dustin and to you Tyler and to you Clay, you will never have to know what it's like to get a call in the middle of the night and a stranger's voice tells you someone who might be your son is being life-flighted in critical condition and to hurry if you want to see him in time. You will never have to know what it's like to drive to Wooster up and down hills with no lights under those conditions not even being able to see and hoping the boy they found laying in the ditch with no ID is someone else's son. You will never have to live with your guilty conscience for praying that the boy in the ditch belongs to a different parent fast asleep in their bed. You will never know the horror of becoming this type of person who would wish a terrible tragedy on another innocent human being, becoming the person who will turn her back on God and tell the sweetest lady in her Bible study group to go to hell. You will never have to push nurses away or call the hospital staff filthy names when they hold you back from seeing your own flesh and blood lying dead on a gurney with his eyes open and pupils rolled back. You will never have to scream Liar! to a doctor doing the best he can. You won't ever be the bitch who doesn't say thank you when they bring Kirk back to life because that's his name, Jared. His name is Kirk. That's his name, Josh, his name is Kirk. Remember that name, Dustin, his name is Kirk. His name is Kirk, Tyler. That's his name, Clay, remember it, his name is Kirk. The court won't say it but I want all of you to say his name.

When you have to look at a face swollen to a purple mash and tubes coming out of his body like a science fiction movie, you won't ever have to be that person who thinks for a moment he's better off dead. And you won't ever have to scream That's not my son! cause you don't recognize his body laying there and falling to the floor anyway in uncontrollable sobs because some part of you knows it's true that the bloody pulp that is not your son is your son. But you call the doctor a liar anyway and you slap him for what he did to your son. You will never experience an onslaught of specialists in white jackets sweeping you against the wall like soldiers with machine guns, the ER doctor, trauma surgeon, brain specialist, cardiologist, all of them poking their weapons at you and you hoping they will just shoot you and get all the suffering over with. You want to die rather than hear that Kirk has a tear in his aorta, severe brain damage, bleeding to the brain, and a collapsed lung. And how he is at the wrong hospital to boot because they aren't equipped to deal with the tear in his aorta but they don't know if he can survive the flight to Toledo. Jared and Josh, you will never have to be the one to make the decision to let your son leave on a flight that will probably kill him. You will never have to drive to Toledo at three in the morning with the window down even though it's winter just so you don't pass out or drive off the road yourself. Tyler and Dustin and Clay, you will never have to look up at the stars in the black sky and wonder why they are so unusual tonight. You will never have to pray that the star you see aiming so brightly right at you is not your son, your oldest child and still your baby boy, added newly to the heavens.

II.

Halloween
A Year Earlier

I Recognized The

site as soon as I arrived. I had followed her.

In the chilled air I breathed in the nearby water, the way it suckled the roots of sycamores, the way it laid a green scent atop the autumn decay leafing its banks. Instantly I was transported. Why had she led me here again? Why now? The one I had failed to cherish was long dispersed in the soil. I did not trust myself. Given free rein, I might have gone foraging for his grave.

Perhaps my sister had taken note in me of visitations by the keeper of melancholia. Perhaps I had leaked too much unease during recent days. Perhaps she worried I might turn to my own moods and neglect her. After several decades her childish attention span had kindly flitted to her twin brother. She must have decided during an unoccupied moment, as all her moments were, that she should do something about me. I will accept this as a genuine fugitive concern on her part.

It was night when we arrived back. Despite the trees whose odors stirred my memories, maple and pine and beech and sycamore, all else was different. The place was overrun with human life. I could smell it. I could taste it. The air burned acrid from giant machinery. The fields had turned into pathways of hardened tar. The withering of mortal lives took place inside vainglorious dwellings meant to celebrate and shelter them.

We were alone. All the humans were encased inside their protections. We strode past dark farms. We listened to the mangling of branches, the deer within. We listened to the steady creek. We heard powered vehicles and watched their bouncing lights disturb the night sky and erase the constellations.

From inside one of the vehicles came screams and the sound of smashes. Pumpkins were being hurled. They flew from the vehicle's open windows and smashed upon the road. These smashes were, I gathered belatedly, not tragedy but comedy. This was the kind of joke that humans lived for as they continued to find ways to honor their own inadequacy. I had watched towns in Italia and Hellas be built and grow into cities that melted into pools of megalopolis, and the bigger and more fiery the concourse, the more the scrambling mortals searched for jokes. We, on the other hand—we were not seeded with humor, and our dreams sprang literal before us. We could not explain our lives even to ourselves. We were left with obliterating ourselves as our only way to adapt.

One of the pumpkins landed perfectly on the road without bursting. My sister drew her bow and let the arrow sing. The shaft sank deep and lit the round fruit in gold. The pumpkin's carved leer flamed at me in the darkness. She must have known beforehand this was the night of some human tradition. She kept greedy track of these things.

Past the treeline we continued. We stood at a farm window. Lanterns cast in yellow the life within. A family ate a meal in rigid silence. The mother at the table turned to squint bewildered at something at the window. My sister clowned before her and tapped the glass with her bow to mystify her further. Her youngest boy sent us a smile but his father's smack upon the table brought him back to the food. We moved on.

We strode across their farm. Inside a barn my sister shed gold on their hay and fed a hank to a depressed mare who pulled back its gums in a loving grin and licked her face.

We stopped. We both heard it. We turned to listen.

Outside the stable came footsteps. Then near the doorway laughter. A youth's laughter. Then the boy himself. He was a big enough boy on his own merits, but against the dainty creature in his arms, he loomed a colossus.

The youth turned and pulled the girl inside. He walked backward into the barn, grasping both her wrists. A loose grasp perhaps but calculated into inescapable shackles. She had no choice but to follow, all while the playful looseness of his grip encouraged belief that her motions were voluntary. Her eyes were black, her eyebrows black, her hair also black and plaited in two stiff tails that brushed the tops of her breasts.

This was our first meeting of the dear pet.

The youth sat her down on a hay mound. He pulled out a can and shook it. Both my sister and I heard the metal ball ricocheting inside and sent each other quizzical glances. He flourished the can in front of the dear pet's face as if in serenade. He even swung his hips to the rattles he created.

The dear pet remained as if a freshly whelped creature, compliant and fazed.

I had seen innumerable boys like this one. There was in human adolescence either a kind of dewy beauty that could briefly sway an older male from his marriage or a god from his assigned travel or this, a blunt coarse prime and a raw face no one would die for.

The barn air reeked of the fetid stink of male youth—a stink he sent our way with each agitation of the can. He played his musical instrument, then whipped off the orange cap and pushed down. A mist hued in orange sprayed the air.

The dear pet watched the tinted fog sink to the straw floor.

Outside the barn arrived careful shouts—raised whispers set on a timer. We left the barn and tracked the sound and found a girl heading our way. She was pretty enough by mortal standards. She had hair long enough and thick enough and flaxen enough to please the gods. Her shouts were nervous queries—Chieko? Chieko?—followed by glances to the farm dwelling. Each time it remained quiet, she dared to shout again.

My sister swiftly went rigid. The animal in her rose up. She rushed back to the stable.

The dear pet's hair had been thrown upon the noisy, loosely boarded stable floor. There in the straw and dirt and bestrewn feces, I recognized it as false hair. The piece of braid posed like an excreted creature, ready to crab away from any attempts to capture it. It appeared to be alive, so precise were its black plaits and ribbons. The dear pet's own hair had turned thin from the damping sweat. Her garb was being ripped from her body and blindly, frantically thrown in a pile where the braided arms of the hairpiece reached out to it.

Had the boy been able to see us, he would not have noticed us anyway. His laughter was drenched with sex. All else was drowned out by what he wanted. He did not bother to remove his clothes but simply dropped his pants.

The pride these mortals took in their pathetic male appendage! So special to them that they had to dress it in a cloak. By the time he finished protecting his small proud sword, my sister was already atop the dear pet. And when he stabbed hard at the dear pet, he met gold. And all he ruptured was himself.

He lay squealing on the barn floor as the flaxen-haired girl rushed in screaming.

The male youth twisted on the odorous floorboards that had embraced goat, horse, pig, dog, and cow. His bloody urine left his scent to join their history. His forearms inched him toward the doorway. He was nearly stepped on by a panicking goat jumping to escape. The moon glow revealed the purpose of the can. The goat's quivering testicles shone a freshly painted orange. Off it ran into the darkness.

The boy writhed out of the barn, holding himself as if his guts might fall out.

The long-haired girl grabbed the blue dress and wig and was brushing off the straw and trying to cover the dear pet when the night brought slamming doors from the farm dwelling across the field. There was no time for the dear pet to dress. She was pulled naked from the stable by the girl. The pet's tiny breasts and curveless body made her boyish, made her into delicious prey, made her the object of my sister's thrall. And my sister responded as the Artemis of old, doing what she once did best: Artemis, the protector of the forest's vulnerable creatures; Artemis, the protector of the young and the innocent. She had saved the dear pet. And now she followed her. She could not let go.

Henry Zimmerman Saw

the dog from the kitchen window. He was standing over the sink with his morning coffee. Gulping it down like he had somewhere to get to. Even after all these years he wondered about the lives of people who got in their cars in the morning and drove to work. Lots of those people, lots more than his type, and there were news articles about how commutes were getting longer and more congested and how to make your commute more pleasant. Sometimes Henry told himself he'd start listening to books on tape the way the writers of those articles suggested. Knew all along he'd listen solely to music, all kinds of music, and then when he was stuck in traffic he'd envision the book still drowning in his head and not inked on the page.

"I've seen this dog before," Henry said.

Ginny came over to take a look. She had pulled a big sweater over a jumper. Under her jumper she wore black tights although he was careful to refer to them as leggings because that's what she told him they were called. Sometimes he felt she'd rather be in that world that so outnumbered them, where she could chat with coworkers about leggings and strategies for the female foot. She had actually mused to him about how she would deal with the rat race. Little things she'd carefully considered, like how she would change out of comfortable shoes right in the lobby of a high-rise. Take off the sneakers and then slip on high heels and then push the button for the elevator to the eleventh floor, where she had decided her workplace was located. The agony of four-inch heels upon a marble floor would be made up for when she got to stand as tall as many of the men, squeezed against them shoulder to shoulder in the elevator so they couldn't help but notice. She could joke about it because Henry was tall. What's your job there on the eleventh floor? Henry asked her. Head of knitting department, she said. Ha ha ha. I'd go global, she told him. Explained why Ginny loved those TV Hallmark movies. They actually had things like head of knitting departments. Sometimes he looked over at Ginny during those movies and he could tell she was dreaming of being in their place, with powerful people calling up and asking if her new knitting design was going to make deadline.

Ginny peered out the kitchen window. Don't see anything, she said. Wait a sec.

The dog trotted back along the driveway, stopping to sniff at tires.

That's Licorice, Ginny said. The Atkins's chocolate Lab.

Oh, lord, Henry said. Don't suppose you could call them.

She's not any nicer to women, Ginny said.

Henry refilled his mug. One more cup and I'll do it.

Thanks, Ginny said. You're a sweetheart.

She left the kitchen and in another minute he heard her on the phone. That was Ginny. His little chuckle almost made him sad. He almost felt tears. Really he did. She would have done well in the rat race. Instead she married him and there it went. She always called it a rat race because that was such a negative term, she wanted Henry to believe he had saved her from the cut-throat treadmill, but he heard the dreaming in her voice.

While Ginny was on the phone, he went outside and called the name Licorice. Licorice bounded toward him and joyfully accepted his pats. He rolled on the ground and offered Henry his belly. By the time Ginny was done on the phone, Licorice was in the kitchen and Henry was sitting at the table with Licorice's head on his thigh. He was nagged by a song snippet about a loyal Irish hound: *The trade winds drove her but he stood guard in the blast.* He couldn't remember the rest, only that it didn't end well for either dog or maiden but was very beautifully sung.

Well, well, looks like you made a new friend, Ginny said. She sat at the table and reached out to Licorice. Licorice kept his head on Henry's thigh, eyes looking up at him. Ginny picked a few burrs from his fur.

He only likes me, Henry said.

Ha ha, Ginny said. Good dog, she said to Licorice.

What's the story? Henry asked.

She wants us to bring him back to her.

She's not going to pick him up?

Nope.

Hmm.

We'd better feed him something first, Ginny said. She got up and started searching the cupboards. What would be good for dogs?

Dog food, Henry said.

Ginny acted like he hadn't said anything smart-aleck. Dog food, she murmured thoughtfully, moving around cans. She took out chili con carne as a possibility.

Henry had to cradle Licorice's heavy head and ease him off his leg in order to stand up. I'm just gonna go into town and buy some dog food before we take him back.

That's way out of your way, Henry. Atkins's is thataway. Ginny's head nodded toward some distant point.

This way I can be sure he'll be fed.

They gave Licorice some water, which he lapped at in a distracted way, those eyes still on Henry.

He's afraid you're going to leave him, Ginny said.

Don't know about that, Henry said. But when Henry went outside, Licorice abandoned his water and jumped right inside Henry's truck as soon as he opened the door.

Henry was sad all the way into town and sad at the way Licorice waited so patiently in the truck. He ran into Freddy Burker in the Walmart, literally ran into him at the end of an aisle. Hard to say whose fault it was but Henry apologized while Freddy stared him down. In addition to the dog food, bags of Baby Ruths and Kit Kats were balanced in his arms (just in case anyone knocked tonight), and though he wasn't much for banter he tried to joke to Freddy that if he ran out of candy for the trick-or-treaters he could spoon out dog food. He waited for Freddy's glare to slack off. Like anyone is coming to your house! Freddy almost yelled at him. You did once, Henry told him. Freddy's childish anger there in the aisle sprang back to life the actual little boy: a perpetual temper tantrum wrapped in cherubic roundness. You were dressed as a ghost, Henry said, his voice trailing into the past.

Here! Freddy called as Henry walked away. When Henry turned, Freddy threw some more bags of candy at him. Henry was so shocked, the scene played out in slow motion. Milk Duds, Skittles, Milky Ways, and Snickers. Henry watched them fly through the air and land against his chest. Here's for all your ghosts! Freddy sneered and kicked down the aisle.

What was wrong with that man!

What was wrong with that child!

Freddy had been in school with Danny. He stood out for all the reasons a boy wouldn't want: bad at sports, a chubby toddler's face that resisted puberty, curly hair, the losing end of playground fights. Freddy had never picked a fight with Danny, however, in fact always vied for Danny's attention. Would do anything to get it. Danny was the opposite of Freddy. Didn't ask anyone to like him; they just did. Being admired by the other boys might have been nice for Danny but in the long run maybe it wasn't so good. Still, any way you sliced it, Danny would not act up like this in the middle of a Walmart—even in his current state. He might embarrass himself showing up to shop high or drunk, might stagger down these aisles, might even pass out, but he would never act like Freddy. Would always say Good Afternoon, Mrs. Fill-in-the-Name. He retained his mother's good manners. Or so Henry hoped. And Freddy? Henry watched him stomp away, that soft muffin butt and girlish thigh meat—if only he could see himself from behind, maybe that would give him a little humility. He remembered that Halloween long ago when Freddy had shown up. He hadn't even asked his mom, the late Mrs. Burker, if he could ruin her nice set of sheets in order to be a lousy ghost. Had just stolen them off her bed and cut out eyeholes. Had knocked on the door hoping to get with Danny's trick-or-treating crew. Danny let him of course. Danny was nice that way. A nice boy. Just one wrong turn by a nice boy, maybe somebody handing him something in the school restroom. Just one little thing, like that poor American kid taking a sign down in North Korea and then he was in jail and then he was dead. One little thing and a whole life unravels.

In the parking lot Henry opened the Tupperware bowl Ginny had fixed up when it became clear that Licorice would be riding along with him. In the bowl were a can opener and a spoon and paper towel. He watched Licorice eat the dog food from the Tupperware bowl. Licorice let him wipe his mouth with the paper towel. They had a long ride to the Atkins place, long enough for Henry to get too used to the heavy warmth on his thigh. He was sadder when he pulled into the Atkins drive and Mrs. Atkins came out and yelled at Licorice, who had no choice but to obey, his head twisted back toward Henry while his paws obediently stepped toward his mistress. Mrs. Atkins grabbed hold of his collar as she talked to Henry. Every once in a while she jerked it. She talked, but he didn't hear a thank-you in whatever she was saying. He found himself thinking, If that's what she does to a dog, her children must be tragic news. Then he caught himself. Folks could say the same thing about him and Danny. What was it that had made Danny get involved in that sort of life? Biology? A hand under the bathroom stall passing him something to try? A body geared for addiction? Or had Henry done something wrong? What fatal mistake had he made in his parenting? No way it could be blamed on Ginny. The fault was his. What was it he should wish to take back? Harsh words? That one time he slapped Danny's three-year-old bottom? The way he and his dad had joked when Danny didn't take to hunting? The way he had forgotten to sign him up for summer baseball?

The way he had made him play soccer instead even though Danny cried and threw up on the field?

He and Ginny had hoped to have more kids. More kids might have given him a clue, maybe put his mind at rest. He'd seen lots of families, kids all raised the same way but one goes astray while the other is pride and joy. Don't blame yourself, the child care expert who was Ginny's sister had told him one too many times. But he did.

Mrs. Atkins's house was wildly decorated for Halloween. Lining the driveway were plastic and real jack-o'-lanterns. Whopper spiderwebs screened the front porch, where ghosts hung within. And the front yard greeted you with a cemetery of styrofoam headstones. The place looked fun. But the tight expression on Mrs. Atkins's face didn't reveal a person who enjoyed things. He guessed she could ably play the part of the witch, the one piece of Halloween decoration missing. The way she considered him, a shrew about to cast a spell, caused him to back away, much to Licorice's distress. She took note of Licorice's attachment to him, said, What did you do to him? and he said, You're welcome and you have a fine dog, should appreciate him more.

That was a lot for him to say.

And she didn't like it.

A cruel accusation was gearing up in her. He could see it coming and fled to the truck. He quickly backed out of the driveway as if from a slingshot. Noises came out of Licorice's throat until the collar jerked again.

It was time, Henry decided as he drove off. As he passed his own house, he stopped right on the road and honked until Ginny looked out. Going to the library! he shouted toward her. Didn't know whether she heard him or not, but she gave him a wave.

IN THE LIBRARY's anteroom, Henry gathered his courage in the restroom. He thought of Ginny changing out her sneakers for high heels.

Both of them were part-time living in make-believe worlds, Ginny with the career she never had, he with his book. Not one word of it written, but already it was a best-seller.

He entered the library proper and forced a friendly nod to the librarian who looked up at him. This town could cast you suspicious looks when you weren't servicing your recognizable spot. The librarian gazed at him like a stranger. Her eyes followed him to the line of computers he had glimpsed. He headed over there as if he knew what he was doing. Once he was seated he dared not look up at her. He felt her gathering up books and then she turned away and he took a deep breath and checked to see she wasn't watching. Before him was a computer. A whole row of them. He stared at the sci-fi world laid out before him. Just let it sink in, he told himself. Let it sink in and it will all become normal.

Fortunately the computers were already turned on. He had chosen a place two empty seats away from a giant boy. Far enough not to infringe, close enough that he could copy what the boy was doing.

Act normal, Henry told himself. His hand poised over the space bar like a concert pianist at the ivories. His fingers tickled the keys. The audience waited. And waited. A cough in the uncomfortable hush. The crinkle of a candy wrapper. Everyone waiting on his artistry to pour forth and nothing happening. Oh, lord, Henry was out of his element.

Was he the only one in the world who didn't have a computer?

He could answer that.

Yes he was.

His hand went limp over the keyboard and fell to his lap.

The boy turned to him. Henry saw shyness on his face. Knew right away he wasn't dealing with the likes of a Freddy Burker.

Hi young fella, Henry said.

The boy relaxed. You gotta type in your password, he told Henry.

Right, Henry said.

The boy scooted back his chair and stood up. Giant was right. The proper description for him. I'll get it, the boy told him. Get what? Henry waited almost excited for the surprise the boy was about to fetch. He watched the boy walk to the front desk. The library was empty except for the two of them and the librarian. The boy could have made noise and nobody would have looked up with a sssh, yet he moved his body carefully and quietly. He reminded Henry of something. He had time to think while the boy spoke to the librarian, and he landed on the image of himself and his dad hunting in the woods, the way their muzzles were pointed safe and downward. The boy walked as if he were a firearm checked on safety. Because he was, with his size, something loaded and dangerous. The boy had learned to step along the paths of the world as if to say, Please, I'm harmless. This analysis might sound crazy—to everyone but his dad. He and his dad used to puzzle out the woods together, piecing together clues. His dad would understand perfectly. His dad was wise and he was curious and it was odd moments like this one, watching a boy walk over to a librarian, when he missed his dad anew.

Here's your password, the boy said. He handed Henry a slip of paper.

Thank you, Henry said. He imagined turning to Ginny. A password! he'd exclaim with a wink. Our treasure hunt begins!

The boy sat down next to him. He enveloped the chair. Henry noticed that he used a bigger chair at his computer spot. The librarian was watching them with a not unkind expression. She was the one responsible for getting the boy a bigger chair. That was the boy's special spot and his special computer. Henry read the scene like scat and animal prints. The emptiness of this library called out as clearly as bird calls. Day after day the repeating orbit of this sanctuary played out before him. The boy was a regular and he kept her company. Nobody else ever came. Not to see the books. Not to use the computer. Everybody but Henry and the boy already had a computer. Henry didn't have a computer because he was a hopeless old man who had just recently learned you could call up on the phone and order takeout and have it ready by the time you got there. The boy, though—he clearly knew computers. If he didn't have one of his own, there was only one reason. The paw print of money was plain on the trail.

Now you can do what you want, the boy said.

Super, Henry said.

And you can print stuff out here, the boy said.

Sounds good, Henry said.

Are you looking to do anything particular? The boy's cheeks turned red with this question. Henry could see it took a lot out of him to ask something that might be interpreted as prying.

Well, I'm writing a book, Henry said. It's one of them kinds will write itself once I get started.

The boy nodded.

Are you writing a book? Henry asked.

No. I got websites I run.

Oh yeah, said Henry. That's good, he managed. The boy waited for him.

The quiet between them grew. Henry heard the turn of a page. The librarian flipping through a magazine.

The outside door opened with a loud pneumatic crack. Henry jumped. Somebody walked in but then didn't walk in.

Probably just to use the restroom, the boy explained. That happens.

Are you usually alone in here?

Yeah, the boy said.

What's a website? Henry asked.

It's like this, the boy said. Despite his size, he stood up with an easy bounce and moved over to his computer. He did this and that and then showed a screen to Henry. This is one of them, he said. I sell sneakers and these clothes. The boy clicked through photos of zip-up sweatshirts and baggy jackets.

Those sneakers are nice, Henry said. Don't much care for the clothes.

Me neither, said the boy. It's the brand that's important.

You got any girl sneakers?

Not really, said the boy.

My wife might like a pair of girl sneakers, Henry said.

I could try to get some for her. Give 'em to you at cost.

That's nice of you, Henry said.

Already Henry was thinking of Thanksgiving. It would fall on Ginny's birthday this year. And already he knew what the birthday card tucked inside a pretty new sneaker would say: Let's go to a lobby somewhere and you can change out of these sneakers into high heels so I can take you out to dinner. Elevator included at no charge!

The Monte Carlo

always found its own way home while Travis daydreamed. The country-side was usually so black, but tonight it was flecked with bouncing flashlights, at least until you got farther out. Houses too spread apart and no point knocking on the Amish doors anyway. It was mostly in town that the kids went begging. Parents monitored from their cars or patrolled along the sidewalks. It was the one day out of the year Travis used to like his mom better than the other moms. She had no intention of escorting him along his trick-or-treat route.

From the Monte Carlo's front seat Travis gathered the first folded pile of clean clothes and brought them inside and laid them on top of the dresser. He went back to the car to get the socks and underwear. Mr. Zimmerman, whom he'd met in the library that very afternoon, had struck a deal that if Travis helped him once every two weeks on the computer, he could use their washer and dryer for free at their house. Travis just happened to have all his dirty clothes in the car. If the first time was any indication, Mrs. Zimmerman was actually going to do the laundry for him, fold it, and then feed him afterward.

Mr. Zimmerman had shown him the notebook he was writing in. He was collecting songs for his book and he had the lyrics half written out and then he was going to include the actual music, too. He still had to somehow hunt down the rest of the lyrics and then find a way to get hold of the sheet music and copy it. Songs like "Greensleeves." Right? Mr. Zimmerman had said to Travis about the daunting task. He wasn't insulted that Travis didn't know "Greensleeves"—that was why he was writing the book. The book was going to be titled "Good Songs." Mr. Zimmerman told him how much work and research it was going to cost him, which was why he hadn't gotten started. Travis decided to keep Google a surprise for him down the line. In the meantime he wrote down a few of the song titles with a line of lyrics and told Mr. Zimmerman he'd research them for him. He'd also Google how to publish your own book and get that information printed out. Mr. and Mrs. Zimmerman acted like they were getting the better part of the deal. Mrs. Zimmerman asked what his favorite food was and he said peanut-butter-and-jelly sandwich and she said, Come on, don't be so polite, so he told her the truth and said beef stew. Oh, my god, if he could get beef stew with lots of beef, that kind where the meat was real soft.

It was late by the time Travis left the Zimmerman house but he nonetheless detoured through town to see if there were any Halloween stragglers. The bigger kids were out roaming. The last of the small kids ran to beat them to the doors. Travis saw classmates from his high school. Some had even graduated, like Kirk and Bratley. Kirk carried a big sword and sliced the air in figure eights when he wasn't trying to lop off the little kids' heads. They were minimum-wage trouble-makers. Had Juggalo tattoos. Travis recognized Corbin and Anisha just from their body types. Corbin was stretched into a skintight Green Lantern superhero outfit and Anisha was dressed as Wonder Woman. It all died out as soon as he left town and it was like it never happened and none of those people ever existed.

Travis swept up the underwear from the passenger seat and balanced the balls of socks on top and the two bags of candy on top of the sock balls. He killed the Monte Carlo's headlights and maneuvered through the blackout, the memorized terrain of a path he had laid down with a couple bags of gravel from Yoder. Then—and what a moment it was— the solar motion detector he had just installed triggered on and Travis stood amazed in its halo. It worked. He reveled in a surge of pride. He had built this very moment a dollar step by a dollar step, from Yoder's gravel to Walmart's solar light. The movie would capture him, Travis Hicks, age seventeen, standing in this spotlight, his eyes a Wyandot's eyes, his jaw a soldier's jaw, his

Darkness.

The motion detector timed out. He was swallowed by impenetrable carbon. The trailer, where was it? Ahead? To his left, his right, over here? Didn't know.

The gravel under his feet was gone. Just dirt. A knob of weed. Couldn't find the gravel. Trying to tread water in a black lake. Scraped forward but found himself back at the Monte Carlo. He shifted in another direction, arms locked by the stack of laundry, unable to swing and trigger the motion detector.

Socks and candy went flying as a body staggered full-bore into him.

Something big tackling him. Travis absorbed it, felt its size and strength. Kept standing although everything inside was hurtled into the occult. Fear rocked him. He swung out for his car, his trailer, the motion light. At his feet lay the heaviness of sorcery, this thing at his feet.

Shaking inside his own paralysis.

Came a voice: Fuck you, Travis. A man's voice tucked inside a high school sophomore.

Instantly calm now was Travis. It was Jared Overholser's voice. Jared's big body had gone sprawling after knocking into him.

Fuck you, Travis.

Jared rolled on the ground at Travis's feet. Whimpering. Panting weird breaths.

Fuck you, Travis.

Jared crawled away from Travis, setting off the motion detector again. Then paused on all fours. There in the light. He stayed like that, like he was playing horse. His pants had slid over his butt.

Some of the ebony beyond had been drained by the motion detector's spotlight and Travis could see some things out there. The brushstrokes of the Keims' farmhouse and then Mr. Keim's shadow dashing across the briefly pale field toward his barn.

Jared crawled in the opposite direction—whimpers, moans. Travis watched him pull himself up like an old lady and begin his caneless stumble, his stumble in need of a cane, down the road into darker shadow. Until blackness swallowed him and distance swallowed his moaning.

Rimming the edge of the bright circle was this: a wiggly big caterpillar. Travis bent to pick it up before the light flicked off. He already knew what it was by the time his fingers touched it, but he powered through and stood up with a condom hanging from his fingers. It was gross but nothing inside so it wasn't that gross. Two people stood watching him. Like that. Two people right there and then the solar light shut off and he couldn't see anything and was too afraid to move. His bladder shuddered. He grabbed at himself to stop the leaking. And then the spotlight rang on and Hannah Kirkpatrick was standing there with a naked girl.

Stop looking, Travis! she whisper-screamed.

Travis was glad for her rage. His bladder retracted. He was okay on that end but still shaking.

Hannah hurried inside the trailer with the naked girl.

Travis used the temporary light to search for his socks and the two bags of candy the Zimmermans had given him He festooned the condom across the top of a weed. When the light went out, he waved around to trigger it again. This time Mr. Keim was standing there. Travis yelped. He grabbed himself, pushing back the pee. The socks and candy fell again.

It was the only time Mr. Keim had stepped onto Travis's side. He stood wordless and staring, boring into Travis a hatred and anger that frightened Travis as much as those two creepy figures. He had imagined them, hadn't he? A man and a woman, an unearthly couple, inhuman killers. He would drive to Walmart tonight and sleep in its parking lot, his car between long-haul truck drivers. Those guys carried guns.

Hello? Travis said to Mr. Keim.

Mr. Keim turned like a military soldier and stomped away.

The light went out and Travis stepped on the candy. He waved the light back on and picked up his by-now dirty socks and the two bags of candy and lunged up the cinderblocks and knocked on his own fragile door.

Come in, whispered Hannah.

Inside he recognized Chieko, the Japanese exchange student.

Did you see her naked? Hannah demanded.

No, Travis said. His mind was not on a girl's nakedness. His mind was on the Walmart parking lot and the big eighteen-wheelers that would keep him safe.

Hannah shook her head at Chieko. It's okay, she told her.

Okay? asked Chieko.

I didn't see anything, Travis said. Nothing, he said loudly to Chieko.

She's not deaf, Travis.

Chieko was dressed in a blue-checked jumper with a short-sleeved white blouse. In her hand were dusty pigtails.

The Wizard of Oz, Hannah explained to Travis.

What's that? He was steady now, calm enough to recognize Hannah's sigh of frustration.

Who are you dressed as? Travis asked.

A witch, said Hannah.

You look like a normal person.

A good witch.

Travis opened the candy bag and handed squished Baby Ruths to Hannah and Chieko. They sat in a circle on the floor and poured out the rest of the candy.

Kit Kat bars. Oh, of course, Hannah said with disgust.

Is everything okay? Travis asked her.

Barely.

Travis said, I have his DNA in case she wants to go to the cops.

Hannah shook her head.

You can't let him get away with it.

Don't worry. Chieko kicked him so hard she ruptured him. Didn't you, Chieko? Nothing happened.

It's a crime.

After football season we can decide.

Seriously? He needs to get kicked off the team.

And then we'll miss the playoffs. It's not just the football team, Travis. There's the cheerleaders to think about. Who will we cheer for?

It's not right, Travis said.

After the playoffs her English will be better and she can explain what happened.

She needs to report him, Travis said.

How do you know? I'm not even sure what exactly happened, Hannah said, except that IT didn't happen.

How do you know that if she can't say it in English? Travis turned to Chieko. Did Jared rape you? he asked.

Chieko gazed mutely about his trailer.

See? Hannah said. She patted Chieko on the shoulder.

Chieko rested her head against Hannah, then took out a joint from the pocket of her blue-checked jumper.

Do you want to smoke dope? Hannah asked him.

If you really want me to, Travis said.

Chieko stood up and searched in kitchen drawers. She found the matches before Travis could direct her.

It's from Amos, isn't it? Travis asked Hannah.

Yeah.

He shouldn't do that to her.

She's got the money. Hannah lowered her voice to a whisper—a lot of money, she said and shrugged. Amos makes her pay for it, even though …

She sent a false smile over to Chieko.

Even though what?

You're so innocent, Travis.

I use condoms, Travis protested.

Oh, my god, Hannah said. Shut up!

Chieko sat down and passed the joint but Hannah shook her head.

Aren't you going to? Travis asked her.

I'm a varsity cheerleader! Hannah told him. She looked insulted. I'm a role model, Travis. And I took a vow to be the best role model I could be.

Travis smiled.

Don't smile! And next year I'm running for head cheerleader and I don't want to have to lie about my conduct!

Travis got up off the floor and went into his bedroom.

Are you in your bedroom so you can laugh without me seeing?

Travis brought out a big box. He pulled out Supreme box logo hoodies, all in gray, and then his prize, a Supreme faux fur bomber jacket. Could only afford one, but if he sold it he could make a lot of money.

Oh! Chieko exclaimed. Then more gusts of wonder.

See, she knows.

She likes that stuff? Hannah cringed at the sight of the boxy gray hoodies and reared back.

It's really popular in Japan and China and Korea.

That doesn't make it not ugly.

Ask her if she wants to buy these from me.

Why?

Just ask.

Do you want to buy these? Hannah asked Chieko.

More gusts of wonder from Chieko.

Do you want to send these to Japan? Travis asked. This clothes? Send? he asked Chieko. Make fly. To Japan?

Wow, you speak Japanese, Hannah said.

Yes yes yes! exclaimed Chieko.

Told you, Travis said.

She pays me and then the Japanese pay her.

Whatever, Hannah said.

They watched Chieko overreact to the dope and pass out on the floor.

Is she for real? Travis asked.

You know she's living with me now, don't you? Hannah said. That other house didn't work out. Their two kids are in grade school. Which would be good for her learning English but they don't talk to her. I don't think she's a fast learner either and I mean, I don't mean that in a mean way.

That's nice of your mom.

My mom doesn't care. My mom fucks high school students, Travis.

No she doesn't.

You're so innocent, Travis. Everybody knows.

No they don't. I don't think it's true. And I'm not innocent.

Okay, Hannah said. She looked over at Chieko prostrate on the carpet. Travis and Hannah bent over close to her face. Her eyes are half open, Hannah said.

Is she asleep?

She told me I could go visit her in Japan.

Are you?

I think the summer between senior year and college.

That would be good, Travis said.

I better get her home, Hannah said.

III.

FEBRUARY

SIX MONTHS EARLIER

What is high school football in a one high school
town? It is what all life revolves around.
—*Anonymous*

On A Night

in late winter, Dr. Devajaran found herself kneeling in an attitude of adoration. She was alone in the cold and dark. She was alone in a ditch along a country road. Legs like prison bars surrounded her; she was alone. Her daughter was with her somewhere in the crowd, her daughter's best friend as well. The lanterns lit her way from one to the other. A circle of lanterns around each one. Her knees were soaked in mud. The mud, turning to ice.

Two boys lay on the ground, fifteen, twenty feet apart. One was moaning. One was silent. She knew these boys. She didn't know them specifically, not their names or the names of their parents, but she knew them. They were children of lowered sights, and she treated their mothers and fathers and grandparents for the illnesses their group most often delivered too soon: chronic bronchitis, high blood pressure, type 2 diabetes, skin carcinomas ignored. Here they were, the two boys, living up (living down?) to the predictable: speeding, no seatbelts, drinking. The town's caste system was at work. It had deposited its lower rung in a ditch.

She dared not speak this. And it was painfully true that it could happen to anyone. But so often it didn't.

If she had one second, if she had one slice of a moment, she would have searched for her beloved daughter in the gathering of Plain men—or at least her pair of Frye boots, the kind Adesh strutted home in at winter break.

Anisha, call Adesh!

It was a Friday night. What was he doing!

She could not calm the crazy thoughts. Adesh at a party, trying to impress the boys as smart as he. *My dad has an apartment he never uses we can party there.* And they would scrape through the snow and slush of Cambridge, he in his prescuffed retro boots he was so proud of, already becoming like them.

Call your brother now!

Her daughter was safe. Just stay clear of the road, off the berm, far back, in case another car goes skidding off the road.

Cross at the lights in Boston! The cars might slip on the ice!

Anisha, stay off the road!

She called in a panic to the legs and knees and the blind spots of their faces. Their lanterns stabbed when she looked up. Their legs imprisoned.

Anisha, do what your mother says. The voice belonged to Miriam.

She was already behind. Two boys were dying. She needed time returned to her. Four minutes was all she asked. Her skills could perhaps return four minutes to these boys. Her hands were speedy and sure. And a flashlight, slim but strong, sucked in her mouth. And Miriam was also there, down on her knees, the two of them. Miriam! How was she here?—a miracle. Four minutes. Together she and Miriam could do it.

The first boy's tibia and fibula were crushed. Thrown free of the car, the limp body had found the one soft spot. Thrown through the air and landed not on road, not on gravel berm, not on the hard frozen field. The body had found the winter blanket of a ditch. It had helped to save him—if he were to be saved. Like an uncleared gutter, the ditch had gathered a season's drift of foliage to receive the flung boy. The car had rolled. It must have glanced a fleeting blow on the boy's leg before flipping across the street into the barren cornfield on the other side.

The traveling moon caught the white of bone.

Her daughter's friend began to scream. An impossibly high octave, almost like the ending note to a song.

Get him away. Anisha. Take Corbin away. It was Miriam again taking charge, knowing beforehand what Dr. Devajaran needed.

The hysterical high notes played out farther down the road, a softer song.

Tell them to stay off the road, she whispered.

Make sure they are off the road, Miriam said to one of the lanterns. My boys, go with Anisha and wait for me. Go now.

The flashlight held in Dr. Devajaran's mouth was slipping. She bit down on it. The drool was dripping from her chin. She felt the tender wipe of a kerchief at her mouth.

The boy was bleeding wildly but not fatally; the femoral artery was safe. Miriam already had strips of towel for her to tie a tourniquet. It was likely he would lose his lower leg. She cut through his corduroy jacket. She would have to leave these wounds to the hospital.

He was dressed too thinly for a frigid February night.

Was Adesh wearing the coat she'd bought him? She knew he wasn't. Not stylish enough.

A blanket, something warm? she asked, not looking up. There was silence above her. Miriam was on her knees. Everyone else above her. Miriam blindly raised an arm and a coat was hung upon it. She covered the boy. Dr. Devajaran didn't have to wave them back, ask them to give her space, allow her to see, give the victims air. The quiet men stood un-interfering and positioned, their lanterns just so.

She and Miriam left the bleeding sites on the first boy's torso and went to the other boy. The blood was issuing from his mouth in noisy yo-dels. The smell of beer or whiskey bubbled out, she couldn't tell which. Miriam was kneeling, already restraining his head between two towels. It seemed so natural to have her here, her children's former childminder. It was as if no time at all had passed. Miriam had children now her-self, three of them, very young but precociously steady and quiet as she had always been, reliable as the two rolled towels she had somehow produced to secure the boy's head. Life had been magic when Miriam had been with them, quiet and magical, a time so charmed that Dr. Devajaran had resisted all her husband's pleas to abandon this nothing town. Her husband had tried other names: backwater, bankrupt, ignorant, racist. Boonies—a new word he came up with one year. She preferred that to his harsher unforgiving words. Boonies—it sounded like a cartoon. Who wouldn't want to live in Boonies.

Miriam took the flashlight from Dr. Devajaran's mouth and shone the narrow cone on the second boy's head, nodding the beam to his chest in sync with Dr. Devajaran's tiny flying hands.

Thank you, Miriam, she whispered.

Some of the men were checking the crash site. The car was upside down They had located it in the stubs of the cornfield. They reached their lanterns through the burst windows. The upturned tires were still spinning. Click click as they rotated. A feeble click, then another. The spinning wouldn't stop but it was weak. Click click: it seemed to count the moments left for these boys. Time was running out. Was it the smell of burned tires charring her nostrils or the kerosene of the lanterns?

The men continued combing the stubby cornfield. They patrolled up and down the ditch on both sides of the road. Now the moon had floated behind a witch's cape. It was black behind the men. Nothing but blackness. Black trees like an army coming to destroy them all.

Is there another? Miriam called to the men who had paused along the ditch to aim their lanterns for a closer look.

No, Dr. Devajaran said. No. No. The four minutes she was gaining would all be lost. These boys in the ditches—that was all they would ever be if there were more. It was how they would end their lives. Thrown in a ditch. Found in a ditch. Died in a ditch.

What? Miriam asked the men.

She couldn't leave this second boy for another, not unless she made the decision to sacrifice his life. A decision based on what? Because the third boy had a better chance, was a better person, was someone she happened to know? She was suctioning the choking blood from the second boy's mouth. She feared a torn aorta. He was trying to move, was agitated, was fighting, but Miriam locked his head. This one might die, would die if she couldn't return the minutes to him. She had already decided to move to the third boy, if there was a third boy.

No one else, Miriam reported softly.

Only these two?

Yes.

In the distance she heard sirens. And now it would be up to them.

How she missed Miriam, she realized. Adesh and Anisha in preschool, their chubby thighs, their loving innocent bodies—how she missed that. She missed the long lists Miriam used to make each day, the obediently complete sentences. She missed taking Miriam home on summer days, almost always stopping for ice cream that they'd sit and eat in the car in front of the farmhouse. They'd watch for purple martins to land in the birdhouse. Miriam taught her the names of flowers and how their borders were believed to protect the garden crops. The first words her children learned to read came from the plain square sign in front of Miriam's house: Eggs Nuts Candy Baked Goods Quilts. Miriam and her Amish life were a children's book the children got to read each day. She missed that. Her medical practice was unthriving those few years but her life just the opposite. Free time. She got to experience what that was like. And she loved it. She felt a pang for her very first patient in this town, now dead, who loved her, who brought in a friend and then another friend—a loyal elderly patient base of three. And she had time for them and how they laughed. The woman—what did she die of? nothing really, which was how it should have been, just the years running out for her—was plump like fresh-made bread, her tiny mouth squeezed by the rising dough of her face. My god, what was her name? And she bought a cherry-red convertible for her eightieth birthday and they both went off for a spin.

When her husband first visited her in the town of Kattoga, he deplored the conditions he found her living in. Deplore—that was his exact verb. Deplorable—that was his exact adjective. What deplorable conditions are those, my love? She always spoke in overly endearing terms to her husband. He seemed not to notice. At the Cleveland airport she would stand on tiptoe and peer as far down the line of gates as possible. She could thus witness the final twenty-five yards of his nine-thousand-mile trek into her arms. He strode as if on a business trip, no anticipation, no dreaminess, no need to neutralize an embarrassing excitement on his face as he drew close. He wore a suit. He didn't bother to look for her until he was outside security.

His infrequent visits made each first night together a repeat of their wedding night—embarrassment, her delays in the bathroom. Her mind didn't typically vex itself with ironies, but she was aware that the young she treated often had more worldly experience than she did. As a doctor she knew all the complications of sexuality; as a woman, she knew a couple of positions. They were nonetheless effective. During her residency at Toledo General she twice became a mother. He stayed at Bangalore Medical College and waited for her to find someplace better than a cold corner of Ohio. Instead she found someplace worse, in Ohio's midriff.

What conditions in Kattoga did he deplore? She had stopped noticing how half the downtown had fallen away into palimpsested shells. How signs hung over the neon tracings of former signs and then those, too, faded into tracings. The hardware store, empty. The empty display window of the formal dressware store sent the kids to Lima for their prom outfits. The Christian video store, its display window still fully on display, was sunbleached and gathering a biblical tide of dust. The town hall itself, for lease. She could buy it, and if her husband would move here, together they could form a doctor's center. Preventive medicine. Education. Complementary therapies. Everyone living happily together. The building stood, months and months unsold, an empty rebuke to her marriage.

But the grand historical courthouse rising on its central hill—this was her glass half full whenever she drove by. For her it was still a thriving downtown. The courthouse that had welcomed presidents was now and then abuzz with its former glory. The Bundt Haus with its daily specials.

The Go-Fer pizza, voted regional runner-up for best milkshake. And the Franklin Art Studio, chronicler of their not-quite-real family life. Always the four of them in the photos she hung. She and her husband and Adesh and Anisha. Always inseparable. For years it was a stilted indoor grouping with the same wavy gray background. For years she and her two children clutched each other on cloth-covered stools while her husband stood behind, touchlessly wrapping them in his arms. Always their eyes were aimed toward something in the upper right corner.

In these photos everyone changed but she. Her children grew up, her husband got heavier and went white at the temples and then unnaturally black. You could see him rearranging his expression by stutter steps as his status at Bangalore Medical College rose, until he no longer looked like a particular father and a particular husband but like the actorly essence of those things. The photo shoots moved from indoors to outdoors, to the stone bench in the cemetery, her children posed back to back, knees up, all gravestones out of frame, nothing but lush greenery behind them. Everything changed except she. She was always the same, simply smiling her big smile. In every photo she was genuinely happy, her mouth large and her teeth very white. She looked much the same, unchanged by time. In the early photos the fatigue tattooed under her eyes made her look older so that in the later photos she had simply caught up.

She did not particularly miss having a real husband. She did worry, however, that her children missed having a real father. Boys without their fathers ran wild. She'd seen it time and again in this town, the search-and-destroy missions of fatherless boys added to their already untamed adolescence. How did her own boy escape? How did he escape this ditch? What was he doing this very moment on this very Friday night? If she traveled to him to make sure he was safe, it would no longer be Friday night and the time she might be able to return to these two boys could never be returned to her own son. He was too far from her. She couldn't reach out to help. Was he still at his desk, still deep in his Harvard studies? Or was he drinking from a keg? Had he been persuaded by the rich white boys that he was one of them now? It would take only a moment for him to learn the real truth of that. It would take only one wrong step. And then her husband would have been right all along.

Anisha, call your brother!

No answer.

She's with my boys, said Miriam, and then she did something she never did. She touched her and patted her arm. She is safe, Dr. Devajaran.

At once her confidence was shaken. She was kneeling in a ditch, two boys were dying, one would die she was sure, one would lose a leg she was sure. She began to tremble. The sirens were here; she held on. One of the paramedics was Gavin. Gavin, who brought his problem with women and authority to work. Even in this situation he bristled under her orders. This one straight to Toledo General, she told him. They usually life-flighted to Lima but Lima wasn't equipped to treat aortic disruption and she was sure this was the issue. Toledo General, she ordered. Gavin appeared not to hear. The boy who might surely die—had her four minutes been enough?—was nothing more than a carcassed gurney he pushed into the ambulance. This is not a pizza you shove into a pizza oven! she screamed. Gavin was short and muscular and what she did admire about him was his strength and his ability to leverage and balance the awkward load of bodies—but that was the only thing she admired. This was the first time she had ever felt herself lose control, and she saw it, she watched it happening, and she was willing to let go if it meant saving a life.

The boy will die if you don't get him to Toledo General!

Gavin did not respond.

The crack of thunder in her chest flung her toward Gavin. Her skin and coat and eyes and long unraveling hair were strobing red. She must have looked a banshee.

Miriam held her back.

The ambulance doors were already shut, the sky was black water, the moon hidden. The lightstreams from the kerosene lamps drained into the night as the Plain men moved on and headed back to their houses. Even Miriam had turned to leave without acknowledgment. Her little boys were riveted by the sight of Corbin stumbling toward them, still crying in high-pitched stammers. They looked at this teenage boy in wonderment as they were led away. Miriam's hand rearranged a little chin face forward, and the staring sweet eyes disappeared.

Just the mention of the hospital in Toledo brought back the secret particulars of her failed marriage, her failed attempts at worldly experience, Toledo, where she had done her residency, where her husband had visited so many times but so few! The sex that was dark as this night and filled with smells and movements that left her baffled but were in the end miraculous. The daughter it had produced was right here, held tight in her arms. They were alone on a dark country road, she and her daughter, and then Corbin running to join them, all of them shaking in their huddle. It was a cold night in February. Nobody could understand how dark it was out here, how alone. The three of them, scared and hugging and crying, I love you I love you.

Call your brother, Anisha!

He already texted.

Is he all right?

It's okay, Mom.

What did he say? Don't lie to me.

Anisha lit up his message on her cell screen. "Yo whattup bruh."

Florence!

Florence was the name of the patient she loved who drove the red convertible, and she had died on the couch after a happy life and been found three days later.

The ambulances drove away. The red lights stayed in sight, then leaped into the black lake and vanished, and they were alone huddled in their bouquet, she and Anisha and Corbin. If He were ever to speak to her, it would be now. She asked Him to please, please listen to her prayers. Please keep her daughter safe. Please keep her son safe. Please protect Corbin. Please let her children live. Please ... and she realized she should not be praying to any god for the reason next in her thoughts: because they are better.

Kirk and Bratley were not high! Check the tox report. The drugs in their system were the drugs administered onsite by the EMTs.
—trollingbutknowing

doctor was impaired.
—*simonkenton*

Hannah Did Not

understand any of the words the disgusting Jared was aiming her way. He was cackling too hard. She did not understand why his friends were laughing so hard, in a way that was beginning to sound dangerous. Something had changed, maybe because of the beer. It was a Friday night in February, and without football they had nothing to do.

Hannah stood in front of her house with Erika and Chieko. She had forgotten to turn on the porch light. It was dark as midnight though only eight p.m.

Come on, said Erika, tugging Hannah to the door. Chieko pressed close to them. Both her arms were wrapped around Hannah. Hannah was afraid if she opened the door the boys would burst inside. They didn't know her mom and Nan weren't home, but Jared would suspect.

It was three girls facing off with four guys. Advantage, boys.

But they were in Hannah's front yard. Advantage, girls.

She didn't know about these other three guys, but she knew about Jared. They'd lived next door to each other all their lives, a country acre separating their houses. On summer nights the fights between Jared's parents arrived as a night forest of insects. In winter the howling winds deposited screams that were long expired. Now the parents were divorced, and the shouting matches were between Jared and his mother.

Why the boys were laughing, Hannah didn't understand but her body shivered harder. Erika was always the first to get scared over nothing although this time she allowed Erika to pull her inside the house and they opened the door quickly and shut the door quickly and locked it to the boys' jeers. Something was thrown against the window, which sent Chieko into Hannah's arms. The thin winter air bared all of Jared's taunts. He yelled nasty words about Erika being black and Chieko being Japanese.

Hannah turned on the porch light and opened the door as far as the chain lock allowed and shouted, She speaks English now and understands what you're saying, asshole!

This amused the boys so much they stumbled over themselves. She saw in the shock of porch light a deer frozen in its tracks. It toppled over when Jared fell against it. He wrestled with it and fake-stabbed it to death.

Erika was already calling her parents.

They're never going to let you come over anymore. Hannah started crying. She opened the front door again. And you suck as a quarterback! Jared, you suck! You won't ever make the NFL! She gave a final slam to the door then opened it and yelled, Loser! but the yard was quiet and the oak trees asleep.

When Erika's parents arrived, Erika gave Hannah a mournful cheerleader kiss and went out alone so she could pretend Hannah's mother and grandmother were inside. Her parents wouldn't want to come in anyway. And if they did come in, they wouldn't be able to unsee Nan's ashtray with its furrowed holder and lipstick-stained butts. Not that Hannah didn't live in a nice house. She did live in a nice house. She was on the good side of the dividing line. Still, Erika's parents weren't the type to socialize with Hannah's family. People like Erika's mother never texted people like Hannah's mother. They didn't hold it against Hannah though. Whatever it was had obviously skipped a generation. They liked Hannah. Hannah was problem-free. But they also had a line they drew.

FYI: School board has called emergency meeting.
—*truebandmom*

I don't see the school board stepping in. They have
a 3/4 percent tax on the ballot coming this fall.
Them not letting the boys play or having a terrible
season would all but ensure the failure of their tax hike.
Just reality. Not taking sides.
—*snackbarmom*

We Watched Them

from the same treeline where I had watched him leap from the fox-covered chasers—yes, I, the great Apollo caught off guard. Yes, the once great Apollo grounded against a beech, the keeper of Sleep paying a short visit. I have never admitted that he put me in mind of Heracles, not Heracles himself, rather some visage faintly akin to Heracles, some torso and mass akin, certainly the difference huge and I am reluctant even to broach such heresy as it was a vague impression anyway, an unformed notion *Heracles bursting through the woods* that should invite eternal ridicule (especial from my sister) were I ever to reveal it. I kept silent for a hundred years and then another hundred and then half a century beyond that, and still I nursed these images. And now I was back, over and over, to relive them. This was the circuit we traveled on repeat: from Caspian Sea to hither local creek, back to Thebes, which lives no more, back to New World marketplaces bigger and showier in their prime than anything Hellas offered yet sadder and more paltry in their decay. There was nothing else in our existence to do. Back and forth. No future did we have yet no end either.

One hundred years earlier I had watched a man finish weeping and hang himself in trees similar to these and I had not interfered. As his spirit departed, I waited for his internal tyranny to pour out in a pestilence of pygmy demons. These enemies I would either vanquish or strategically observe for later skirmishes. But the world had pivoted once again. The body swung on its own in this new era and what lay inside was not a pagan itching for a sword fight, was not a keeper of Tenebris, was not. Was neither. Was not a thing or person at all. Was not even a logos. It was an immateriality without name or substance. In this new era, armies of despair had begun their slaughter within. Artemis might draw her arrow, but against what?

We could not understand. Nor did we dare try. It was not in our nature.

This, however, we could perceive—the scene before us: five bory-eyed boys, tumbling under their encounter with Dionysus, Silenius, the satyr and his nymphs.

Five mortals acting idiotic. How relieved we were to have our attention directed to manifest displays we could apprehend.

Among the five boys was one who shone golden. My attention distracted, I almost did not recognize the boy we had previously encountered, the one my sister had gifted with a damaged male appendage. He was the one who dragged a stiffened stag onto the road and arranged it—my attention still drawn to the golden one who lingered back in hesitation but who, when a powered vehicle swerved squealing to avoid the stag, tumbled in hilarity with the other boys. All were stumbling drunk from the satyr's visitation. They watched as another vehicle passed, barely righting itself on the road, its horn blows vehement and the boys half hidden and delighted. And then an angry shout You! came their way and they sprinted across the field, deserting the stag to his troubled destiny.

This was not a pumpkin on a tarred path sending me its leer but one of our sacreds set up for scorn and gauntlet.

This was not comedy but tragedy.

My sister drew her arrow.

He's a nice boy, the wide receiver. It's a shame he was drawn into it.
—*MomWhoKnows*

Unfortunately they listen to their quarterback even off-season.
—*towncrier*

He also broke the state record in track and field if we're talking
about the same kid.
—*fanboy*

The whole track and field record? He broke it?
—undefeated

It's Just Me

said a voice outside the door of Hannah's house. The knocks that persisted were light, but the voice louder and louder. It's me! It's just me!

Who is Just Me? asked Chieko.

Who's Just Me? Hannah asked the peephole.

It's me, said the voice. It's Josh. Come on, it's me, Josh.

Why are you here?

The eye came close to the peephole. The pupil magnified all of the blue iris away.

Are you on drugs?

No!

Prove it.

Because I can't run track if I'm on drugs.

I can look at people's eyes and know they're on drugs, Hannah said.

I'm not on drugs, Hannah. You know I'm not.

How do I know it's really you?

You're looking through the peephole.

Prove that it's you.

I asked you out on a date once.

Not good enough.

You said no.

Who wouldn't! Everyone would say no to you!

(This was not true. He was singularly handsome. But he was thinner than Hannah and, at the time he asked, shorter.)

I pooped my pants in first grade.

Everybody knows the poop story, Josh!

I pooped at your house, too. You hid me in the bathtub until my mom came.

Hannah opened the door until the chain balked. Chieko's chin was on her shoulder, trying to get a glimpse of the handsome golden boy. What do you want?

Jared wants to apologize?

You said that like a question! Hannah slammed the door.

Hannah ordered Chieko to the couch and they both sat. Hannah reached for the TV control.

Please Hannah, said Chieko.

No.

Come on, Hannah, it's Josh! His voice was loud but the knock still polite

I'm not listening!

I like Josh, Chieko said. Please Hannah.

Come on, Hannah!

Stay here, Hannah ordered but Chieko got up and followed her. Hannah opened the door the length of the chain. Did he call you up to do his cleanup? she screamed at Josh. Quit doing his dirty work! She slammed the door, then opened it. Are you a man or a mouse?

Hannah, just listen—

Why are you his slave? She closed the door then opened it again. What does he really want?

To apologize, Josh said.

I'm gonna call the police, Hannah said.

Because Jared wants to apologize?

Okay Jared the asshole say you're sorry! Hannah called out to the blackness.

Sorry! came a voice.

You scared Erika!

Sorry!

Hannah slammed the door.

When she looked out the window, Josh was still standing on the lit porch. Chieko tapped on the pane. Oh, Josh! she said. I like him. He is kakko ee.

This was the Japanese Chieko had taught her so they could comment on boys in secret.

Josh is like beautiful Japanese boys, Chieko sighed. Other than yearning for boys, Chieko didn't express many interests. She was slow to learn while Hannah, at least for a while, had been eager to teach. "Some kids" at school and not just boys had begun to mimic how Chieko misspoke, but fortunately Chieko didn't catch on. In fact, it seemed to make it easier for her to understand them. It made Hannah sad to realize that her mother and grandmother would have been "some kids." She was glad they had taken in Chieko, but she began to dread dinner when her mother and Nan entertained themselves with snark that they thought oh so subtle. Her mother loaded up on wine. Her grandmother on beer and coffee and cigarettes. Imagine a grandmother acting like that. Hannah bet Chieko's grandmother wore a kimono and bowed politely every time she spoke.

There were times when Hannah wanted to escape into homework, but it was hard with Chieko sitting on the bed. Sometimes Hannah wanted to escape into her own private cave and bring a candle to her unlit fears, to uncover her own despairs, but even at night Chieko's breathing paused her. Sometimes she sat up and stared across the room until Chieko's sleeping mound came into silhouette. She couldn't think straight. Not with someone there. She couldn't find out what was on the other side of these dark feelings. She knew it was better that she didn't.

Chieko tapped on the window again. Josh waved to her. Kakko ee! squealed Chieko. She shook Hannah's arm. Kakko ee, Hannah! Kakko ee! Chieko shook her again.

Okay, kakko ee, said Hannah.

Standing on the porch, Josh looked small in his regular clothes. He went up to normal size in his football uniform. He was a little orphan in his tracksuit. He looked best drenched in a swimsuit with his abs gleaming like cut glass. Yes he was gorgeous. His hair was beautiful and golden, especially during off-season, when he let it grow long. When they were younger and hung out, men looked at him. Hannah thought it would stop after he reached puberty but Josh was still compact and porcelain, his hair a shiny yellow compared to Hannah's dirty blond, and it was embarrassing for Hannah to be with a boy more attractive to men than she was. And she was pretty! And boys liked her. Boys did, but men liked Josh.

Chieko had thrown on her coat and opened the door. I'm going to see Josh, she said. She was outside before Hannah could stop her.

There is more to this than meets the eye.
Ask the Amish. They were all there.

—anon

She did not recognize the palpable injuries
—simonkenton

Travis Could Not

pinpoint the date that he first noticed the undrawn curtains. It had to be fall or winter. Probably fall, at the time change. The Keims' house stood proudly nude. Protest against the unfair early evenings? Against the season's gloom? Maybe they were exhibitionists.

It was unjust that coming home in the afternoon was the same as coming home at night. Travis delayed at school. Joined the Shakespeare club yo. Sought delays at the post office. More delays at the town library. Checked his storage unit behind the Marathon station. Got a pizza at Walmart and they heated it for him and he chewed it in the darkness at the edge of the parking lot. He used the Walmart bins to dump his trash. Once every two weeks he was treated to clean laundry and dinner at the Zimmermans': beef stew, pot roast, Swedish meatballs, spaghetti and regular meatballs, pea soup (good taste, horrible color), homemade biscuits, chicken pot pie, crumb cake, potatoes and a lot of other vegetables that made Mr. Zimmerman laugh for some reason. Travis ate it all. He kept a list of what Mrs. Zimmerman cooked. Mr. Zimmerman's book was coming along. He had his research spread out on a big table in the sewing room. One half was Mrs. Zimmerman's fabrics, the other half was music sheets and lyrics. For the moment Mr. Zimmerman seemed to enjoy the look of that busy table; Travis would save scanning as a surprise for later. Mr. Zimmerman still thought there were little people inside the computer doing the work—not that clueless but almost.

He showered at the travel center gas station in Lima. That was more than forty miles round trip with the speed limit mostly forty-five and he worried about the mileage on his car but he liked the way it ate up time. He drove by the Taco Bell to see if there were classmates inside. If he saw Kyle or Anisha or Corbin or Hannah, or even Kyle's sister Kassadee slash Elsa and her mom, he would wander in as if by chance and even if he'd already had his pizza he would order more food off the dollar menu and eat again. But life for them was shutting down, too. The Taco Bell in February was cold and empty. All day on Friday he waited for someone to ask his plans. Why did everyone always say TGIF? It was a nightmare the way the winter weekend loomed. It was wrong. Wrong the way he was shut inside with nothing; he was down to a BarcaLounger and a mattress. Often he stayed standing for hours so he wouldn't turn into a loser growing mold in a BarcaLounger. Often he sat on the floor. Or lay back in contemplation, just lay on the carpet. Pushing up weights, staring at the ceiling. Did the top of a trailer count as a ceiling? It looked like something a bird could peck through.

He was afraid to jerk off for fear that someone outside was watching him the way he had begun to watch the Keims.

The way he was watching them now. He could view them from far away. He could do close-ups. He could walk along the little road and watch the scenes as a bright as a fire, watch the scenes shift as he passed to and fro, safe because he knew they could not see out. Then he got more daring. He moved closer, right up to their window. Right at their window, where he was tonight.

He loitered outside so close his nose brushed against the pane. His feet were huge.

They would leave tracks. The prints would suggest a bear had been stalking. Except it was clearly human. Except it was clearly Travis.

Except it was clearly too early to go to bed. Except he had winter spying missions to do. Except he could behave himself.

Except he could not go back inside that trailer.

The Keims' kitchen glowed a deserted amber. Where was she?

And what if she came and she took off her clothes?

What if she started doing a striptease?

He would run away. He would not let her shame herself out of desire for him.

So why was he doing this?

Because maybe he would stay.

Shadows flitted across the field. Travis twisted from the window. A line of them, one by one. When he turned back, Mrs. Keim was in the kitchen. He flopped to the ground, frantically crawled. Caught, had he been caught? The front door opened. The answer came: Mr. Keim was storming out in attack mode. Travis was safe behind a bush but it wouldn't last long—

people don't take off their clothes in the kitchen so why do you keep doing this?

the shadows dashed back across the field.

Kind of like a cyborg reacting, Mr. Keim jerked toward them. Shadows frolicking and stumbling. The cyborg's head snapped in place. Located them.

You! yelled Mr. Keim. You! he yelled.

The shadows choked, their laughter choked them. Frightening and cyborg-unreal how Mr. Keim clicked in on their location, how his military strut gathered speed as he zeroed in. The chase was on. The shadows loved it. Travis ran the opposite way.

He was on the road. The safety zone of his trailer lay behind him. He couldn't get to it without passing the Keim farm. It was black and he couldn't see. The running had disoriented him. He heard stifled noises and every few beats a hoot of manic laughter and Mr. Keim bellowing You! but their jungle combat was growing distant. He could feel the ditch wanting to suck him in and he could follow the ditch and wait for a car to light the way and regain his bearings that way. That's what he would do. He would keep going along the road until he met the path that led to Yoders'. Then he'd circle back, the long way, across the little wooden bridge.

A car swerved and squealed and the horn blared and something in the road lit up and Travis jumped away and was nearly hit by the zagging car that farted apologetic smoke and charged back into the night.

Coming: another set of headlights. Travis stepped back this time and squatted in a knot of barbed weeds. The thing on the road lit up. Travis froze at its glow. The thing leaped high in a line of flame and landed at his feet. The eyes of a wounded deer stared up at him, long lashes blinking. An arrow burned to ember in its flank. Its head turned with a dying snort toward the car. Travis had barely registered the car. It was plowing right over him in a blinding light. He raised a protective forearm to his face.

The car flipped in the other direction. It flipped fast, over and over.

Everything was quiet.

Travis ran.

The one defendant comes from a good family. He's a football player because he's talented. Talent to excel not talent to cause trouble called him to the gridiron. His brother is one of the nicest kids you'll ever meet. There are bad apples, sure, but a lot of good ones too.
—*kattogacitizenoftheyear*

I had a really good apple once. I left it up in the guest bedroom by accident. It went bad.
—*undesignatedsurvivor*

I assume you mean "nicest" brother as code? He is a treat, that one. Check into the "nicest" brother n you'll find out he runs with the daughter of the doctor, suspicious just a little? The two of them run the marching band like little hitlers. They not the band director determine who gets the leads n guess what, it's always that girl. Nobody else can play Taps? Much as I hate to see one of our local heroes go down, I hate it more knowing I'll have to sit through another of her tributes.
—*truebandmom*

That's what happens when misfits get power.
—*truemisfit*

They were both there and picked up by the police
for questioning. Doesn't anyone here read the paper
or do you prefer to get your news through Russian bots!
—*snackbarmom*

We Watched Him

as he wept. Golden in his beauty, he shed tears that should pelt the ground and be reborn as laurel. This boy whose beauty lifted him like air. He would be a feather in my lap. A breath upon my palm.

Your lust for beauty trots the same furrow, mocked my sister.

And only one time was that not the case. The one in animal leggings, chased by the fox warriors. He was not tender. He was not a golden sprig. He needed no help from me but accepted it with a smile that might have been amused, might have been fatherly but was not, even in memory's exertion, one of love. He was a man who expressed no hunger but might agree to a feast put before him. He might sample ambrosia the way one might pick up this rock instead of another. Even before the great Apollo he was not visited by temptation. He listened only to the siren whispers of the forest, which lured him away from me time after time until time ran out. He never turned to me with greedy eyes for the life-saving succor I could provide; he never watched his own mortal sunset with fear.

What do you say? my sister demanded. Behold how exquisitely the lad shines. Let us a roast him and take a bite.

Your wits are slaked by a moldering aqueduct, I told her.

Ha! she laughed. She knew my insults arrived as shields to my true nature. How much she was enjoying my distraction.

The golden boy cried into his device and called for it to rescue him.

His wet lashes left such a polish on his cheeks as to render him a subject for white marble. Only his mouth had turned ugly, deformed by the entreaties that passed through his lips. The image of the man hanging in the trees sent worry to keep me company. I had learned of the Within these past scores of years. I had learned what it does to humans. I knew that within this boy an army of demons waged war. I stood helpless to render aid as the boy wept. Trouble and plague I could still manage from time to time. But this other realm, Within, was a place I could not tread. Good was a thing I could not accomplish. Good was a thing I could not even define.

Drum major and doctor's daughter have been arrested
and charged. Get over hating on the football players,
irrelevant since they had nothing to do with the prank.
—*simonkenton*

Not true. Read the Columbus Dispatch, not the local rag!
—*truemisfit*

Drum major and female accomplice
are 100 percent nerds. The prank was much too awesome
for a nerd to carry out. Not possible.
—*okiefromkattogie*

Quite possible actually. A nerd's bitterness at the world cannot
be underestimated.
—*freedomlover*

They do not have the skill set.
—*okiefromkattogie*

Nerds are usually extra smart and can think up things.
—*rover*

Have to agree with okie about lacking the skill set.
A nerd would never look at an empty grain unit and
think how they could steal corpses and hide them
in there. Not possible.
—*dreamcatcher*

I am a nerd and I'm always thinking about where to hide
the corpses I steal.
—*undefeated*

Her Flashlight Scoped

along the perimeter of the yard. Hannah had chased them from the back, where they had set up along the flagstones beyond the deck the fake deer and beside it cans of paint. Paint couldn't be scraped off flagstones, and flagstones were the kind of thing her mother cared about.

Jared lived right next door. Why couldn't he do whatever he was doing at his own place?

Hannah's flashlight found them in the stand of shivering trees and comfortable evergreens that separated their properties. Three of the boys were asleep or passed out on the ground no matter the cold, although it was warm enough under the spruce canopy that they probably wouldn't freeze to death, not that she for one second cared. She recognized Dustin Crosby as one of the sleepers. Knew him from the football team. She was forced to cheer for him whenever he caught a ball even though he took all remedial classes. He was just about the stupidest person she'd ever met and he liked it that way. She aimed the flashlight right at his face. Strobed it. Nothing.

Jared, however, was wide awake. He was holding a can of paint for Chieko and guiding her. Josh was awake, too; he sat back on his haunches, elbows on knees and head on fists. His butt didn't touch the ground. He stayed in that position as if entirely comfortable. As if thinking great thoughts, not as if he were watching Chieko dip a brush into a can of

Rustoleum and paint the letters Jared spelled out to her:

P, Jared said.

U, he said.

S, he said.

S, he said.

Y, he said.

Chieko looked over to Josh for approval. Josh tipped over trying to control himself. Jared shook himself into the fetal position and lay there in hysterics.

You're so funny, Hannah said.

Doctor misdiagnosed leading to a several hours delay until they life flighted him yet again to another hospital, a fatal delay resulting in brain damage.
—*realcitizenoftheyear*

They're still alive so fatal delay wasn't fatal.
—*anon*

It's still brain damage!
—*realmom*

The other victim was unnecessarily tourniquetted resulting in a near amputation.
—*citizencane*

Does a near amputation mean that it wasn't amputated? Almost as if he still has his leg because the tourniquet saved it?
—*undefeated*

Shawnee and Wyandot

once clashed on this road, which back then was a trail that followed the creek and they could run along its banks in the dark because their moccasins had eyes. They were magic skimmers of the night and quiet as bobcats. Their feet landed on the ground like soft paws, all communication was through their paws. The ground told them everything they needed to know. Travis used to pretend each of his toes was tipped in an eyeball, which meant he had ten very large eyes guiding each of his steps. He was a Wyandot who scouted the enemy surefooted through the trees and brush, day or night, it didn't matter. His seeing-eye feet rendered darkness a useless weapon.

And so he had defeated the night on this night. Had resisted the black magic the Shawnees had thrown at him, the demon trying to possess his spirit animal, an innocent deer; the medusa charging him with her multiplying bright eyes. But he did not look, he forced his own eyes away from her thrusting, compelling headlights, did not look into them, did not turn to stone, and he ran surefooted through the trees and found the path that shortcut to Yoders' and now he was on the single-lane trail that the Wyandots had once sneaked down while the Shawnees were encamped. All was quiet. The dark magic the Shawnees had sent after him had been sent howling back into the woods. When he got to the little wooden bridge his feet told him where he was, he could hear the echoless percussion of soft wood and feel the aging fungus under him, and he knew in fifty more steps he would turn the corner and be home in fifty more. And then the moon came out of the clouds and told him he was right. Even showed him the path to his home. Even showed him that a person was waiting for him outside the trailer.

Josh.

Or Corbin.

Their silhouettes were the same.

The moon picked up longer hair.

It was Josh.

Josh was crying and pounding on the walls of the single-wide. He was a star wide receiver and state champion in the 3200 meters who was too defeated to climb up three cinderblock steps and knock on the door that Travis realized he had left unlocked.

Josh collapsed against the trailer, weakening, until he toppled to the ground and continued to cry.

Travis backed away. Yoder's meager gravel crunched under his feet exactly in the midst of one of Josh's quieter sniffles. Josh scrambled like a maniac toward the scuffle of pebbles.

Jared? Jared come on help me man!

Travis felt his chest drain of its blood.

You are a Wyandot. Turn off your toe lights and stay still.

Jared? Jared Jared come on!

The motion detector flipped on. Josh screamed as the harsh light burned him. He jumped back and hunkered into a ball. He looked like a movie-monster insect lasered into a dying glob. It was an awful sight. Embarrassing for Josh, who would never live it down if someone like his very own friends caught sight of him.

Lucky for Josh, Wyandots did not spread rumors.

Travis took a backward giant step into the safety of the blackness. Jared was still curled up and weeping when the spotlight timed off.

At each rising hiccup of a sob, Travis had time for another giant back-step. He waited for the next gulp of sobbing, took a step. There was a beat to it. Even in crying there was a beat to be discovered. Kyle Jenkins would discover it immediately and tap it out on his snare drum. Corbin would direct with his mace, his mace thrust high to signal the fermata, brought low when it was time for the band to hit it. Travis was marching to a safe place to keep watch until his trailer was free. He had to get off this path before Jared and the others showed up. The enemy was out there and he had to hide before the enemy descended in a shrieking attack. But he could not see. And he had lost his powers. And something about it was real now, like when his mother had burned down the house. It was a joke, it was funny, the *licking flames dancing*. But then it was real. And his mother was real. He had always dealt with her like a black magic spell he could defeat with a Hogwarts transfiguration potion from Professor McGonagall.

He could not see at all. He had fifty steps to the bridge but was he even going in the direction of the bridge? He had to scrape his feet to make sure he stayed on the path and that caused noise so he had to be careful but luckily there was Corbin raising his mace, *follow me and keep to the beat.*

He followed Corbin. When Corbin raised his mace, Travis stopped. When Corbin brought it down, Travis took a step.

Even from this distance he could hear that Josh had started to hyperventilate. His breathlessness squalled across the dead landscape. He sounded like the end of one of his races. Josh did the distances because Corbin could beat him in the sprints. Travis was on the field that day, having been conscripted for the shot put *just throw it that's all*, and they lined the track as Josh flew by to begin the bell lap. Corbin was there, screaming at his brother. Travis was smothered into nerve-wracked silence. He could not find his voice as Josh flew by. He could not cheer at the history being made. First place was not what Josh was after. He was already alone in first, any challenger way behind. Josh was so far ahead he could walk it in, yet he was desperate, his face contorted. He was chasing glory and his breath came as a gale, obliterating the very body that was exposing the nineteen-year-old state record as something set by mere mortals, the very idea of mortality; his blistering pace was out to destroy the notion that life had limits. Travis remembered how sure he was that Josh was going to die. That phrase *die trying* suddenly made sense. It was a real thing.

Corbin was signaling for him to take a step. Another giant step. Corbin scoped his flashlight. Corbin had a flashlight. It was Corbin. Actually Corbin.

Travis did not ask himself why Corbin was really there. He was in enough trouble on this night. When their house had burned down, Travis had been living in three worlds. Only one of them was real and he had learned not to ask questions but to figure it out. He had three columns listed in his mind: Unreal Unreal Real. He had to figure it out.

Think.

Travis made himself think.

The cellar has a single window where the hill slopes down. You already know this.

He was used to this, finding that window in the cellar of his imagination. He could crawl out and land on grass on the side of a hill and the real world would begin. He was sorry to say good-bye to the Shawnees and Wyandots. He much preferred their world to this one that had only flashlights and things, a mattress, a BarcaLounger.

Travis knew he was visible in the margins of Corbin's flashlight; another bob of the light and he would be caught, a deer in the headlights—but then came another of Josh's sobs, a terrible sob—and the flashlight bobbed in another direction and a second person entered the scene and pulled Corbin toward his trailer, and Travis knew by process of elimination it was Anisha because there wasn't one without the other.

He heard them find Josh. His motion detector lit up the stark trees and turned them into tall branched angry men. The men hissed and cried out and then they calmed and then became just whispers, just three kids crying together.

Travis could walk normally now to the bridge, where he would wait. His feet scraped against wood and he waved his arms until he found the bridge railing and he followed it up and there he stood, his hands pressed into the splinters of the rickety structure that cars avoided, that buggies and horses still crossed. The whole night was caused by him. He had caused his mom to lose boyfriend after boyfriend, he had caused her to take drugs, he had caused her addiction, he had caused her poverty with all his excessive needs. He had ruined his mother's life and driven Mrs. Keim into a sordid world of striptease and pole dancing and if he ever felt for one second that he was superior because his mother's cigarettes had burned down their house, he should take a look in the mirror, Bub. And now he had caused death and murder, had driven Mr. Keim to kill, had caused a car to crash. It was almost too easy to forget that the car included people inside since they had reacted so silently to the destruction of their lives.

That's right, Bub. All you.

The overgrowth below him—a wild churning.

Oh fuck oh fuck oh fuck!

Fuck!

Are you there?

The desperation vibrated through the wood. They were directly below him.

Jared Jared oh fuck man!

Now a hollow reverb. The voices had found the culvert pipe.

Jared Jared Jared

JARED!

Help me!

Come on man HELP!

Travis staggered back, gained control, kept stepping backward eyes on the bridge he could not see Yoder's farm but he knew it was there and he knew that at the front corner of the yard closest to him was their telephone shack. He could squat behind it and hide. He could make a call from there. He could call the police. He could do his civic duty.

And now a line of lights was coming.

We would not be faced with the epic proportions of this tragedy
if not for the epic proportions of the injuries, due in large measure
to incompetent on-scene care bordering on malfeasance.

—*lifelongkattogie*

Even if the two kids were high and drunk that's a holy different
case. Deal with this recipe that cooked up 5 teens who put a deer
on the road that caused serious permanent injuries, for crying out
loud they could of all lost their lives. Thats a holenother disaster
not a prank gone wrong.

—*resident*

If you are going to get the story straight you must listen to all EMS
responders on the scene and when they are stating in a public record
that one of the victims was sent to the wrong hospital despite protests
of EMS personnel who saw what the doctor did and recognized but
could not override her authority.

—*JudgeMissMyMommyHerrick*

Drippings Of Lava

had begun to pour down the road. A steady ooze not fast not slow not stopping, there to help but not benevolent either, it was the fire-and-brimstone underground of the Old Order called to emerge from their places of rest. They were climbing out, they were here, they were set in motion and the lava rolling toward Travis was inevitable and one of neutral vengeance. And the lava fired up not the whole sky but the basement of the sky—lit it yellow, lit it red, streaked it white. The impenetrable blackness paled. The moon found a gap between charcoal clouds and shone above them. The smell of kerosene was strong. And Travis found the telephone shack and hid behind it.

Younger and older men moved with deliberation down Yoders' driveway. Yoder was there. As well as a woman extending her apron sunken with supplies. Unlike the others she was running. She moved fast. Little boys followed but couldn't keep up. Yoder grabbed one of the little boys by the collar and lobbed him in another direction. The boy came running—toward him.

The walking men with their lanterns were almost to the bridge. And now squeezing through their ooze came an eye-set of lights, same low intensity as the lanterns but deadly in its pace.

The reckless vehicle negotiated the dark with only its parking lights.

It bounced by the silent men, who kept moving with their lanterns.

The men did not turn aside or take note of it. It nudged the woman running ahead with her laden apron. Vehicle and woman both hit the little wooden bridge at the same time, but the vehicle stopped and the woman kept running until she got to the corner and turned right, down the road where Travis's trailer sat, where the Keim farm sat beyond that, where the state route sat beyond that, where the crashed car lay. The tires upturned in the cornfield were spinning viciously as Travis ran away. So vicious—it would have shredded a human being down to nothing.

The woman had run out of sight. The vehicle had stopped on the bridge. Headlights flashed on. Headlights flashed off. On and off, three, four—seven, eight—eleven times the headlights flashed, the car idling there.

It was Jared Overholser who stepped out of the car. The walking men were passing him. Jared ignored them. They ignored Jared.

Hi, Travis.

Travis jerked toward the little boy who had arrived at the shack.

Oh, Travis said. Lucas?

Noah, the boy said.

Noah was the baby. Time passed even for the young.

And Travis wouldn't be hiding in the dark in someone's yard forever.

The boy politely edged his body between Travis and the shack, opened the door the crack allowed by the shift of Travis's body. Even that crack brought to Travis the smell of barn though there was nothing but a telephone inside. Noah squeezed inside and Travis heard the little voice saying, Is this 911? I'm supposed to call 911.

On the bridge Jared had reappeared. He pulled a friend and pushed him into the car. Then two more friends bolted for the car's shelter like movie stars covering their faces from the lanterned paparazzi.

The car eased down the road. It gunned its engine but went slowly. At the corner it turned left as the lanterns turned right. Another person came running. The leg speed would have given away Josh but he knew it was Josh anyway. The vehicle paused, collected him, and roared into the countryside.

Travis remembered to move his body so the little boy could get out.

Noah said thank you to Travis.

You're welcome, Travis said.

Noah pointed toward the shack and tapped the air like a woodpecker. Travis opened the shack's door. Noah lingered, his curious eyes back and forth.

Travis? asked a voice.

Travis saw a shadow he knew was Hannah. He saw another shadow and he could guess that one, too.

Thanks, he said to Noah.

I've heard from good sources the coach of the football team
has hired hackers to influence social media. The lawyers for
the football players are in on it too. Don't let them turn the
tide of public opinion.

—*kattogacitizenoftheyea*r

Coach McManus saved my son's life. He was going bad but the
coach set him straight. He's now second year at Lima State.
—*proudLimaStateMom*

There would be a necktie party if the situation was
reversed and it was Kirk and Bratley put out the deer decoy
and hurt the star quarterback.
—*okiefromkattogie*

Why did one of the football players go around bragging a
few days later about causing the crash? Because that seems
pretty incriminating. Not taking sides, just genuinely confused.
—*cookiejarhandler*

Because his name is Dustin Crosby and he's an idiot.
—*undesignatedsurvivor*

Finally something we can agree on.
—*trollingbutknowing*

The Commotion Outside

kept Travis and Hannah and Chieko cowering inside the trailer. The motion sensor had tripped on, nothing to be done about that, but they were quick inside and plunging to the floor as if on a military exercise. All lights off so they couldn't be seen. They pressed against the wall, ducked under the curtainless window, and felt their way in the pitch dark to the mattress in the bedroom. Nothing else in the room. His grandmother's dresser gone by Thanksgiving. The mattress like a piece of toast tossed to the floor. Chieko hung on to Travis's forearm. He could feel his forearm vibrate from her wild trembling.

The only window in the bedroom was on the opposite side and it pressed against feral thickets. That side was his grandmother's property, which neglect had turned into a solid blockade of weed bushes and weed saplings and poisonous growth. Travis turned on the light and shut the bedroom door.

Are we in trouble?

Maybe.

I think so.

We're in trouble.

What do we do?

Hannah, I made paint with Jared. Hannah—

Shh.

Do we go out there?

No.

No!

What happened, Travis?

I don't know.

Did you see?

A car crash, I know that.

Something really bad has happened.

Maybe.

I think somebody is dead, Travis.

What should we do?

Go out there?

No.

Hannah you help me please, said Chieko. I'm sorry to go with Josh.

Hannah lay down on the mattress and turned toward the wall. Oh, my god, she whispered. She sniffled.

Hannah please help us, Chieko said.

Can you take us home in the morning? Hannah asked the wall in a lifeless voice.

Okay, Travis said.

There I've helped us, I've solved all our problems, Hannah said and continued staring at the wall. She whispered, I need to pray but I don't know how.

Hannah you're scaring me, Chieko said.

It's her bedtime, Travis said.

Hannah's chest moved in a burp that might have been a chuckle. One of those end-of-the-road chuckles a guy in the electric chair might make. Something flared in Travis's body seeing Hannah turned away from them, facing the wall like that.

Chieko laid herself down next to Hannah. Travis turned off the light and was leaving when Chieko called, I'm so scary, Travis!

Oh, god, Hannah sniffled. Go to bed, Travis. Go on.

Travis please you stay, whined Chieko. You tell us a story.

Leave him alone, Hannah said, still talking lifelessly to the wall.

I'm scary without him.

I have to think, Hannah said. I have to pray.

You have to close your eyes, Travis said. He turned on the light.

Whachu doing! Chieko screamed.

Quiet! warned Hannah.

I'm sorry Hannah, okay Hannah okay? I'm sorry I was to go with Josh.

Oh, my god, whispered Hannah.

I have to make sure your eyes are closed, Travis said. Before I can tell you a story.

Chieko's whole face squinted shut.

Travis plugged in the nightlight he used to keep the bedroom from entering the black gates of hell whenever he slept in there. He turned off the overhead. He sat cross-legged on the floor like the Wyandots did during the powwow where they passed the peace pipe to him and welcomed him into their tribe. He sucked it deep into his lungs and the braves waited for him to cough and hack and for the tears to spring from his eyes. But none of those reactions came to pass. He was the first white man ever to suck in the peace pipe and call it home. The braves watched in awe. You are one of us, they said.

What goes next? Chieko asked.

Next is this: just as he was about to accept Chief Wyandot's necklace to become his honorary son, a wild dog jumped into their midst with a terrifying snarl! And dripping sharp teeth!

Oh no! cried Chieko. Oh no wild dogs!—very dangerous in Japan. So scary. My friend have two times—

Shh shh shh, said Hannah. Be quiet and listen. Hannah turned away from the wall and said to Travis, I bet it's not really a wild dog. I bet it's Chief Wyandot's biological son dressed up as a wild dog.

Travis hadn't thought of that.

Oh no! What is biological son! exclaimed Chieko.

Not so loud, Hannah said.

Good guess, he said. The wild dog *is* actually the chief's real son wearing a disguise. But that's only half the story.

And he went on to tell them the rest.

The brother and his fag hag were brought in for
questioning and pointed the finger at the quarterback
because of long-standing grudge.
—*5thcolumn*

You seriously don't think band geeks could have broken
into a barn and stolen a deer decoy and painted it
with obscenities I'm sure they don't even know
the meaning of.
—*wildernessvoice*

Yes a band geek could of. Depends on what instrument they play.
—*tbdbitl*

Said obscene words were misspelled. Nerds would not misspell.
—*1988champ*

Hardly Past Dawn

the flimsy door shook. Travis jerked in the big BarcaLounger. Middle of the night he thought. His head stuffed solid with untapped sleep. The door shook again. The knocking came fast and demanding. Not the middle of the night. The curtainless windows said the dreary day had begun.

Travis bounced up when he saw Hannah's panicked face peek around the doorframe. He motioned her back. He shut the bedroom door, then thought better and let it swing out a casual few inches.

He opened the trailer. A police officer was standing there on his cinderblocks, one leg up, one leg down—the way police officers posed on steps.

I'm Officer Johnson, the man said.

Travis said nothing. His head fully stuffed with the sleep he needed more of. Could not think to say hello. Made himself resist the urge to turn and check the bedroom. He was thinking of them hiding in the bedroom and if he said something, the word he uttered might be Hannah instead of Hello.

I'm making the rounds, the officer said. Am I bothering you?

Travis shook his head.

It sure looks that way.

No.

What were you doing?

Just sleeping, Travis said.

Kind of late to still be in bed.

What? Travis said.

Wake up. Get rid of the words you shouldn't say. Clear your head.

Almost eight a.m.

What is? Travis said.

Just kidding you, man.

There's no school. Travis stumbled over the words.

Just pulling your leg, guy. I know it's early for you kids.

Kids?

No kids!

Just me!

Shut up till you get to the meadow.

The officer tried to peek through Travis's body into the trailer's insides. An impossible task. The officer rocked back on the cinderblocks, one leg higher than the other. He lingered there at the ready. He pulled out a notepad from his back pocket. He opened it and studied his notes. He unzipped his puffy cop jacket and fished out a pen and wrote something and clicked the pen as if loading a bullet into its chamber. Then slapped the notepad shut and shoved it back into his pocket. He lifted his gaze to Travis. Those were dumb moves on his part. Meant to be official gestures, like he was mulling the details of a criminal complaint that could land Travis in jail. It was meant to intimidate him, but all it did was give him time to wake up.

No kids just Travis.

No kids just Travis.

Your name is Travis.

There are no kids.

Simple.

Did you see what happened last night? The officer settled on riding his thick belt, like it was his saddle or something.

I heard stuff, Travis said. The winter air hitting him. Sticking his head out for more. His brain on chill.

What kind of stuff?

I know there was a crash.

How do you know that?

I heard it.

What does a crash sound like?

It didn't sound good, Travis said.

Not good like how? the officer asked. Didn't you go check it out?

They told me to go back inside.

Who?

The ambulance guys.

What'd you do then?

Went back inside.

Here?

Yeah.

Mind if I step in? The officer had already raised his back foot. Was about to thrust himself through the doorway. Travis would have to move his huge body for that to happen. He did not move.

My mom doesn't want anyone coming in.

Where is she? Can I talk to her?

She went to a friend's house.

Good move.

Travis Hicks is waking up!

Was she here last night?

No.

Where's her friend?

Urbana.

Slick.

What's the friend's name?

I think …

Any name. Any name will do.

I think it's Willy.

Willy what?

She just calls him Willy.

You sure it's Willy?

No I'm not sure, Travis said.

Turn it to your advantage. You just fucking read Shakespeare and took a vocabulary test!

I stopped listening to her dating stuff.

Nailed it.

I see. You alone in there?

Yeah.

Simmer down.

Don't shake!

When the officer leaned in, Travis took a closer peek at the badge—*that's it, go through the motions that present themselves*. The jacket parted and Travis could spy the identity bragging upon the left shoulder. *Good calming moves, learn the details of your surroundings.* It said Erly Johnson. *You've got Name!* Travis almost laughed because he remembered that name but then the mindfuck came back, his bottomless anger—*No.*

Save it for later.

Look at the bright side.

This very cop just a few weeks ago had taken a photo of his mom passed out in a car and now he was too dumb to put the pieces together.

That's funny actually.

I don't think your mom would mind too much if I stepped inside.

Go find her in a car and ask her.

She told me not to. Sorry. You can't come in.

Thank him for ruining your life.

The whole world in on it.

This Erly Johnson officer actually kept coming as if to burst through the door until he met the wall that was Travis and his head landed between Travis's breasts, not that Travis had cleavage, not like this officer who was soft enough to have a couple of mounds protruding.

Travis felt bold.

There was nothing the officer could do in the face of a flat refusal. Travis knew that. Everyone watched enough TV to know their rights by now.

You are bold. You are a bold man.

You are twice his size.

Own it.

Travis stepped outside and shut the front door. He was in Goodwill sweatpants and a sweatshirt, limited-edition Nike socks in Cleveland Cavaliers colors, and no shoes. He didn't feel the cold at all. The crash was over there, Travis said.

How do you know?

That's where the road is.

How do you know the crash was on the road?

Travis got to experience the thrilling superior rush of raising his eyebrows at someone. He towered over the pudgy officer.

Did you see it happen?

No.

Didn't have anything to do with it, did you?

No.

Come here, this Erly Johnson officer said. Travis followed him in his socks to the police cruiser, where the man popped the trunk. Inside was a wooden thing. *Hit Me! Pussy!* were painted on it.

Know what this is?

No.

You're looking right at it. You don't know what it is?

I sorta see what it is, Travis said.

But you don't know what it is?

I don't know.

But you see it.

I see it, Travis said.

And what do you think?

I think it's …

What?

It's not real.

But real last night. And bright gold. And it blinked up at you with haunted girl eyes.

You want to take a guess who this belongs to?

Him? Travis pointed over to the Keims' place.

No, Officer Erly Johnson said.

Yoder? Travis said.

No.

The police officer tried to stare him down, a hard thing to do when he had so far to look up.

Like Kyle Jenkins does except a joke.

What's the weather up there?

It's not mine, Travis said.

It doesn't belong to you?

No.

You're Travis, aren't you?

Yeah.

You're not surprised?

About what?

Travis, you know how I know you're Travis?

Because that's my name?

Sarcasm! Bold!

Don't you wonder how I know it?

People at school? Miss B told you?

Who's Miss B? The officer shrugged his shoulders.

He's lying. Everyone knows Miss B.

Henry Zimmerman gave me your name.

Travis didn't say anything.

Henry Zimmerman hunts with this deer.

Oh, Travis said.

You know Henry Zimmerman?

Who is Henry?

I know the Mr. Zimmerman part, Travis said.

Figure it out. Mr. Zimmerman is Henry. Even old people have first names.

You been to his house, haven't you? Erly the officer said.

Yeah.

Not too nice of you to steal his stuff.

I didn't steal his stuff, Travis said. Did Mr. Zimmerman say I did that?

The way Officer Erly Johnson wasn't quick to affirm it gave him his answer. Travis was feeling more and more comfortable as the conversation wore on. The officer was not the dumbest person he'd ever met, that title belonged to a couple of teachers, but he was dumb in a way that restored equilibrium to Travis's congested mind. Travis felt like this conversation could go on forever. The longer it went on, the more it would soothe him. *You've reached the meadow, the grass between your toes.* He was starting to enjoy it.

Would you mind calling Mr. Zimmerman on your phone? Travis made his request sound as polite as possible. I want to make sure he doesn't believe that about me. Could we call him on your phone, please?

My phone is for police business only.

This is police business.

No, we're not going to call him on my phone, Officer Erly Johnson said.

IV.

PRESENT

Amos Goetz Pulls

out of the Zimmermans' driveway as Travis pulls in. Amos is still driving the same cart with the same rundown horse. Travis isn't a horse person but the mare looks tired and sad. Her head hangs. Travis blocks the drive with his Monte Carlo and gets out.

Hey Amos.

Oh yah, Amos says.

Travis eyes Amos. He has time to take a good look. Amos won't break the silence. Won't offer conversational help but won't talk back either. Travis can relax, idle in place, find his voice. He knows exactly what he wants out of Amos. In fact, he's been keeping an active eye out for him, but Amos has become impossible to locate. He isn't at his family farm, and Yoder didn't answer him when Travis asked his whereabouts. It's been over a year that Amos has been out on his own. He should be back at the Goetz family farm by now. But Yoder didn't answer.

Travis pets the mare's forelock, runs his fingers down the bony forehead. He sees that Amos is still wearing commercial Dickies and that his bowl haircut is so long he ties it back. His personal hygiene has always come and gone and today it's gone. Travis smells the horse, overworked and unclean, its odor strong. But horses always smell good. Amos, his odor strong, overworked and underfed, doesn't come off as well. He doesn't quite look Amish anymore. He looks more like what he also is: a drug dealer.

I'm looking for my mom, Travis says.

Oh yah, Amos says.

Do you know where she is? Travis asks.

Oh yah. No, Amos says.

A sharp sweet smell of hay pinches the air. The horse relieves itself on the driveway. Amos jumps down and grabs a shovel from the cart, scoops up the manure, and throws it on the other side of the road.

You get a chance to say good-bye to Chieko? Travis asks.

Oh yah, Amos says.

Travis says no more. There's a lot to say about that topic, but that's not why he needs to talk to Amos. He grabs a friendly hank of the horse's mane. Amos checks the sky. The September sun is dropping faster than it did just a week ago. Amos needs to get a move on to beat the dark, but Travis knows he won't say anything.

Mrs. Zimmerman is at the door and waving to Travis with a smile. Mr. Zimmerman watches directly behind her. She looks like she has two heads, the one below for cheerful, the one above for serious.

They won't hire you if I tell what you do, Travis says.

Oh yah, Amos says.

The Railroad Tracks

converge in a cityscape of grain elevators. Tall grain units, fat ones, alpha and beta ones, sky transports between their steel architecture. Their gleaming cluster stands as the entrance to town. Its portals bustle with trucks and Amish buggies kicking up dust.

Travis drives behind the grain elevators and follows a utility road down a spurline. The grain elevators stairstep down from silos to tanks to bins until they spread out into single-story storage facilities, corrugated setups of deserted offices and supply businesses. Then a scrap-metal yard with no discernible access; its outside wall is constructed of side-by-side U-Haul trucks sealed together. The wheels and axles have been knocked off the U-Hauls so that they sink into the ground, no access under them or through them, a clever postapocalyptic barricade.

Some of the back doors to the U-Hauls are flung open. Inside sit a few loungers.

Here? Travis asks.

Yah, Amos says.

Travis gets out. His tires are low, he sees. The treads almost gone. It's either new tires or ride the school bus. He can't take the school bus. It'll make it official where he lives and he doesn't turn eighteen until March. No telling where they'll make him move once they know, even though they already know, they just prefer not to know, but then they'll have to stop pretending and do something about it. All of this will happen if he can't get some decent tires for his car. He can't take the bus. It will ruin everything. Besides, he's got a business to run and he needs his car. Besides, he's a senior. Seniors do not ride the school bus.

I'm looking for my mom, he tells the guy dangling his legs over the yellow rental truck.

Me too, the guy says agreeably. His face catches a sun ray. His blue eyes are really really blue. His cheekbones poke out smooth and burnished against the beard and matted hair.

Jackie Hicks, says Travis.

Good luck, man.

Travis waves to Amos. Amos steps out of the car.

You got anything for me? the guy calls to Amos.

We're looking for Jackie, Travis says.

You won't find her here. Jackie don't like urban living, the guy says. She ain't a city gal.

Travis and Amos

leave the railroad tracks behind and drive deeper into the countryside for several miles. A road Travis has never been down takes them by a lengthy tangle of forest so entwined it looks untouched since the Wyandot era. On the other side sits a misshapen cornfield—a patchwork of high stalks, low stalks, and bald spots of no stalks. A path leading through the cornfield into crossed swords of junk trees and silver maples might actually be a driveway. There might be a house back there but Travis wouldn't want to venture in to find out. That man, Spalding's dad. Someone like him would live there doing their freaky things. Something off about this place. The sick cornfield says it all.

What's with the cornfield? Travis says.

Yah, Amos says. For once he's genuinely agreeing, not just saying his weird yah to everything anyone says. Travis senses a connection.

Are you living at home? Travis asks.

Yah no, Amos says.

Do you want to?

Yah.

Do they want you to?

Yah no.

Are you being shunned?

Yah.

Are you sad?

Yah.

The road swings round a bend and they speed out of this otherworldly capsule and return to civilization. Back to normal with grain storage units ahead and a house with a lake and parkland.

Yah okay, says Amos.

Here?

Yah.

Are you sure?

Travis has his doubts but swings into the dirt apron in front of three squat silos with cone tops. Their steel shines in the sun. Travis gets out of the car and walks over. The corrosion of the seams and bolts and welded ladder rungs becomes visible. The storage spouts are open and Travis takes a peek into empty darkness. A rusty hopper sits on a track that leads to a loading site. It almost could pass for normal. Much like his Monte Carlo. It almost passes for a normal car. Mr. Zimmerman has talked about needing a new pickup and selling his old one to Travis. Travis tried not to act excited. Whatever the cost he'll do it, as long as he can pay monthly with no money down.

Across the street is the parkland where foments a lake and a dock and an endless meadow of private land. The place almost looks affluent but not. Maybe it was once affluent but always weird. Travis is glad he's not by himself. He would already be back in the car and barreling down the road. He says to Amos, You know where I live.

Yah.

In case you need something.

Travis wouldn't mind actually. He hates sleeping in the trailer alone.

Travis steps across the street to what he presumes is the owner's house. He and Amos stand before a two-story white clapboard farmhouse. Looks decent at first until he takes a second glance.

In the downstairs windows, sheer curtains hang like a long dirty wig: an old hag standing in each one, stroking her white hair.

Travis is about ready to call it a day.

Amos points down the long driveway. The driveway becomes a lane that opens up into some kind of vacation spot, a lake with a dock and a pleasant picnic shelter and cement restroom. That's what it looks like at first. Travis has learned it will all turn into some kind of haunted alternate universe.

They start down it.

A few steps bring them to a No Trespassing sign. Then to a No Swimming sign. Then to a No Hunting sign and then to a No Fishing sign. And then to a This Means You sign.

I'll wait here, Travis says.

Amos marches ahead. Travis watches him pass one structure that has burned to the ground, leaving only posts and the scorched concrete foundation. Past a field of farm equipment and silage forks rusted to a rich cinnamon. Amos arrives at a long maroon barn and walks to the front and waves. It's safe. Travis joins him.

The front of the barn is long and open and it faces the desolate lake and offers complete visual protection from the road. There are no doors. It's a carport barn.

Hey Bub! says his mom. She's sitting in a lawn chair, enjoying the day. Amusing herself with her long hair, which she is braiding down her chest. She makes the braid wave hiya! to Travis.

That same guy as before is at a folding table, playing cards. It's not solitaire he's playing. He's just spreading out the cards and looking at them. His mom has to blow on a plastic whistle to get his attention, even though he is six feet away.

Look who it is, his mom says.

The guy gets up and gives Travis's hand a shake. He notices Amos and gives his hand a shake. Amos, he says. You got something for us?

Danny, come on. My son's here.

He sits back down and slides cards.

How are you, Bub? his mom asks.

Let's make this fast, Travis thinks. The Whoevers who staked the No Trespassing signs might return. The old hags might come floating down. His mother might make him remember things.

I hear you're doing great, his mother says.

Travis pulls the pen and papers from his back pocket. He unfolds the papers. I need you to sign this, he says.

Anything for you, Bub. You know that, don't you? Danny, are you paying attention? She blows on her plastic whistle, which makes a half-clogged sound. Danny, listen to this please. My son has papers.

Yep, the guy says.

What are the papers for, Bub?

Financial aid. To college.

Dang, Bub, you're in college already.

Something Travis has never noticed before: his mother is not a big woman. She's on the small side. And his grandmother is small. And his mother is reddish-blond and very freckled. And he's dark-haired. He's never put two and two together before. His size and ability to tan come from the other half. If Miss B is out there looking for his father, he should be easy to spot. Look for a seven-foot-tall Wyandot.

I'm really proud of you, Bub. Aren't I, Danny?

What are your papers called? the guy asks.

Brag on you all the time.

FAFSA, Travis says.

Yeah, I've heard of that, he says.

Do you live here? Travis asks.

We're the caretakers.

Right on cue several geese land behind Travis and he turns around and notices them all over, flapping in the lake, their filth everywhere. Beyond the brackish water he spots a tan dog, mangy and skinny even from this distance. It's prancing around the restroom shelter. Then, as if it knows Travis is watching, it squats and does its business. He wishes Miss B were here to witness this, proof that he is not obsessed with poop but that poop is obsessed with him. Maybe Desdemona's scarf is Shakespeare's human condition, but this is Travis Hicks's human condition: just a whole lotta crap wherever he goes. He'd like some scarves, he would. Like to find some scarves on the ground instead of shit.

Travis kicks away a couple of geese. Great job, he says.

His mom hacks into hysterical cackles.

I don't appreciate that, the guy says.

Oh, come on, Danny, he's making a joke. I can't help it I've got a comedian for a son.

He's insulting me.

Travis waits for him to go back to his cards. His mother whispers, You take after me. Her thumb jerks toward Danny and she mouths, No sense of humor.

Travis shakes the papers and says to his mom, They wanna know if you're married, divorced, widowed, or single.

I'm single and I'm loving it.

Also if you graduated from middle school.

With honors.

Also if you graduated from high school.

The guy flips up the table and the cards go flying.

Are you going to stand for this, Jackie?

Travis points to the question on the form.

You got something to calm him down? Jackie says to Amos. Bub, pick up those cards while I get Danny settled.

Amos pulls out a baggie of pills. His mother unbuttons the thigh pocket on her camo cargo pants. She fingers out some loose bills and counts up to six dollars. Also from the pocket she takes out a pill bottle and holds it out to Amos, who shakes out six pills, careful not to touch them with his fingers. Travis remembers now his mother's random fastidiousness. She reaches for the hand sanitizer in a wheelbarrow and freshens her hands, then pours out two pills for Danny, who gulps them down with the stagnant dregs of a bottle of Crown Royal peach. His mom buttons the pill bottle in her cargo pants.

I'm sorry I missed your graduation, she says. Missed my own, too. Was right on track. She air-draws a big belly over her stomach.

Don't pamper him, the guy says.

I thought it was a Saturday. Danny, remember? It was a Friday. All dressed up and there I was, party of one. Really sorry, Bub. But I was so proud of you.

I haven't graduated yet.

I withdraw my apology, his mother says with a barking chestful of glee.

Travis tosses the papers to her.

She wide-eyes the foreign objects on her lap. Her hands still work the braid. Travis grabs them back and shuffles through the pages for her, holding each one up to eye level. Her braid flaps hiya to each page. Each page responds with small print and checkboxes and cramped spaces for fill in the blanks. She offers a long meaningful gaze and then a shake of her head. I don't know, Bub, she says. Seems like a lot of work just to go to college. Sounds like it might be a scam. She messes with her braid while thinking about it.

Did you file an income tax return last year?

His mother blows on the plastic whistle. Did I file an income tax return? she asks.

What was your gross adjusted income? Travis asks.

What was my gross adjusted income?

Last year? the guy asks.

Both of them stare at Travis without answering.

Just sign and I'll figure it out. Travis holds out the pen to his mom.

Sounds like a scam, Bub, she says. Really sounds like a scam. I don't want you getting in trouble.

Sign it, okay.

One hand leaves the braid and takes the pen. Travis points to the signature line.

Don't sign it, Jackie, the guy warns.

Making it sloppy so they can't read it, she says. Scam protection. Bub, you're gonna have to play a round of cards with Danny before you go or he's gonna be upset.

Travis sits on a barrel on the other side of the table. He spots his grandmother's dresser they took from his bedroom.

Where's my BarcaLounger? Travis asks.

That got sold, Bub.

Grandma bought that for me.

No, she didn't, Bub.

Travis turns back to the table. He waits for the guy to deal out the cards but his chin has tipped to his chest and he's fallen asleep.

Tell Us Something About Yourself

Okay, sure. I'll get started with the information that my name is Anisha Devajaran, and what sets me apart from your other applicants is that I play the E-flat cornet in the marching band and I do my homework at my favorite booth in Taco Bell and enjoy lots of unstructured time, which has led me to interesting prediscoveries. I like to call them my 40-watt moments because they could use a little more voltage but they're getting there. So, what I mean about unstructured time is that it's like sitting under a tree but *aware*, so that if an apple falls in your hand *voila!* 40 watts to 100! and you discover gravity. I'm 17 so I'm giving myself 10 more years to get to the full falling apple/lightbulb discovery.

Unstructured time has not made me into a slacker. Ask my teachers who are always telling me to slow down. I've made a flow chart of all my unstructured v. structured time which I can show you if you'd like. Keep in mind that band practice is very structured and requires two-a-days in August just like the football team, and four times a week once school starts. Then there are game days and when those are away games it requires at least an hour on the bus because we play other country schools and some of them you wouldn't believe the distance. I'd say cities are lucky because you just go down the street to play another school except that some of my best memories are the late-night bus rides in the dark. I'm embarrassed to say I used to really take it to heart when our

Cougars lost. Now not so much. I can even see it in the cheerleaders in the way they shake their pompoms. Win or lose, it's the same kind of perfunctory jiggle. I never really understood that term "phoning it in" until I watched those pompoms shake in the air and then drop to the ground and the cheerleaders step away. It's exactly the same as last year, exactly the same movements, the same shake, the same count, the same jump, but it's all different and it's not my imagination. This is how DNA works, is what I'm thinking. It all looks the same, it all looks the same, it all looks the same, and then it's not. It's a prediscovery I'm working on.

A lot of my unstructured time is spent with my best friend Corbin. Corbin is the drum major in our marching band. Last summer we did a massive fundraising drive for new uniforms and now you should see Corbin. He looks glorious in his red and white tailcoat, cummerbund, epaulets, spats, and boot top tassels. He looks like *Vogue* magazine's "New Face of the Revolutionary War." Even the few liberals in our town, like my mom and me for example, get a surge of teary-eyed patriotism when Corbin takes to the field. By the way, a group in Cambridge, MA bought some of our old band uniforms. Thought you would be interested in that. They are reenactors. Also, a group touring as Paul Revere and the Raiders. They are music, not reenactors. They bought ten uniforms. I know Paul Revere is big in Boston, but read on, I think you're going to be surprised about our little town's own Paul Revere.

Back to Corbin. Corbin's brother Josh is the wide receiver for our football team. Last year Josh broke the state track record for the 3200 meter run. That's a big deal in this state because Ohio thank you very much has brought you Jesse Owens and Edwin Moses and Tonja Buford-Bailey and Dave Wottle. These are all Olympic champions who once went to high school in Ohio and set unbeatable records. Even after better shoes and better track surfaces came along, it was a long, long time before those records could be touched. This is all information we were made to learn after Corbin's brother became state champ in order to best appreciate his accomplishment. It's not like Josh stood up to Hitler or anything, but Kattoga High is still really proud of him.

So when I tell you that Corbin's state-champion brother runs the distances because Corbin can actually outrun him in the sprints!!! like really??? like yes!!! you'll have some understanding of Corbin's miracle of speed. So that is an amazing fact about my friend Corbin. So when I say that watching Corbin sprint all alone down the football field in his new band uniform is a rare sight to behold, you can put it in a little more context and understand how amazing it really is when I say amazing. I mean, it's amazing.

It's our tradition to march from the high school to the stadium on game night. The stadium crowd can hear us coming. Giant Cougar paw prints painted on the road lead us to our destination. When we enter the stadium from behind and prepare under the bleachers, the crowd can't see us but they know we're there. Everyone starts stomping their feet and we can feel the vibrations above us. We let the crowd get good and ready. We wait until the stomping is about to bring a whole section of bleachers down.

Then Corbin gives the signal.

Like swifts in flight, we soar out from the bleachers and take to the field. We blast our entrance march anthem above the crazy wild cheering until the whole band is lined up at the end zone. The instrument players gradually stop playing section by section until only the drummers are left, only the drummers and the cymbals. We wait until the crowd noise drops off the bleachers section by section, and then when it's quiet enough the cymbals peter out and then the bass drums get softer and softer, and then it's silence and it's just the snares. They sound so light in one way, so fragile and vulnerable, and the crowd stays quiet to listen to them because it's like listening in a way to a history lesson, this is how our nation began, snare drumming like this, marching like this, standing straight and proud to meet the opponent at the other end. Sometimes the sky is bright when we enter, sometimes there is a pink sunset, sometimes there is already darkness. The season takes us from heat to pleasantly chilly to downright cold. Through it all we stand at attention, me first in my row, cornet snugged under my arm. It's one of the most important moments of my whole high school career, standing there like this, honoring something that I know is real but can't ever explain.

Let me tell you what comes next. Corbin, who has sneaked inside our ranks to hide himself, suddenly punches through our lines and begins his sprint across the field. You should hear the people! From absolute quiet to absolute insanity in one half second. One hundred yards in a backbend goes Corbin, his baton held high in the air and the plume from his busby touching the ground. He's fast, so fast, and the crowd is going nuts. When he gets to the other end zone, he pulls himself to attention. Stony-faced, he accepts the crowd's adoration. I know how much Corbin loves this moment because he's my best friend, but you'd never know it from the way he stands riveted at attention, heedless of their cheers— until he dips into his ceremonial bow.

In case there are any former baton twirlers on your committee, you might be interested to know that Corbin uses an all-metal Strutter, not a rubber-tipped rod, for his baton performances at halftime. According to our band director, Mr. Hurd, Corbin is the fastest baton twirler he's ever seen. Which is great because Corbin has dreams of becoming the drum major at The Ohio State University. I have dreams of becoming a typical freshman at Harvard, but I think you already know that, and I am so honored that your committee is reading this. I have made 15 copies in case everyone would like their own printout, or maybe you'd rather have one person read this aloud. That's fine, too. Thank you very much in advance for considering me.

Use a Separate Sheet if Necessary
As in a *single* separate sheet? I will assume you meant plural. Now I will try to answer your questions one by one.

Tell Us about Your Perfect Scores
I have translated your question *Tell Us about a Challenge You Overcame* to mean tell us about your college entrance exam scores, which were

perfect 800s on the SAT and a perfect 36 on the ACT. I know that information is listed in my application but I thought I would mention it again because the only other person to have accomplished that in the history of our town was my brother two years ago. Now he's at Harvard. I hope you don't mind family members at the same school. If you kind of do, please keep in mind that we would overlap for only two years.

How Long Has Your Town Been Around?

Basically ever since Simon Kenton slung Daniel Boone over his shoulders and outran the Shawnees. That was in 1777 although the town wasn't an official town until 1845. George Washington was once here before that, FYI, as a 17-year-old surveyor. But give or take 250 years, including George Washington, no one's gotten into Harvard except my brother.

Also, no fault of his own, but my brother didn't have to deal with some of *the challenges I overcame* (see previous question) on the way to perfect scores. For more than a year I fretted over my calendar, worried that my SAT exams would fall during my menstrual cycle and I'd blow it. I am usually a very happy person, "cheerful Anisha" is what I'm often called, but on the first day of my period I am the opposite of cheerful Anisha. I bleed a lot and I am in a terrible mood. For 8 hours I care about nothing, whether I live or die, stuff like that. Doesn't last long and my optimistic nature takes over by day's end, but it definitely lasts all morning and the SAT and ACT tests are in the morning so if an exam fell during that first day of my period not only would I do awful, but I'd *want* to do awful. If the exam fell during the subsequent two days, my mood would be fine but there would be the delicate issue of a bloodbath. My mother assures me all of this will get better. I know from her (she's a doctor) that sometimes women don't menstruate at all or they experience it to a negligible degree. I'm pretty sure Queen Elizabeth I and Harriet Tubman and Clara Barton and Sacajawea did not experience monthly bloodbaths. Call this another 40-watt realization moment, an area of study I'd like to pursue for a paper at Harvard. This is not to diminish Sacajawea's achievement. Even without a period, I could not lead Lewis and Clark through the wilderness for 7000 miles—in moccasins—plus I would get lost. However, this private medical issue I've entrusted you with would never ever stop me from missing class. If you check my transcript, you will see that I have perfect attendance, and I will have perfect attendance throughout my college career.

Who Is Simon Kenton?

I knew you were going to ask that. Everyone does. And guess what, this is what I was promising when I mentioned Paul Revere and how proud Harvard must be of their local hero. Simon Kenton is our local hero.

I guess if someone on your committee says he prefers Daniel Boone over Simon Kenton, it's no big deal, but keep in mind that in today's world Daniel Boone is the type who would be constantly working the media, Facebook, Twitter, cable news appearances, etc. Simon Kenton? No, just the opposite. He didn't need the cheers of the crowd. He didn't need a thousand likes for hitting a bull's-eye at half a mile away with musket fire. He didn't need to feed off fame. Simon Kenton saved the life of Daniel Boone. Can you imagine if it was the other way around? Daniel Boone would be on *60 Minutes* and every talk show there is, telling that story, a little more embellished each time, until it had little relation to what actually happened. But Simon Kenton wouldn't utter a word of protest even as the story got crazier and crazier and Daniel Boone more of a hero each time and Simon Kenton more and more like a grateful puppy.

As I said, it's actually Simon Kenton who saved Daniel Boone's life and he did it at the very spot not far from where I sit in the Taco Bell writing this essay. Our town is named after him, after Simon Kenton's Shawnee name of "Cuttahotha," which means "condemned to be burned at the stake." This is something the Shawnees tried to do three times but failed. I don't know the particulars of this. Frankly it's hard to figure out how exactly you can get loose from a pole you're tied to while a fire's going on at your feet without a deus ex machina to get you out of it, but he did, three times I guess, and he wasn't the type of person to lie or exaggerate, and that's how we named the town, although Cuttahotha got mistranslated as Kattoga.

Kattoga, Ohio. That's us. One high school. One football team. One marching band.

And also Simon Kenton could load his Kentucky long rifle on the dead run. Which I mean, I'm 1000 percent for gun control, I really really am, and have written to my congressman about it, but that was a different time back then. I thought I would mention it because this ability to run and load—remember it's one of those old guns where you have to pour power from a horn and then churn it with a metal rod—this might be something your committee members have heard of and attributed to Daniel Boone, but again, not to belabor the point but don't listen to every talk show you hear. It's Simon Kenton who did that. As you can see, I aim for historical accuracy, something I would bring to my classes at Harvard.

What Are Some of Your Talents?

Obviously, loading a Kentucky long rifle on the dead run is not one of them. But Simon Kenton didn't get an 800 on his SAT either.

What Is Your Favorite Word?

Cornet.

Why Is That Your Favorite Word?

Thanks for asking. The easy answer is that, as you already know, this is the instrument I play in the marching band. It reminds me of good times. When I see my cornet case sitting at the front door almost like a golden retriever panting to go out, my heartbeat picks up. It's at the front door waiting for me and we're both at our happiest when I take it outside and let it loose.

You have to understand, the K-High marching band is not just a band, it's a way of life that probably involves half the town if you go by who's a band alum or who's a sibling or a parent of a band alum. The rate goes up to 98 or 99 percent if you go by 6 degrees of separation, the point being the band is much bigger than its 103 members. The band is almost the biggest thing going in this town. Almost.

What Is Your Least Favorite Word?
Pigskin.

Who Is a Hero to You? A Mother or Father or Grandparent Is Not Considered a Good Answer
My mother.

Please Elaborate
I'm sure at least half this town would say Coach McManus is their hero. He gets us into Sectionals every year and this year we've made it into Districts. And yes, we won the Division IV State Championship not too long ago. We're kind of on the map. I am at the Taco Bell right now trying to finish this essay before Friday so I don't have to report the district scores to you. It's not that I don't want us to win. But I don't want us to win. Not with that quarterback. He's got another year to play anyway; he can do it when I'm out of here. Every Friday this season, despite what happened, I've been a professional. I do my job, heading up my row as first cornet. The trombones do their job; the flutes and clarinets do theirs. The cymbals have a job to crash at the right spots. Assistant Band Director Miss Stacy does double or triple her job. This Friday she'll be screaming "Good luck don't suck" until she's doubled over in pain. I think she suspects what's going to happen and she won't be able to stop it. We've got it all secretly planned out. We're going to mess up one of our songs—on purpose. We chose "Secret Agent Man" as our suck-'n'-squawk song because we do it every year and the crowd counts on it and they know how smooth we deliver it. So of course they'll know we're doing it as a protest, but you know what I'm really thinking now that

I'm thinking about it? The crowd won't get it at all. They'll just think we suck. It'll be a long bus ride home in the dark after that performance.

A lot of the blame will be directed at Corbin and me, I'm sure. The newspaper led the way by calling us the "town's two misfits." They also went after my mother. But as for the actual people who actually caused it?

If You Could Choose to Be Raised by Robots, Dinosaurs, or Aliens, Who Would You Pick?

The aliens already live here. The dinosaurs are playing this Friday night at Districts. I guess that leaves robots. (Is it *whom* would you pick?)

How Would You Cure World Hunger?

With the superhero power you ask me to choose in the next question. So I'm skipping that and going straight to this:

Tell Us Something Funny about Yourself That Will Make Us Laugh

That you'll think my photo is a mug shot and then you'll go online and then you'll see me and it is a mug shot.

Tell Us about Something Ironic That Happened to You

Do you know who that actor Bill Murray is? He was in an old movie we were watching and he shot me a look right through the TV screen, right at ME, right as the cell rang that changed everything. And then he just shook his head like Boy, are you in trouble now. But aren't we all? he seemed to say and Good luck, kid. When I told my mom about it later, she said, Don't take that seriously because he used to be a comedian and he meant it as a joke.

Tell Us Something You Do for Fun

When my mom and I need to stock up on Indian food, we take a drive to Columbus. It's about an hour and twenty minutes to get to the Indian grocery we like the best. We also load up some canned goods for the food bank nearby since curing world hunger is something I worry about. Most of the way there she is very quiet. She is decompressing. My mom can be extremely tired and not even know it. She's like a humming-bird. There's a quiver inside her body even as she sits motionless, hands locked in steering position, and drives, rigidly drives, almost frozen at the wheel. The quiver skims across the surface of her skin, clue to a dis-turbance below. It requires at least 40 minutes of her sitting calmly and clearing her head before that vibration fades out, and that never happens unless we are driving a lot farther than usual. So I love it when we pull out onto the state route and head south of town, over the two railroad crossings and past the grain elevators where the Amish are usually lined up in their wagons.

"How can they load enough for a grain elevator on a horse-drawn wagon?" I always ask my mom (because these are giant grain elevators we're talking about), but our trip has just begun and she doesn't usually answer. She doesn't even hear me yet.

Listen: They'll tell you the road is curved. They'll tell you about hills. They'll tell you about steep climbs that wind and twist and deliver sur-prises. They'll tell you anything to make you think it wasn't their fault. It's flat out here, flat and straight. Don't believe what you hear.

At the 40-minute mark I watch my mother's face begin to relax. What-ever it is she's worrying about, usually a patient, I can visualize the mo-ment it's exhaled from her body in shadowy wings. It flies away, clearing all worry nests in her body. Then her grip on the steering wheel loosens and one hand falls to her lap. She turns to me and smiles as if only 30 seconds have elapsed, and we begin to talk.

If it's a day when Corbin is accompanying us to Columbus, I turn around in my seat and chatter away with him, one eye on my mother, who doesn't seem to notice we are there until the shadowy wings fly off and then she cocks her head, catching the end of something we're saying, and laughs out loud at us. That is the best, absolutely the best, when the three of us are together and my mom is laughing.

Take Us Back to February

So listen: It happened on a Saturday night. Five boys put a deer decoy on the road. Five boys; one of them was Corbin's brother. It was February. It was 23 degrees out and the two guys who crashed used to go to our high school.

Isn't This a Challenge You've Overcome?

I really had nothing to do with it despite what the papers say.

Who Else Was There?

My childminder was there. I remember that. I recognized her in the dark after all these years. There's something so otherworldly about Miriam. She seems above it all. She was completely calm and completely authoritative. She told Corbin and me to step away, which we did. But if we hadn't stepped away ... She told me to take Corbin where my mom couldn't hear him crying while she worked, so we went off to the field holding our cell phones as flashlights and that's when Corbin's brother called us again. This time he was hiding somewhere and he needed us to help him. And we did. We found him hiding by an abandoned trailer and we got him into a getaway car, I hate to use that word, it sounds like a movie—getaway car—but that's what it was, a getaway car, and nobody ever knew about it. "It" meaning they didn't know about us. They still don't know. One of the five guys bragged about the accident a few days later. I mean, that's not exactly Harvard material right there. There's a lot of those types in our town.

The Committee Remains Confused and Uncertain

I will take you through it step by step. Imagine that it is February, that very day in February, and we are headed to the Indian grocery in Columbus (and the food bank). Corbin has removed the down coat he hates and rolled it next to him on the backseat. He tells my mom they should go to LensCrafters and he will help her pick out designer eyewear. He's really on about her getting more stylish glasses. He thinks Versace or Burberry would look good on her. Stylish and doctorish at the same time, he explains.

Corbin believes that everybody everywhere outside of Kattoga can identify every brand of clothing and accessory at a glance. So it's very important to wear the right things that everyone is immediately identifying and scoring in their head whenever they happen to glance at you. Corbin tries very hard not to let them discover he is a farm boy from a small country town with modest parents who do not have as much money as he needs them to have.

I always know what Corbin is thinking because he always tells me what he is thinking.

A finger pokes the back of my head. I turn and send Corbin a smile. My mother sends him a smile via the rearview mirror. This is not our last happy time together, but it is our last uncluttered happy time together. Corbin is wearing a trim velvet jacket, size 36, that couldn't fit over most girls. Underneath is a striped blue shirt with a contrasting white collar and white French cuffs. The cufflinks for this we found in an antique shop in Mount Liberty. He likes places that are 90 percent junk because he feels it gives the discerning eye a better chance. His soft blond hair is blow-dried out of the curls he hates. It's February and it's cold. There's no reason for Corbin to wear a velvet jacket that will only be obscured by a coat, especially a shapeless puffy down coat. But I know what he's thinking. He'll leave the coat in the car and hurry into Nordstrom, where he is convinced everyone will watch, listen, and judge. I already know this but he tells my mom and me anyway. It's like he has to keep accusing the world of inspecting him down to his socks so that repetition will make it go away.

"Don't be ashamed of who you are," I tell him when he finishes.

"I am ashamed," he says.

"You are wonderful the exact way you are," my mother consoles. She is always kind, my mother. Her kind words fall like petals.

"No I'm not—what word did you say I was?"

"Wonderful."

"No I'm not wonderful." He leans forward and knocks his forehead against the back of my seat. "But I like the way you say it."

"You have an amazing talent," my mother tells him, "like nothing anyone in this town has ever seen."

"As long as you like batons. What word did you say again?"

"Amazing. You are amazing with the baton. Incredible and beyond belief."

"Beyond belief?"

"Breathtaking," my mother says.

"As long as you like batons."

"And I do. Very much. Who doesn't?"

"A lot of people."

"People who don't like batons don't even know enough to think about that," I tell Corbin. "I've heard a lot of people say they don't like Indian food, but I've never heard anyone say they don't like batons."

"Yeah I should shut up," he says.

"Oh, Corbin, no. This is your safe space. You say whatever. I will not be shocked. I promise." My mom sends him another smile via the rearview mirror.

"I love to hear you talk," he says to my mom. "Especially when you're saying nice things to me."

"You are the major general of all drum majors."

"You're joking with me."

My mother chuckles. "I might be lighthearted, but I only tell the truth, Corbin. You know that."

"All the time?"

"All the time."

"Even to your patients who have a really bad disease?"

"Even to them."

"Let's say they have to get an arm cut off."

"I break it to them as gently as possible."

"Finger by finger."

"Yes, so to speak."

"Do you think blue velvet is me?" he asks.

She expels Corbin's anxiety with her laughter.

"Do you think I'll be the drum major at Ohio State?"

"I will love you no matter."

"Do you think Anisha will get into Harvard?"

"I will love her no matter."

"What about Anesh?"

"I will love him no matter."

"What if he's in a frat where they get drunk and rape girls?"

"I will visit him in jail and love him no matter."

"Will you come see me at Ohio State if I'm the drum major?"

"Of course."

"Anisha won't be able to come because she'll be at Harvard."

"Maybe I'll be at Columbus State instead," I say. "And then I can come see you."

"Your mom won't even begin to talk to you if you go to Columbus State."

My mom says, "Don't put anxious ideas into her head, Corbin. I will love her no matter."

And then we all laugh because none of these bad things will happen.

Listen: this is the before scene when all we are worried about is Corbin's velvet jacket and what designer glasses my mom should get. By the end of this day our lives will have flipped into shadows. For years to come the stealth inner workings of a crushed soul will stand ready for a surprise visit, to deliver a crack to our crystal-clear moments of joy. In a few hours Corbin's brother and four others from our school will set a deer decoy on a country road and make a car fly into a winter cornfield and nothing will ever be the same, for the boys who will suffer, for the boys who do it, for all of us. My mom will save the lives of two people and all they will say about her is that she was a drunk Indian and almost killed them.

But we still have time to enjoy this last day. We are still part of this town and not their two misfits. We are the Ohio State drum major and Harvard frosh and we return from Columbus in a mood of celebration and rent a movie and make popcorn. We start a fire in the fireplace. My mother has successfully not worked or thought about work almost all day and tomorrow is Sunday, another day off, and that will be two days in a row for her, something she really needs because I can tell she is exhausted and doesn't even know it. With just a few hours' rest her skin shines. Her eyes are peaceful and moist. She pours herself a glass of wine. I make hot chocolate. Corbin models the two pairs of skinny jeans he bought at J. Crew and we applaud and then we sit back, all three of us on the sofa, and pull a blanket over us. We have less than an hour left before our names in this town will be forever changed to the "girly baton twirler," the "little Indian girl trumpeter," and the "town's third-world doctor from India." Those are our names now. Those are the good names.

And then while we're sitting on the sofa, the actor Bill Murray pauses in the movie and looks at me funny through the TV screen and Corbin's cell phone rings. You're in trouble now, Bill Murray says. But aren't we all. Good luck, kid.

I can't make out the words that Corbin's brother is screaming. The screaming is enough. It tells us everything. My mother has grabbed her medical bag and stands over Corbin, who is stuck to the sofa with a frozen expression. I get lost in time during these moments. My body is moving, I believe, but my brain is paused and it seems I have enough time to read a book before we leave—leave where, I have no idea. I just know we are going somewhere bad and Act I of my life is over. Corbin has managed to stand. His hands are thrust into his new J. Crew skinny jeans and he looks as good as he can look, which is to say handsome but not like his brother, Josh. He has a slightly hawkish nose to Josh's Roman nose. A slightly weak chin to Josh's muscular jaw. He can be photographed out of these flaws (flaws to him, flaws that have created obsessions), and I have no doubt his senior pictures will be elegantly angled and shaded. And I know without him telling me (although he will tell me) that he fully intends to commit *seppuku* before setting foot in Franklin Art Studio, where they will take you to a stone bench in the cemetery and have you hug your knees and grin. He's already got his eye on a photographer in Cleveland. And I know what the upshot of this will be. In the photos he will look unqualifiedly handsome. He will look like his gorgeous brother.

I have always wished that Corbin could have been given his brother's beauty. It would mean so much more to him.

We are just over a mile or two from the site of the accident. Nothing distinguishes it from anywhere else. It's blackness, pure blackness. Nothing announces itself out of the blackness. There are no streetlights out here. No lights of any kind. The Amish houses are dark. We drive right past before my mother hits the brakes. A solid glint over in the stubs of a cornfield. She backs up until the headlights can be of help. A car is upside down, its wheels still spinning.

There is no point in us asking her anything; she will not answer. Her mind is now far away, which is to say her mind is *here*, right here, it doesn't go beyond this upside-down car, and everything else is erased.

She jumps out with her medical bag. We jump out.

But where do we go?

And after all that sobbing on the speakerphone, Corbin's brother is not here to show us where to find them. We cannot find them. Corbin and I have to get on our hands and knees and crawl forward. My mother is in the cornfield by the overturned car. Me on the edge of the road. Corbin on the other side along the ditch. And no cars come.

As we work we hear the sounds of each of us breathing. The bodies are hidden from us like lost friendship rings, like lost contact lenses— things. Things we need to find.

"Where are they?" I yell.

"Ssh," my mother calms.

Then we hear it. A moan. A rustle.

Corbin yelps.

"What?"

"Something is squirting out!" Corbin screams.

"You found someone?"

"It's squirting!"

"I'm coming. Put your hand on it to stop it."

"I can't!"

"Put your hand on it. Press."

"I can't!"

"Press, Corbin!"

Corbin's hyperventilation guides me to him. My hand is upon the squirting, and then my mother's hand is atop my own, pressing it down.

And still no one comes. All I hear is the drone of insects. But it is February and the drone is inside my head.

And then I look up. Swaying lanterns illuminate a line of slow-moving figures. Of all the things I see that night, this string of lights penetrating the darkness frightens me the most. They appear as creatures arising from their graves. It is all I can do not to jump back in fear. I cannot run away and desert my crucial job of pressing upon a bleeding thigh. I feel the loss of blood myself, am feeling faint, and then my hand is gently lifted and another takes my place, and it is Miriam, my childminder, and I am a child again and she tells me to go, to take Corbin and follow her own little boys to a field and to keep quiet.

Some of the Amish men sway through the fields, their lanterns on the lookout. Some stand over the two bodies with their lamps, the vapor of kerosene strong, while my mother works. They are already walking home in a long straight line of swinging lights by the time the ambulances howl down the road with the two bodies loaded. A hand circles around my upper arm and pulls me away—a policeman who has just arrived. Late, after everything has already happened.

Why Did They Take Mug Shots?
I don't know. Really, I think just to be creepy jerks.

Did They Arrest You?

No. They gave us corn chips and sugar-free peppermints and asked us questions. They separated us and questioned us for hours. We had blood on our clothes and I guess they expected us to freak out and start squealing. I suppose we acted guilty because we were keeping it from them that Josh was involved, that we had actually seen Josh. They played good cop. They played bad cop. They needed a scapegoat because they had no idea what had transpired at the scene because they are a well-known joke as a police force. Really, I think it made them think they were doing their job since they'd obviously completely failed in their real job, which was getting to the accident scene on time. If one of those boys hadn't bragged about doing it, they never would have solved it.

Please Elaborate

They can't or won't understand that an Indian girl who wants to go to Harvard and spends most Saturday nights with her mother wouldn't be out painting dirty words on a fake deer and putting it out on the road to scare the cars. I'm sorry, that's just not an Indian girl's idea of fun. They press me further about the dirty words I didn't write. They seem most interested in the dirty words, where did I learn them, do I do any of those things with boys. They act like there's no correlation between a perfect 800 on the SAT and proper spelling of obscenities. They tell me maybe I misspelled the words on purpose to throw suspicion on someone else. Like who! I almost yell at them (I'm getting tired). There are too many people with bad spelling in this town. Everyone would be a suspect. They tell me there are witnesses who can place me there. They tell me Corbin is already confessing, that is will go easier on him should one of the accident victims die. Me? I'm looking at a murder charge unless I start singing.

They give me 15, 20 minutes to think about that and I fall asleep at the desk (I'm really tired). When I raise my head, a policeman is looking at me. "How long has your mother been an alcoholic?" he asks.

And then when they finally arrest the real guys who did it, it's like Go Cougars! Great prank, guys! Hand slap, high five, write an essay, get out there and make us proud.

Do You Think You've Gained a New Perspective on Life from Your Experiences?

No, not really. I'm still me, even if people don't see that me anymore. I'm still me, that's all I can tell you. I wish I could be like Miriam, rising above it all. She wouldn't go to Harvard, wouldn't go even if you offered to pay her way, including first-class transportation and catered meals. She's just above all our earthly strivings. But I'm not like that. I don't have perspective. It's out of proportion how much I want to go to Harvard. You wouldn't even have to pay me.

Who Comes Running

late on such an important evening? Dr. Devajaran bolts from the hospital, stopping at her car to grab the little-bit-wilted bouquet of flowers. No point trying to drive there. She would lose time. Everyone has already parked their cars all the way up to the ER, where signs warn them not to use the hospital lot. Well, she's going to be the exception. And she knows there will be people criticizing her for it. She sits sidesaddle on the passenger seat long enough to slip out of dress flats and change into sneakers and then off she flies from her illegally parked car. She likes running. Within a minute a smile is on her face and nothing but good thoughts in her head.

Hannah Kirkpatrick's mother leaves the snack bar for a smoke, goes into the car of someone who calls to her, and loses track until Hannah's grandmother phones her, texts her, then pounds on the car window. Kyle Jenkins's little brother, Kody, isn't standing outside the elementary school with the basketball coach/eighth grade teacher, as ordered. Of course he isn't because he's too much like Kyle. Mrs. Jenkins finds him kicking soccer balls with friends.

Corbin Greesley's mother is trembling in her car until the last minute, having avoided this season's football games altogether. How cheated she feels. Cheated out of her son's ramp entrance and halftime show. Cheated out of the crowd screaming "Gree-eee-sed Lightning!" when her other boy catches a ball and races downfield. She has a son on either side of the battle line. She herself is a compromise state and one son is Johnny Reb and the other Billy Yank. All she wants is to wake up from this nightmare. Her husband arrives, weaving through the packed Goodwill lot of Football Friday vehicles and locates her huddled in the backseat, where the tinted windows are darker. He's dressed in a sports coat and tie, and he proffers his arm to her like a wedding escort and says, Hold your head high.

All of the parents scurry onto the field just in time. All seniors and family members accounted for.

Except Travis Hicks, who stands alone in line.

Except everyone knows this was coming. Except everyone has forgotten to account for it. Except Travis could drop out and help everyone pretend. Except Travis doesn't want to drop out. Except everyone will be embarrassed if he stays. Except Travis wants to stay. Except he might make the parents feel bad. Except Travis is a senior, too. Except it might ruin the parents' evening. Except Travis wants to hear his name called.

Mrs. Jenkins says, Travis, I can escort you and run back for Kyle.

Travis shakes his head. Kyle is one back in line. There won't be time.

Kassadee/Elsa jumps beside Travis and holds up her letter K. I'm going with Travis, she declares. She pokes her letter as high as it will go, up to Travis's head. Look, she says.

Good riddance, says Kyle Jenkins.

Mrs. Jenkins says, Let the announcer know.

Who the fuck's the announcer? Kyle asks.

Kyle, says Mrs. Jenkins. She never bothers to raise her weary voice any longer.

And now Mr. Hurd and Miss Stacy have taken an alarmed step onto the field, and then another step. And Miss B comes trotting to join them. Dr. Devajaran is motioning to Miss B that she'll circle back after Anisha to escort Travis.

Travis sees Miss B and can't help the smile he tries to bite back. He sees Miss B shake her head at someone in their line and then it is Miss B herself who strides forward. For a moment Travis realizes it will be all of them, Mr. Hurd and Miss Stacy and Miss B and when everyone sees what is happening, others will join, and the crowd will empty the bleachers and flood onto the gridiron to help escort "Senior and Marching Band Member Travis Hicks!" across the field, somebody will be filming, it will go viral, Travis will be on the *Today* show in New York City, the host will say we have a special guest who wanted to be here with you and then Yoder will step out and there will be a movie made of their friendship.

Three steps in Miss B stops, gives a nod and one of those smiles of finality, a fare-thee-well-my-friend ending smile, and she turns away and that is it, he is never going to see her again.

Kassadee/Elsa's hand is tugged around his forearm. He turns to see Spalding's mom there. May I have this dance? she says.

Travis doesn't say anything.

My son looks up to you, Travis, she says.

He does?

And not just because you're a senior. We all do. We're all very proud of you.

Travis wants to say, Tell me more about that please, but he's unable to speak. When he catches his breath, Anisha's name is already being announced. Dr. Devajaran presents Anisha with her bouquet and they step across the field together.

Corbin's named is called along with his mother and father and brother Josh. The ones cheering for Corbin try to outdo the ones cheering for Josh with "Gree-ee-sed Lightning!" and for a moment Mrs. Greesley thinks, All is forgiven.

I love you, Travis! cries Kassadee/Elsa.

Get a room, Kyle Jenkins tells her.

Travis strides across the field with "Family Friend Mrs. Roxanne Burker!" while Mrs. Burker tells him, Listen to those cheers, Travis. Everyone loves you! and Travis thinks, Really? I guess they do. When he gets to the end, he turns to watch Kyle Jenkins and "Siblings Kody and Letterette Kassadee-Elsa!" announced. Somehow they forget about

Kyle's mother so the family goes ahead and starts to walk and then the announcer corrects himself and adds her. Kyle does not disappoint. He has strapped on his snare drum and does his own entrance march. At the end, to frenzied encouragement, he does a mic drop with his drumsticks. He jumps in the air to high-five Travis. Savage! he screams.

Travis waits until "Senior and Varsity Cheerleading Captain Hannah Kirkpatrick!" is called. She gives a friendly wave of her pompoms and steps between mother and grandmother. Her mother is dressed like a teenager and her grandmother is dressed like someone her mother's age. Her mother leaves to go back to the snack bar and Hannah waits alone for "Senior and Varsity Cheerleader Erika Williams!" the last one to be called, the gulf between them never wider. They are apart now, almost like lovers forced asunder. They have been kept apart until they were simply apart, and Erika never runs up to hug her in school or pulls back her hair when she thinks she is sad, which she would have to do constantly if they were still friends like in the old days, like six months ago, like ancient times. Hannah is on her own now and she doesn't know how she can move forward. If she can at all. One foot in front of the other is too much, is a cliché. The ten-thousand-mile journey beginning with a single step is something that sounds totally ridiculous.

Congratulations, Erika, Hannah says, hugging her on the sidelines after Erika waves her pompoms and glides across the field. I love you, she says, and she says it right in front of Erika's parents. I love you, she says, meaning, Good-bye.

Freddy Burker Is

in attendance on Senior Night, and that sets Travis on edge. Travis hasn't seen him for weeks but during the third-quarter stretch, when he gets to leave the band and sit in the stands and eat a footlong that Hannah's mother has saved for him, he catches sight of a head with a thick wavy bulk almost like a woman's wig. Freddy Burker's shapeless face is almost like a woman's, too. But his expression is neither male nor female. The lips are pressed into a tight smile between inhalations of French fries, a smirk people would call it, but it goes beyond that. It's the kind of smile that stops teachers in their tracks and they call it out. Teachers get aggressive when they see that expression, but really they're unnerved into overcompensating. It's nothing like Kyle Jenkins's idiot grins or the recent grim boredom he's noticed behind Hannah's polite flash of amusement when the teacher's eyes find her after a lame funny remark. Travis has seen Freddy Burker's smile before, a couple of times—on Jared Overholser—and it has scared him each instance. Travis can't help the rush of blood he feels, the breathlessness. The hotdog feels too heavy in his hands. He sets it on his lap. He takes another peek. Freddy Burker is eating his fries one at a time, daintily selected from his little cardboard sailboat of fries, daintily tipped with ketchup. He eats slowly enough that the smirk has time to reappear between bites. He is wearing his murder outfit, big cowboy belt buckle and cowboy shirt.

Coming off a fresh kill, Travis thinks.

Freddy Burker sits up high in the stands, the last row all alone, and gloats with his secret. He's not here for senior night; Spalding's only a junior. And Mrs. Burker has kicked him out of the house and no one knows where he's staying. At least that's what Spalding has told him. Hannah said the whole thing was going to escalate if cable streaming documentaries and podcasts were any indication. How could it not? she asked him. Would you be content just to kill dogs your whole life?

After the game, in which Jared throws an overkill of five touchdown passes, Travis finds Hannah at the snack bar and he's happy to have a reason to talk to her. Your podcast prediction is coming true, he wants to tell her. Guess who's here? he actually says. He nods meaningfully toward Freddy Burker. Hannah gives a hasty glance to nowhere and says Oh, yeah and turns back to her mother. A party isn't a good enough answer, young lady, scolds Mrs. Kirkpatrick. What party whose party? she demands. It sounds like fake mothering. So much of life is about not doing your homework and finding a way to get credit for it anyway. Travis can picture Mrs. Kirkpatrick so clearly in high school and not because she appears to be wearing one of Hannah's tops. He can see the sun freckles across Mrs. Kirkpatrick's tanned cleavage and muscular chest as he leans down to Hannah and whispers, Freddy Burker is here.

I'm going with Travis, Hannah announces.

Mrs. Kirkpatrick pulls a face. She's still in high school, Mrs. Kirkpatrick, she's never left and Travis knows it's all she can do not to mock him and make sport of her daughter, too. At least I know you'll be safe, she laughs.

As if she cares, Hannah says and sweeps into the departing crowd. Travis lingers long enough to collect a free box of leftover popcorn, then follows.

Travis will remember the hand he places on Hannah's arm to stop her from pushing through the gates and running away. He'll remember how much it took out of him to make that gesture. To swim his hand through the current of limbs until he finds Hannah's cheerleading sweater, the way that sweater feels, smooth and light but heavy. Durable. Red and durable, with victory V stripes of black and white. Hannah twists back at him but she keeps going. Tries to keep going, tries to pull away, but Travis has stopped her and she says Travis let go and for some reason he doesn't let go even as a few of the adults spin round with warning glances. He doesn't let go and he will remember that he doesn't let go, and he will remember why he doesn't let go because it is so unlike him but it is so unlike Hannah as well. What is playing through his head is Hannah always calling a friendly hi to him, what he is seeing are the snapshots of Hannah on her thick-tired bicycle, are Hannah and Chieko riding bikes in the countryside and running into him and how Chieko burst into near hysterics when she first laid eyes on him and covered her mouth and giggled things in Japanese that must have been things like Oh, my god! He's a giant! What's wrong with him! and how Hannah just waited her out, didn't correct her even though you could tell it wasn't respectful what Chieko was carrying on about, and then Hannah modeled good manners and introduced Chieko to Travis and Travis showed them Yoder's farm and they went behind it into the woods and how Chieko said in English she was scared but then she wasn't scared because Travis was there. It was the way Hannah had made them friends that day, the way that Hannah had cared, the way that Hannah's head-shake during Chieko's impolite hysterics firmly planted her on Travis's side—all of that versus this moment's behavior where Hannah doesn't care at all, has become just like everyone else disappearing into her selfies and unbothered by her own uncaringness. Not stopping to give a hug of encouragement to the JV cheerleader obviously standing there waiting for a word of praise from the varsity captain. Travis has watched Hannah so closely all these years and every shadow across her face he has spotted and taken note of. And this is not Hannah.

What do you want, Travis? she demands, trying to pull away again.

You told your mom you're going with me.

I'm not going with you.

You told your mom you were.

So?

Night, Hannah! The junior varsity cheerleader calls to her and Hannah gives the freshman a quick hug and says You did great, Sky and moves on before Sky can respond but the look of happiness remains on Sky's face, the varsity captain who knows her name.

This is not Hannah. This is Hannah imitating the indifferent way everyone else treats everyone else.

Where are you going? Travis calls to her.

Leave me alone.

Where are you going?

A party.

I'll take you, Travis says.

You're not invited, Hannah says. It's for the popular kids who aren't embarrassing.

Somehow the insult is so lame out of Hannah's mouth that it has the opposite effect. It empowers Travis. He feels a command in their relationship he's never felt.

I'll just drop you off, Travis says. I have to go to Walmart anyway.

Despite herself, Hannah laughs. Oh, god, shut up, she says.

The night has that pleasant feel as they walk to Travis's car. So much screaming and horn blowing and drum pounding and touchdown after touchdown has worn everyone out, has worn the night out in fact. Tired adult feet on the sidewalk is the biggest sound. A quiet remark here and there is like a rushing stripe across the sky. Hannah stays silent and so does Travis. In the quiet everyone can be overheard, so everyone keeps quiet, which deepens the quiet.

Good job cheering tonight, someone says. It's sincere and softly spoken. Offered by an older woman with white hair. Her arm is wrapped in her husband's. The night is so quiet, so pleasant with the scrapes of their shoes.

Thank you, Hannah says.

Who was that? Travis asks when they get in the car.

I don't know. Hope it's not one of Nan's friends. She seems too nice.

Your grandmother's nice.

Uh-huh, Hannah says. She slumps in the passenger seat like a rescue kitten. The obvious reaction is What's wrong?

Travis asks instead, Do you want to go by the haunted house before the party?

You're not going to the party.

Before I drop you off.

Whatever, Travis.

They drive by the haunted house with the turret where the judge lives with his dead mother, and they park and stare at the light in the turret where the dead mother lives.

Can you see her? Hannah asks.

Not yet, says Travis.

Nan says she's seen her.

Travis has never actually kept watch at the haunted house before this. Alone, it's the kind of thing that would send him to the Walmart parking lot for the night, tucked between eighteen-wheelers and truckers with their guns.

Remember when she came to our school and we thought she was the substitute teacher?

Oh, yeah, Travis says.

It was right before she died.

She was ... Travis searches for the right word ... pretty talkative for someone who was about to die.

Everyone was laughing at her.

I didn't laugh, Travis says.

I didn't either. I don't think most people laughed actually. I guess there wasn't a lot of laughter. I think they felt sorry for her.

I thought she was pretty talkative.

God I would hate to be that old.

She's not that old anymore.

That's a good point, Travis. Very good. And if you die sooner, you don't ever get that old.

Are you thinking of dying sooner? Travis asks. Because suddenly he gets it now.

I'm thinking about it.

Like how soon?

Hannah shrugs.

You want someone there with you?

I don't think that's the point.

Why?

Just let me think about it, Hannah says.

Travis follows Hannah's directions and drives to the party location and they sit outside a house that's mostly dark.

Your car smells like fresh laundry, Hannah says

Yeah.

I expected it to smell bad.

I might be getting a new car soon, Travis says. A pickup actually.

Hannah doesn't say anything.

What do you think about that?

I can see you in a pickup.

Me, too.

I can't stop seeing you in a pickup.

Travis points to the dark house. Do you want to get out and go to the party?

That's very funny, Travis.

Who lives here?

We can leave now, Hannah says. I just wanted to say good-bye.

I have an errand I need to do, Travis says.

I am not going to Walmart.

It's not that, Travis says. He backtracks through town and follows a short street until it ends in a field, cuts through an apartment complex strewn with plastic tricycles and miniature shopping carts, and pulls into another street that ends in a field. This one has a wide paved path. The pedestrian path pushes all the way through the field to the beginning of the train tracks and grain elevators. Travis points down the path. See that third house?

I guess, Hannah says.

See it?

The one after the first and second houses?

That's where Spalding Burker lives.

Travis parks the car and turns off the engine. I'm keeping watch, he tells her.

Hannah doesn't say anything. She slumps down and rests her head against the window.

Are you going to college next year? Travis asks her.

Obviously not, Hannah says.

Did you apply?

That's right, keep me talking, Hannah says.

Well, did you apply?

Yeah.

Where?

I want to go to Ohio State.

What about Kent State?

No.

Why not?

Not interested.

What about Bowling Green?

No.

Why not?

Not interested. Travis, why are you keeping watch over Spalding Burker's house that's the third one after the first and second ones? Are you trying to delay the inevitable?

What's the inevitable?

I thought you wanted to keep me company.

I'd like to go to Ohio State, Travis says, but maybe junior year. Miss B thinks I should go to community college first.

That sounds so fabulous, Travis. And what is your field of study going to be?

Cinematography.

That just sounds so great.

I know you're making fun of me.

I don't have to. You're making fun of yourself.

If it doesn't happen, it's not like I'm going to kill myself over it.

I've never heard you talk so much. I thought you were shy.

I never heard you … like this before. I thought you were happy. And nice.

Hannah starts to cry. She rocks and cries. I used to think I was happy. I used to be nice. I don't have any Kleenex! she screams.

You can talk to me, Travis says.

I have been talking to you! You know more about this than the whole rest of the world! They're going to be so surprised, their perfect little Hannah.

Then tell me why.

You have a job to do for me, Travis, after. Okay? My mom and Nan won't do it. I can't trust them.

You won't always have to live with them. You're going to Ohio State next year. Just like go and don't come back until Thanksgiving and then just for the turkey.

It's always food with you, Hannah says. And then she says, I'm sorry. I know you have to think about that stuff.

That's okay.

Hannah reaches into her tote bag and pulls out a letter. It's addressed in English with a return address in English, but Travis can see it's foreign. You have to write back to this person, she says.

Who is it?

I don't know.

Travis holds the letter in his hand. It's a little bit thick but not too thick. It's politely thick. Not brush-off thin but not chock-full of all kinds of news. It's from Japan. It's still sealed.

You haven't opened it, Travis says.

I can't. I know what's inside. It's been over two months and I haven't heard a thing from her. I can't do it.

Travis pulls the letter from her hand.

You know what happened over there, Hannah says. And nobody even cares.

It didn't happen.

It was all over the news. I know nobody cares here, nobody cares about anything except their stupid little world. But it happened.

It didn't happen to her is what I meant to say. He holds up the letter. I'll open it for you.

He lightly pecks at the corner.

Don't tear the return address, she warns.

He pecks and pecks at it. It feels like it's been sealed with superglue.

Could you not get popcorn grease on that please?

The back of the envelope looks like the teeth of a comb when Travis gets through with it. He snaps on the overhead so they can both see what he's pulling out. Two sheets of paper, a page and a half of writing. All of it in Japanese.

They stare at it.

Now what? Hannah finally asks.

We read it.

Shut up.

I can speak Japanese, Travis says.

You can speak Japanese?

I learned it last year with Chieko.

Say something, Hannah says.

I can't speak it, Travis says. I can only read it.

You can read that? Hannah asks.

Yeah, Travis says.

It's hard for me to believe Chieko could teach anybody anything, and I don't mean that in a mean way, but really? That's impossible to believe.

She didn't teach me. I used the computers at the town library. I would just learn some stuff and read it to her and she'd say yes or no.

Yes or no what?

Yes if I got the translation into English right, no if I got it wrong.

What would happen if you got it wrong?

She'd say no.

Then what?

Nothing.

She wouldn't tell you what the real word was?

Not usually.

That sounds like her. She didn't have a very large vocabulary. Hannah points to the letter. Read that line, she tells him.

Dear Hannah.

What's the next line?

Please excuse my sloppy handwriting.

It doesn't look sloppy, Hannah says. It looks like art.

It's pretty sloppy, Travis says. Based on my studies. Hold on.

A pickup rushes past them, barely slowing for the path.

Shit, Travis whispers.

What's he doing?

That's him! Travis calls out. He jumps out of the Monte Carlo and runs toward the white pickup that straddles the path, the smooth black-top under its carriage, the wheels bouncing on the grass and dirt. Travis didn't expect Freddy Burker to do this, to go commando down a pedestrian walk. He didn't expect him to show up at all. He's just been sitting here night after night, *some* nights after some nights, not expecting anything, feeling useful while passing the time, feeling that his life matters because he's keeping someone safe, wondering if it really does matter since weeks have gone by and the Burkers seem safe with or without him. Does it matter? Does he matter? He's determined to keep going with his life to find out. Why did Hannah ask the same question and get such a different answer? Freddy Burker has never asked himself this question, he is a marshmallow of evil, and when Freddy opens the pickup door and bumps into Travis, Travis feels his softness and lack of strength and he thinks of Spalding, who is spread wide to look strong but who has no physical strength either. Travis has always felt sorry for him. With Spalding's father in his grip he realizes there is nothing to be done for Spalding and he's glad he doesn't know his own father, the limitations his own father has given to him, limitations that might stop him cold. He can proceed in ignorance with high hopes.

The rifle in Freddy Burker's hands is now in Travis's arms. There by accident, having been transferred by Freddy Burker's clumsy fat. Now Freddy Burker wants it back and is grabbing at it but he's way too loser weak. Spalding and his mother run out of the house and Travis wonders why they are rushing out. It's been a silent struggle between him and Freddy Burker. Neither has said a word.

He hears Hannah yelling and turns to find her. Freddy is already back in his truck and peeling away. His turnaround in the field might have done some damage to the Ford. Hannah is jumping this way and that to avoid him. She guesses wrong and the pickup knocks her down. Travis runs to her side. Hannah keeps saying she is all right she is all right. He is kneeling at her side. She is shaking and Roxanne Burker is shouting, We need an ambulance! I'm okay, Hannah says. Calm down, everyone, I'm okay I'm okay. She's okay, he calls to Roxanne Burger, who stays in her yard. It's okay, Roxanne is saying. Everything is going to be okay. You're going to be okay, Spalding. You're going to be okay. Travis goes over there and Spalding is on the ground. There's blood on his torso and Spalding is weeping uncontrollably. He shot me, he sobs. He shot me. He shot my son, Roxanne screams into her iPhone. He shot my son! He shot me! Spalding weeps. Travis kneels down and touches Spalding's shirt. Oh, my god! screams Spalding. Travis lifts the shirt. He sees some blood. Not too much. He feels underneath Spalding, finds something sharp, and pulls out a pocketknife. What's this? Travis says. Help me Travis, Spalding sobs. He shot me. The gun didn't go off, Travis assures him. I took the gun away from him, he soothes. I don't care, Spalding cries. He shot me! I'm going to die!

Travis holds up the weapon to Roxanne Burker. It's just a pocketknife, he tells her.

The bastard shot my son! Roxanne Burker screams into her iPhone.

News Travels Fast

and by midnight Miss B is sitting in the waiting area of the ER. One by one members of the football team filter in and are led through. There is Dustin Crosby, whose long disposition she suffered through. He doesn't even glance her way. There is Jared Overholser, who sees her, looks right through her with that frightening smirk. There is Josh Greesley, who hangs his head when he catches a glimpse of his old English teacher, who like it or not he's going to get again next year. She almost expects Judge Merle Herrick to walk in next. At length Coach McManus arrives, his hair still damp from a shower. He comes over and shakes her hand and says, Any word, good of you to come, have they found him, none of it a question that needs an answer, and then something about one of our own and by then he is already looking away as he speaks and then somebody motions to him and he disappears into the back with a wave to Miss B.

She has never felt so much like less than nothing. She knows this isn't a time to think about herself. But she feels like nothing. And she wonders if that is why she is a teacher, because left on her own she is nothing to anyone. She can perhaps take some pleasure in the fact that a coach might suffer from some of the same importance/lack of importance phenomenon. The coach won't want to hear that it was not one of his own who saved the day, not a powerful determined football player, brave the way all football players are, showing strength of character the way all football players do, who stood in harm's way and grabbed a rifle from a shooter's hands as they are all taught to do because of their strength of character. It will be Travis Hicks the newspapers will fawn over, not only the local paper, the big ones, too. Coach McManus won't be involved. No one will talk about Coach McManus instilling lessons of courage in his kids. No one will have to hear Coach McManus say, These kids have so much heart, so much determination. I couldn't be prouder of our quarterback, I couldn't be prouder of our wide receiver and tight end. At the very least the coach will have to choke on pebbles just to get the words Spalding Burker out of his mouth. *Rusty Pocketknife Hysteria* would read the tabloids. *Does Football Make Cowards of Us All?*

There's some comfort in knowing that.

And now Travis has a real story to tell and when the colleges hear about it, his heroism amid his hardship narrative, the fact that he's six foot eight and bench presses the weight of the world but takes an extracurricular Shakespeare class ... the colleges she could never convince to visit K-High might suddenly be interested in visiting. Nobody cares about people like them. Oberlin, Denison, Kenyon—elite private schools only an hour and a half away, and not one K-High student has ever gone there, has ever been invited to apply, has ever bothered to apply, has ever heard of these schools. And that makes Miss B sad. That makes her want to cry.

She looks up to see two new people in the ER. The automatic doors usually make a whoosh when they open, but she's heard nothing. The couple are middle-aged. She presumes them to be middle-aged but they might be younger and look older because of the life they lead, or older and look younger for the same reason. It's unusual to see Amish in their medical centers. Perhaps they aren't Amish. She didn't hear them walk in. She didn't hear them check in at Registration. They are just here. She's not even sure they are real. And they seem to be smiling at her, having a good laugh.

Travis Hicks Sits

with Hannah Kirkpatrick. She lies on a bed in an ER cubby, curtain drawn back. She's asked Dr. Devajaran not to call her mother, not just yet, to give her a minute. Dr. Devajaran says, She's on her way so we can X-ray your hip. Hannah says, My hip is fine. Dr. Devajaran says, I know you're anxious to go home, and Hannah says, No, I'm not.

Dr. Devajaran steps out, her eyes on Travis this time, and skates the curtain shut.

Why did she look at you so weird? Hannah asks.

I don't know, Travis says.

Maybe she wants your autograph.

Travis starts to laugh. It feels like a giggle. He's wondering if guys his size can do giggles. It's never happened to him before.

Down the corridor they can hear the sounds of celebration. Through the curtain cracks Travis has spied them, the stars on the team come to briefly validate Spalding's existence. Each one ambles with the slight limp of the athlete, a hitch he's seen Spalding try to imitate—a valiant muscular resolve as each tested and worn-out player makes his way to Spalding's cubby to pay tribute and soul slap one of their wounded. Travis overhears Spalding acting the hero. News isn't out yet that an unspent rifle lay on the ground. Travis feels bad that in less than twenty-four hours Spalding will go back to being a joke. Still, the march of football comrades makes for a pretty good comedy show especially because everybody is trying so hard to ignore the everywhere smell of beer.

And then the curtain skates back and Coach McManus is standing there. Under the lights his hair is streaked yellow, is streaked brown. It's damp. He smells good, and he's wearing a black Ralph Lauren polo shirt with that same logo staring him down.

You took on somebody, Coach McManus says to him. You and my player, you guys took on somebody. You're one of us now, Travis. Coach McManus reaches in for a soul grip. The horseman logo charging at Travis grows so tiny it disappears.

And you, young lady, Coach McManus begins. And then he says nothing else.

Travis buries his head after Coach McManus departs. His whole body shakes.

I've never seen you so goofy before, Hannah says.

Travis tries to stop laughing. Can they hear me? he asks.

Go ask them, she says.

You were right. You told me it was going to escalate.

I don't remember saying that.

Yeah, you told me. You said if cable and podcasts were a clue, Freddy Burker was going to escalate.

You should have listened to me.

I did listen. That's why I was keeping watch.

Really?

Yeah.

You were keeping watch because of me?

Yeah.

So, Travis?

Yeah.

I want some credit when you start doing your hero interviews.

I'll give you all the credit.

Hoots and eruptions down the way.

Oh, my god, Hannah says. Can you imagine what tomorrow's gonna be like? She nudges her head in Spalding's direction. Oh, my god.

He wants it so bad, Travis says.

I hope he wants to be a buttwipe. I've never heard anyone be such a screaming crybaby, oh, my god. Not sayin' nothing though. My lips are sealed. Can you say I jumped in front of the pickup trying to stop it?

Isn't that what you did?

That's what I did.

I thought so.

So can you say it?

Yeah.

So practice it. Here's the camera and the reporters. Talk to the camera.

Travis looks straight at Hannah's palm and says, After I got the rifle away, I don't really remember doing it, it was all chaos. But then the rifle was in my hands and before I knew it Mr. Burker was in his pickup trying to get away. The only person who kept a cool head was Hannah Kirkpatrick, our varsity cheerleader captain, who was jumping and dodging in front of the pickup trying to get the vehicle stuck in the mud so he couldn't escape. And she almost did it, too. She's the real hero. She put herself in harm's way.

That's incredible, Travis. Really incredible.

I practice that kind of stuff a lot.

Can you say it again? This time maybe put *She put herself in harm's way* before *She's the real hero.*

Good idea, Travis says. End on *She's the real hero.* Nice punch.

Do you really think I was?

Yeah.

Maybe I was, Hannah says. I wasn't scared. I really wasn't.

You were amazing. And Spalding—here Travis lowers his voice—is crying and screaming I'm shot I'm dying, and you're like I'm okay I'm okay calm down everyone.

Really? I was really like that?

Yeah.

I was calm?

Yeah. Calm and brave. Really brave.

Brave. Yeah I guess so, maybe.

And I'm going to tell everyone.

Okay. I'm going to be embarrassed but … that's okay. Travis, she says. You need to read me the rest of the letter before my mom and Nan get here. Do you have it?

Yeah I have it.

Did you leave it in the car?

No I have it.

Don't get it dirty.

Travis pushes the wall pump for three glops of sanitizer. He kneads it through his fingers, waves his hands in the air to dry.

They're on their way so, maybe, hurry?

Travis pulls out the letter from his back pocket and opens it.

But don't leave anything out.

Dear Hannah. Please excuse my sloppy handwriting.

You read that part already.

I hope you are doing good. I hope you are happy. I want you to be happy and not do anything you'll regret.

That is a fucking lie, Travis.

I'm just repeating what's here. I can't help what it says.

Keep reading and stop lying.

I miss you so much, Hannah. I love you. I love you so much. I love you. You are like a sister to me. You are so beautiful. You are the sister I never had. I love you like a sister and I miss you so much. I miss your long hair. I love your long hair so much. You were so nice to me, Hannah. You are so nice to everyone. You are the nicest person I've ever met. My life is so boring without you here. Please come visit me in Japan like you promised so I can introduce you to all my friends and I will tell them, This is Hannah and she is my beautiful American sister and I love her so much.

Hannah has turned away from him. She is crying.

I can stop, Travis says.

Hannah keeps her face turned away, a fist pushing at her mouth.

Do you want me to stop? Travis asks.

I want you to keep going, Hannah says.

ACKNOWLEDGMENTS

I owe a great debt to Greg Michalson for his help in making Black Road a reality. He was Nancy's editor throughout her career. She would be so pleased to know he helped bring this, her final novel, into being. More than that, Greg was a long-time writer's workshop colleague and--most of all--a treasured friend.

· JIM ZAFRIS

NOTES ON THE AUTHOR

 Nancy Zafris has published four previous books of fiction: The People I Know, winner of the Flannery O'Connor award for short fiction and the Ohioana Library Association award for best book of fiction; The Metal Shredders, a New York Times Notable book; Lucky Strike; and Home Jar, a collection of short stories named one of the year's ten best books by Minneapolis Star Tribune. In addition to her own work, Nancy long served as the series editor for the annual Flannery O'Connor Award for short fiction. Prior to that, she was the fiction editor of the Kenyon Review. She was also instrumental in developing the generative model for the Kenyon Summer Writers Workshops, where summer after summer she led sessions in fiction writing.

CPSIA information can be obtained
at www.ICGtesting.com
Printed in the USA
JSHW021628030223
37271JS00002B/4